THE Pecos Kid

BEGINNER'S LUCK

JACK BODINE

HarperPaperbacks
A Division of HarperCollinsPublishers

This is a work of fiction. The characters, incidents, and dialogues are products of the author's imagination and are not to be construed as real. Any resemblance to actual events or persons, living or dead, is entirely coincidental.

HarperPaperbacks *A Division of* HarperCollins*Publishers*
10 East 53rd Street, New York, N.Y. 10022

Copyright © 1992 by Len Levinson
All rights reserved. No part of this book may be used or reproduced in any manner whatsoever without written permission of the publisher, except in the case of brief quotations embodied in critical articles and reviews. For information address HarperCollins*Publishers*,
10 East 53rd Street, New York, N.Y. 10022.

Cover illustration by Paul Bachem

First printing: September 1992

Printed in the United States of America

HarperPaperbacks and colophon are trademarks of HarperCollins*Publishers*

❖ 10 9 8 7 6 5 4 3 2 1

CHAPTER 1

THE OLD CONCORD STAGECOACH RUMBLED across the trail, lanterns gleaming into the night. The driver flicked his whip across the horses' haunches, as moonlight reflected upon buttes, spires, and caprock escarpments on the distant horizon.

Inside the cab, a salesman, two soldiers, a lawyer, a cowboy, and a hatless young vagabond sat with knees jammed together, enveloped in the fragrance of springtime. They'd been on the road five days, sleeping in ramshackle roadhouses, alert for Indians.

The young man was nearly eighteen years old, tall, with black hair and ill-fitting clothes. He peered out the window at a town down the road, glittering like a sprawl of diamonds across the valley. His name was Duane Braddock, he had thirteen dollars and change in his pocket, and was on the first journey of his life.

He didn't know a soul in Titusville, and had heard that big towns were sinkholes of sin and depravity, with drunken men shooting each other at random, and scarlet women luring lovelorn males into the fires of hell. Paradoxically, he was eager to see these harrowing prospects; they provoked his youthful curiosity and sense of adventure. For better or worse, he'd lived an unusually sheltered life. Until two weeks ago, he'd been sequestered in a Benedictine monastery high in the Guadalupe Mountains. An orphan, he'd been brought there an infant, and raised by the brothers and fathers.

Duane had spent his brief life praying, studying, and singing Gregorian chant, planning to become a brother, and then possibly a priest, but it started unraveling two weeks ago. He'd been forced to leave for fighting with another acolyte, beating him rather badly with a frying pan. The old abbot had said: "If you can't live in peace with us, you'll have to go somewhere else!"

Duane had never known peace, as if he didn't quite mesh with the world. Even the tranquillity of the monastery hadn't subdued his inner demons, and often he'd doubted that he was truly called to the religious life. He'd longed to see the outside world, and he'd experienced weird stirrings concerning certain Mexican girls who'd come to the monastery to pray.

The abbot had made the decision for him, expelling Duane from the monastery in the clouds. A roof every night and three regular meals a day were things of the past. Whatever he needed now, he'd have to tear out of the world with his bare hands.

The end had come suddenly and with stunning forcefulness. An orphan bully named Jasper Jakes had learned the truth of Duane's parentage from records in the abbot's office, which revealed that Duane was the bastard son of an outlaw killed in the Pecos country, and a prostitute who'd died shortly thereafter.

Jasper Jakes had made painful remarks concerning Duane's ancestry at every opportunity. After several days of mounting anger, Duane lost control in the monastery kitchen, and attacked Jakes. Before the fight could be stopped, Duane had broken Jakes's jaw, shattered his nose, and knocked out a tooth. He himself had taken one hard shot to the forehead, but that was his total damage.

Duane shuddered as the memories flooded his mind. He would've killed Jakes, if they didn't stop him, and he knew that a dangerous beast dwelled within him, which was frightening to contemplate. But he couldn't bear the shame of his deepest embarrassment revealed to the world. Duane had felt like dirty, damaged goods, and no matter how hard he struggled, he'd never wash off that indelible stain—the devil's brand on his soul. Other boys had lost parents to wild Indians, disease, floods, and outlaw raids, but at least their parents had been married, and their fathers hadn't been killed by lawmen.

Duane had vague recollections of his father, who'd smelled of whiskey and tobacco, and wore a black mustache, but was it memory or hallucination? He had been less than a year old when his father was shot, and his mother expired soon thereafter, so how could he remember her blond curls and gentle kisses? But they couldn't've been *that* bad, he said to himself. And even if they were, surely God would forgive them, for aren't we His Children?

His body ached, crammed in with the others, and he wanted to stretch his long legs, but across from him sprawled a sergeant in the 4th Cavalry, snoring loudly. During the trip, Duane had examined his fellow passengers, and most interesting, in his estimation, was the droll, lanky cowboy named Lester Boggs.

Boggs wore a wide-brimmed hat, a drooping, tobacco-stained sandy mustache, and a green bandanna draped around his sunburned neck, but his most arresting feature was the six-shooter gleaming evilly in his holster, slung low and tied down. To Duane, Lester Boggs represented the epitome of what a real man should be, a far cry from the monastery's solemn-faced brothers and fathers, who were always doing penance for something they considered vile.

Duane had tried to strike up a conversation with Boggs, seeking to draw stories and information out of him, but the cowboy fended off all inquiries, sipping pale amber liquid he referred to as "medicine," out of a whiskey bottle with the label partially torn off.

Boggs was tanned, with callused hands, and moonbeams emitting from his eyes. Duane wished he could be a man of the world like Boggs, not a solitary kid of dubious parentage, and ignorant about life.

Duane would be eighteen in only three weeks, and was anxious to realize his potential, although he wasn't quite sure what it was. His education had been good and evil as interpreted by Jesus Christ, Saint Paul, Thomas Aquinas, Augustine, Saint Benedict, and all the other luminaries of Holy Mother Church. Brother Paolo, his teacher and spiritual advisor, had told him that he could accomplish any goal, if he kept his mind pure, but Brother Paolo had once served time in a California jail for being a *bandito*.

The horses plodded toward the end of their day's labor, and Duane heard the driver joking with the shotgun guard atop the coach. The buildings of Titusville loomed closer, with lights aglow in the center of town. *Crack*! went the driver's whip over the horses' flanks. "We'll have us a good steak at the Crystal Palace Saloon," the stagecoach driver said to the shotgun guard. "And a bottle of Old Crow."

Duane had read about far-off exotic lands, and now at last was free to travel anywhere. He was tired of reading books and singing in the choir, and didn't feel qualified to deliver sermons to men and women twice his age. He also wanted to get married as soon as possible, because strange internal physical events were occurring beyond his control.

The sergeant twitched his nose, opened his eyes, and looked out the window. "Thar it is," he muttered. "'Bout goddamn time."

The lawyer awakened next to him, a sleepy grin on his face. "Which way is the cribs?"

The stagecoach rounded a bend, and rocked on its leather thoroughbrace suspension. A whiff of chimney smoke wafted through the window, and Duane's mouth watered with anticipation of his next meal. He always seemed hungry, and hoped he could get a job before his money ran out.

He had no idea where he'd sleep that night. He had no poncho in his sack, not even a blanket. The abbot, furious at the outbreak of violence, unceremoniously chucked Duane out the front gate without supplies, despite Brother Paolo's ardent protestations, citing Duane's age, inexperience, but the abbot refused to change his verdict.

Duane wasn't remorseful about leaving the monastery. He'd endured enough sanctimonious piety and ecclesiastical platitudes to last a lifetime, and didn't want to become a dried-out old buzzard like the abbot. But he still believed in God, the Gospels, and Holy Mother Church. You don't have to live in a monastery to be a good Christian, he told himself.

Something wild dwelled inside him, and he'd yearned for an active outdoors life. Many times, studying in the scriptorium, he'd wanted to run alone in the ponderosa pines, to let off steam, but all he could do was turn the page. In Ecclesiastes, he'd read: *In much learning, there is much sorrow,* and Duane couldn't agree more. Some writers said it one way, other writers declared it differently, but it all boiled down to one principle: *Honor truth, love justice, and walk humbly with thy God.* His only regret was that he'd never see poor, tormented Brother Paolo again. That devout ex-bandito had wagged his finger in Duane's face and said in a grave voice: *Beware the temptations of the secular world. At first it looks like a garden, but then it becomes an oven.*

Across the seat, Lester Boggs drew his gun out of its holster, spun the cylinders, and returned the weapon to its position of meditation on his hip. Then he bit off a fresh chunk of tobacco and worked his jaws like a cow.

The stagecoach arrived at the edge of the town, and Duane perceived outlines of two- and three-story wooden buildings, some with lamps glowing in the windows. A dog ran out of the darkness and barked at the spokes of the stagecoach going round and round.

The driver steered onto the main street of Titusville, and the first building was a saloon, with horses lined up at the hitching rail, and raucous laughter floating through bat-wing doors. Next came a hardware store closed for the night, a barber shop, and then a private home with no lamps on. Men strolled on the planked sidewalks, wearing boots and wide cowboy hats, carrying guns and knives, smoking cigarettes.

Duane wanted to be manly like them, but he felt like an overgrown boy. The faint stubble of a mustache grew on his upper lip, but he'd never been alone with a woman since he entered the monastery. He was conscious of his monk's sandals, old brown pants, dirty white shirt, and no hat.

He was scared and exhilarated as the stagecoach rolled down the wide, potholed street. Three cowboys on horseback galloped past, waving their hats in the air, yipping and yelling like madmen. Duane stared at hotels ablaze with light, saloons full of roaring men, restaurants packed with diners, horses drinking from troughs. The tinkle of a piano came to his ears, and a woman laughed throatily in one of the saloons.

Duane broke out into a cold sweat, and felt uncomfortable in his hand-me-down clothes. In only moments, he'd be on his own in a strange town, but Brother Paolo had given him the basic guidelines: *Don't gamble, don't drink whiskey, and stay away from women.*

Duane spotted a woman waving from behind the front window of the Cattlemen Saloon, her face garish-

7

ly painted, wearing a low-cut dress. He realized that
she was a prostitute, and wondered what horrible circumstance had brought her to such a wanton state.

The mere thought of women made him feel as if he
were covered with ants. He'd enjoyed disgraceful
dreams about Mexican girls at Mass in the monastery,
and reproached himself for licentious imaginings. A
man should be more than a pig rutting among the
sows, he maintained.

Meanwhile, his fellow travelers conversed in scur-
rilous tones about whiskey, women, and cards, the
very items Brother Paolo had told Duane to avoid, and
Duane coughed on the thick tobacco smoke roiling
inside the cab. They were big, rough men, except for
the salesman, who had smooth hands, big ears, and a
beatific smile. "You know what's the best hotel in
town?" he asked Sergeant Cutlowe.

"I ain't never been in Titusville afore, but a troop-
er told me that the best whores are at Miss Ellie's."
Sergeant Cutlowe turned toward Duane and shook his
finger. "Now you stay out of there, boy. Yer too
young fer that shit."

Duane's ears turned red in the darkness, as the
stagecoach veered toward an immense building that
took up nearly the entire block. The sign above the
porch said:

CARRINGTON ARMS

Lights blazed from its windows, spilling onto the
veranda, where men drank leisurely at tables. Someone
fired a shot on a nearby street, and Duane jumped
three inches off his seat. The sergeant leaned toward

Duane. "You'd better git you a gun, Sonny Jim. Otherwise yer liable to git a bullet up yer ass. Some of these cowboys come to town after three months in a line shack, they git a few whiskeys in 'em—they go crazy as injuns. It's always best to be heeled, know what I mean?"

Duane nodded solemnly, as the stagecoach slowed in front of the hotel. He looked at his raggedy clothes, and feared that he'd appear outlandish to the citizens of the secular world. He knew he'd have to get some new clothes as soon as he found a job

The stagecoach came to a stop, attracting the attention of everyone in the vicinity, and on high floors of the hotel, guests looked down at the vehicle pulling up to the door, bringing visitors from beyond the mountains, along with newspapers, mail, merchandise, and warrants for the arrest of certain individuals currently on the dodge.

The stagecoach driver bounded to the ground, wiped his hands on his pants, and opened the door. Duane moved off his seat, squeezed through the narrow opening, and landed on the ground. He felt a crick in his back, and his right knee was sore as he unwound in front of the hotel. Lamplight glistened on his aquiline nose and high cheekbones.

He was fascinated by the ornately gabled hotel before him, the largest building he'd ever seen, and wondered if he had enough money to stay there. Reaching into his pocket, he took out his coins and counted them in the palm of his hand, as if hoping they'd gained interest during the trip, but they totaled the same old thirteen dollars and change.

"What're you doin', boy?" asked Boggs, who

exuded the fragrance of fermented beverages. "Don't show yer money in the middle of the street. There's people here who'd slit yer throat fer what yer got thar. Whar you stayin' tonight?"

"Don't know yet," Duane replied, "but I figured I'd find out what they charge at the Carrington Arms."

"The most 'spensive spot in town—hell, you don't want to go near that place. My advice to you is look fer a boardinghouse run by a fat lady. That way you can be sure you'll eat good."

"I was wondering how to find a job as a cowboy."

Boggs took a step backward, placed his fists on his hips, and regarded Duane. "You don't look like no cowboy to me."

"I'm not yet, but that's what I want to become."

"Wa'al, there's lots of ranches around here, and one of 'em might want a wrangler."

"But I don't know how to ride a horse."

Boggs stared at him in disbelief. "How come?"

Duane didn't want to admit where he was raised, so he shrugged and said mysteriously, "Been busy."

The cowboy scrutinized him carefully. "Where's yer hat?"

"Haven't got one."

Boggs examined him again, as if trying to reach a decision. "I ain't got no dinero either, but there's a feller here what owes me ten dollars. Suppose I meet you at the Crystal Palace in about an hour? I'll buy you a steak, and we can talk, okay?"

"That's all right," Duane replied proudly, reaching into his pocket. "I can buy my own steaks."

The cowboy appeared exasperated. "I told you to put yer money out've sight. Kid, you don't keep yer wits about you, you won't have 'em long. I'll be lookin' fer you by the chop counter at the Crystal Palace."

Boggs walked away on his long bowed legs, and Duane felt as though a great man had just bestowed special honor upon him. He picked me out of the crowd, he thought, like John the Baptist finding Jesus, except that Boggs is a drunkard, and I'm the son of . . .

He didn't want to think about his parents, but had a story worked out in case anybody asked. He knew it was wrong to lie, but sometimes the truth was too brutal to contemplate. Maybe I can become a cowboy, and have some respect, he speculated. Duane watched Boggs lope along the boarded sidewalks, spurs jangling with every step, and he couldn't wait for dinner at the Crystal Palace. He wondered what to do with himself until then.

Meanwhile, the stagecoach driver passed the luggage to the shotgun guard, who handed it to passengers. The sergeant carried his belongings across the street to Sullivan's Saloon, and disappeared into the smoke and laughter behind the bat-wing doors. The driver sauntered toward Duane.

"Got someplace to stay?"

Duane cleared his throat, and tried to speak deeply, like Boggs. "I'll find a boardinghouse, I reckon."

The stagecoach driver raised an eyebrow. "Ain't you got folks?"

"Killed in an injun raid."

"They got a good parson in this town, name of MacDuff, and if you ever git the miss-meal cramps, I'm sure he'll give you a bowl of soup. He might even have somebody in the congregation who can find you a job. Life is what you make it, boy. Don't take no shit from nobody."

The driver patted him on the shoulder, then climbed back to the top seat of the cab. The horses strained as they pulled the stagecoach toward the livery stable. Duane stood in the middle of the street, dumbfounded that the highly respected driver had noticed him.

"Git out of the road!"

Hoofbeats pounded toward him, and he darted toward the sidewalk. Three cowboys galloped past, yipping and yelling down the main street of town, colorful bandannas flying in the breeze. Duane's eyes fell on a sign that said:

HATS

The store was closed for the night, but moonlight illuminated a display of headgear with wide flaring brims and crowns dented in numerous interesting configurations. Duane's eyes widened at the sight of a white ten-gallon sombrero with a neat dent in the middle of the crown. That's the one I'll buy, soon as I find a job, he promised himself.

He became aware of running footsteps, and turned toward a gang of boys not more than ten years old, charging toward him. Barefooted, filthy, ragged, they dove through the air, clutched at him. Something came down on his head, and he saw sunbursts.

He staggered on the sidewalk, trying to make sense of what was happening, when another boy smacked him in the cheek with a rock, and Duane went sprawling backward. A hand groped into his pocket, as the rock hit him again.

"Won't go down," one of the boys lamented.

A voice came from the other side of the street. "Hey—what's going on over there!"

A gun fired, and the boys scattered. Duane tripped over an empty whiskey bottle, fell to the floorboards, his head whirled. He rolled onto his back and looked up at a man with a bony angular face and a six-shooter in his hand. "You okay, kid?"

Duane touched his head, and blood came back on his finger. His nose felt smashed, and more blood showed. "What happened?"

The stranger had a thin black cheroot sticking out his teeth. "Guess they figured you had money."

"I did." Duane reached into his empty pocket. "And they got it all."

The man was tall, in his forties, with blond hair and long sideburns, wearing a ruffled shirt with black string tie. Duane gave him his hand, and the stranger pulled him up. The stranger wore his six-shooter in a holster beneath his frock coat.

"I'm much obliged to you, mister."

"You've got to get yourself a gun, boy."

"I will, soon as I get some money. Do you know where I can find a job?"

"Not offhand." The stranger looked Duane up and down, and his forehead became wrinkled. "What's your name?"

"Duane Braddock."

The friendly expression on the stranger's face changed to something more thoughtful, as he submitted Duane to another appraisal, noticing tattered clothes and sandals. "My name's Clyde Butterfield. Where'd you say you're from?"

"Didn't say."

Butterfield reflected for a few moments, absentmindedly scratching his chin. "If I needed money in a hurry, I'd find a cowboy job."

"Can't ride a horse."

"Can you do carpenter work?"

Duane shook his head.

"Well, if you don't want to rob the bank, you might go to every saloon and restaurant in town, and ask if they need a dishwasher. Where're you sleeping tonight?"

"Don't know yet," Duane replied.

Butterfield paused, as if making a decision. "Watch your step, kid. As soon as you get fifteen dollars, buy yourself a Colt."

Butterfield touched his forefinger to the brim of his cowboy hat, and strolled off into the night. Duane watched him go, certain that Butterfield was an important man about town. He looked at me awfully funny, he thought, and I must be a disgrace in these clothes. Duane smoothed the front of his shirt, wiped blood from the corner of his mouth, and headed for the nearest saloon, to search for a dishwashing job. Nothing can stop a determined Christian, Duane reminded himself.

He thought of acetic Brother Paolo fasting, praying, and suffering, trying to atone for his wicked life as a *bandito*, while Duane had studied in the scriptorium. The monastery had been filled with brooding, gloomy monks like Brother Paolo, who'd talked incessantly about the joy of God's creation.

Duane worked himself to a high pitch of self-confidence as he approached the front of the Longhorn Saloon, where men congregated in groups on the sidewalk and street, passing bottles of whiskey, laughing loudly, gesticulating drunkenly—countless conversations taking place simultaneously. Some dressed like cowboys, but others wore frock coats and stovepipe hats, with brocade vests, gold chains, and diamond tiepins. Horses plodded down the center of the street, and a small shellacked black carriage with two white horses rolled past, its passenger shrouded in shadows.

Duane stared at the carriage, because it resembled an illustration he'd seen in an old magazine at the monastery, about how rich folks lived in the East. But now at last he was seeing the world through his own eyes, instead of from the printed page. He turned toward the Longhorn Saloon, and prepared to push open the bat-wing doors, when suddenly they erupted in his face. He dodged to the side, as a crowd of grim men poured outside. No one spoke, and they resembled monks going to Vespers, except that they carried no cross, and no hymns were sung.

Duane stood near the window of the Longhorn Saloon, as men continued to stream outside. They grumbled to each other, a few passed money from hand to hand, and it looked like a major event was about to occur. Duane peered inside the murky window, saw a bar to the left, countless tables, and women wearing low-cut gowns. A group of them approached the window, and Duane ogled their bare shoulders. He'd never seen such things before, and was transfixed. The women drew closer, motioning for him to get out of the way. They pointed over his shoulder, and he turned around.

Two men faced each other in the middle of the street. Crowds lined both sidewalks, and Duane climbed onto a nearby barrel for a better view. The adversaries were tense, knees bent slightly, hands resting above their guns.

"Make yer play," said the one in a black leather vest.

The other cowboy was younger, leaner, and more nervous. Curly red hair furled beneath his white cowboy hat, and he appeared as if he wanted to be somewhere else. A man wearing a badge stepped out of the crowd, holding both palms out, and his voice broke as he said, "We don't allow no gunfightin' in this town. Why don't you boys sleep it off?"

"Light a shuck," said black vest. "This is between him and me."

The lawman opened his mouth, but no sound came out. A man in his sixties, wearing a business suit, stepped from between two horses. "Deputy Dawson," he said, "I think you'd better move out of the way. You're liable to get shot by mistake, or on purpose."

Someone in the crowd laughed nervously, and Deputy Dawson eased backward, leaving the two men alone in the street. Duane felt as if his hair was standing on end. They're really not going to shoot each other, are they?

"I'm a-waitin' on yuh," black vest said, "and I'm a-losin' my patience. You can apologize, but I ain't got all night."

"You insulted my woman," the young cowboy

said evenly, trying to be brave. "I got nothin' to apologize fer."

Duane heard a new voice on the far side of the street. "It ain't worth dyin' over, cowboy. That's Saul Klevins, and he's the fastest hand in these parts. You walk away, no one'll think the less of you."

"I don't walk away," the cowboy said stubbornly.

"Then yer a-gonna die," replied Saul Klevins.

The young cowboy licked his upper lip, and went into his gunfighter's crouch. Light glanced off his burnished spurs, his pants were cut tight to his legs, his eyes steely. Saul Klevins hunched his shoulders, and his right palm hovered above his gun grip. The night was silent, and Duane held his breath. He didn't know whether to say a *Hail Mary, Our Father,* or a *Glory Be.*

The combatants were frozen like statues in the moonlight, then the young cowboy's hand darted suddenly toward his holster, but Saul Klevins already was hauling iron. A faint smile came over Klevins's face as he aimed down his barrel and fired. The explosion shattered the night, and Duane flinched. Gunsmoke billowed in the middle of the street, and the cowboy's knees locked together. His gun couldn't clear its holster, as he tried desperately to raise it, and a dark stain spread over his shirt.

Klevins narrowed one eye and fired again. The cowboy was rocked on his heels, as his gun fell out of his hand and his hat dropped off the back of his head. His red hair glowed like fire as he staggered in the middle of the street. A woman shrieked, as the cowboy's legs gave out. He fell like a sack of potatoes at the feet of the man who'd killed him.

A smile played over Saul Klevins's face, as he twirled his Colt around his forefinger, then jammed it into his holster. He snorted derisively, then headed back toward the front door of the saloon. "Good shot, Saul," someone murmured. The crowd parted like the waters of the Red Sea, as Klevins approached the door. "Lemme buy you a drink, Saul."

Klevins pushed open the bat-wing doors, and the crowd followed him into the Longhorn Saloon. Duane turned toward the street. A woman in a bright red dress kneeled beside the dead man, her face drenched with tears. "Why didn't you stop them!" she screamed at the deputy.

The lawman was freckle-faced, with a nose like a finger. "Saul Klevins is the fastest gun in this county, and I ain't a-gonna die fer some stove-up cowboy what didn't know how to keep his mouth shut." The deputy wiped his mouth with the back of his hand. "I'll git the sawbones."

He walked away, and the woman gazed at the dead cowboy. A sob escaped her throat, blood dribbled out the corner of the cowboy's mouth, and a gay tune was played on the piano in the Longhorn Saloon. Duane crossed himself and prayed, "May the Lord have mercy on your soul."

The woman's head snapped up, and she looked at Duane. "What're you want?" she asked. "You need to see some more blood—you ain't got enough—you goddamned buzzard!"

Duane looked away, as he reflected upon the sudden destruction of a life. *From dust thou came, to dust thou shalt return.* It had been unexpected, brutal, and shocking, but yet everyone had behaved as if it were a normal activity, like eating a meal or going to Mass. Duane had read about killings, but no description could duplicate the real thing. *Holy Mary, Mother of God, pray for us sinners now and at the hour of our death.*

He looked through the window of the saloon, and saw Saul Klevins at the bar, center of adulation, drinking whiskey. He'd killed somebody, and become a hero in the secular world. It was just as Brother Paolo had warned: moral values extinct in the secular world. Duane sat on the bench in front of the saloon, and watched the deputy return with a dignified man in a suit and shirt, his hair mussed with sleep. Duane guessed it was the sawbones, who kneeled beside the dead cowboy. The sawbones felt the cowboy's pulse, held a mirror in front of his nostrils, and pronounced, "He's dead."

"Well, who the hell didn't know that?" asked the deputy.

The deputy grabbed the cowboy's arms, and the doctor took his ankles. Together, they carried him toward the far side of the street, as the dance hall girl followed, head bowed in sorrow. The street became still as before, and Duane wondered if the gunfight had really happened. He recalled Klevins's speed, like a flash of deadly lightning.

Duane still felt the passion of the duel, and it reminded him vaguely of euphoric feelings that sometimes came over him when the abbot placed the Host on his tongue, during the Holy Sacrifice of the Mass. And he died like Jesus, Duane thought, mocked in the middle of the street, while Deputy Pontius Pilate washed his hands of the deed.

That's the way my father croaked, more or less, the orphan figured. Or maybe he was shot out of the saddle as he was rustling cattle. Duane had no idea of how his father died, as a brave man or coward, outgunned by one other man, or strung up by a posse.

Duane wondered who was responsible for the death of his father, and whether he or they were still alive. He was headed toward the Pecos country in search of answers, because an orphan needs his history, as another man needs food and drink. He couldn't believe that his parents could be so bad. Whatever the truth, he wanted to know it.

The reflection on his parents was interrupted by a woman's laughter behind him. He turned, and saw, through the front window of the saloon, a prostitute squirming on a man's lap. Duane's eyes widened as the man snaked his hand up the woman's dress, and she shrieked with delight. She was fat, her face painted grotesquely, and her breasts surged out of a red satin gown. Near her, men gambled, drank, and hollered at each other, while couples swayed together on the small dance floor, and a man in a striped shirt pounded a piano. In the light of coal oil lamps, it looked like the bowels of hell.

Duane noticed that some of the people were eating from big wooden plates, and realized that the saloon was also a restaurant. He was reminded of his plan to become a dishwasher, made a motion to stand, but something held him back. *You go in there,* said the voice of Brother Paolo in his ear, *you might never come out.*

Duane stared through the window fearfully. Nobody could make me drink something I don't want, and I'm not looking for a fight. He rose to his feet, slapped dust from his jacket, and smoothed down his unruly hair. I can be anything I want, he said to himself.

Someone cackled nearby as he pushed open the bat-wing doors. The panorama of the saloon stretched before him, and the first thing that hit him was a cloud of cigar smoke blown from the lungs of a freighter just in from El Paso. Duane coughed, his eyes watered, his face went red. Beside the door, a man in a string tie spun a giant wheel covered with numbers. "Round and round she goes, and where she stops—nobody knows!"

"Could I have a word with you, sir?"

"Just put yer money down, boy."

"Could you tell me where the owner is?"

An arm draped over Duane's shoulder, and a cloud of flowery fragrance enveloped him. He turned, and his eyes bugged at a half-naked woman whispering in his ear. "Wanna go fer a walk?" she asked, pressing her breasts against his arm.

He was unable to speak, and the sound of a drowning bird emitted from his throat as she wormed her tongue into his ear and maneuvered him toward the back door. "I'll show yuh a real good time," she said. "You just leave everything to LouAnn."

She looked about fifteen years old, with brown hair, brown eyes, long eyelashes, and a few freckles on her nose. He realized that she was the one who'd peered at him through the window. "But I don't have any money," he protested.

Her arm left his shoulder as quickly as it had appeared, taking her smile with it. "If you ain't got no money, what the hell're you doin' here?"

"I'm looking for a job. Do you know where the boss is?"

"The kitchen."

She turned away from him, and dropped onto the lap of a cowboy trying to read a newspaper. "How's about a drink?"

Duane stared at her in fascination. His eyes widened as she wiggled her fanny in the man's lap. The man pinched her bottom and chortled happily. That's a scarlet woman? He wondered how she could sell her most precious gift for a few coins.

I could have her for only a few dollars, Duane realized. He'd never thought that paradise could be purchased so cheaply. The Mexican girls at the monastery had been unapproachable, but for only a few coins . . . ? He felt ashamed of his lascivious thoughts.

"Git the fuck out'n my way!" somebody bellowed.

Duane felt as if a stagecoach had crashed into him, and he went sprawling against the wall, his head narrowly missing a coal oil lamp hanging from a nail. He turned and saw a cowboy in a green and black checkered shirt stalking toward the chuck-a-luck wheel. Duane heard the voice of Brother Paolo in his ear: *Even if you are angry, you must not sin. Never let the sun set on your anger, or you will give the devil a foothold.*

It was a line from Saint Paul, and Duane tried to calm himself. The orphan carried a low opinion of himself, and didn't like it when others confirmed his worst doubts. The big cowboy threw coins onto a colored square, and the man with the bowtie spun the chuck-a-luck wheel. "Round and round she goes, and where she stops—nobody knows!"

The hulk in spurs leaned forward, squinting at the spinning wheel. His head rolled round and round with it, and finally the wheel came to a stop.

"You lose," shouted the man in the string tie, scooping up the money.

The big cowboy grabbed the croupier by the front of his shirt. "This goddamn wheel's fixed!"

The hapless croupier struggled to get loose, and men nearby scooped whiskey and money off the tables. A painted woman screamed, as the cowboy leaned the croupier over the table and drew his fist back for a solid punch to the teeth.

The twin barrels of a shotgun appeared through the crowd, carried by a stout man in a dirty apron, with waxed turned-up mustaches and a bald head. He placed both barrels against the big cowboy's ear. "Let 'im go, or I'll blow yer fuckin' head off!"

The hand of the cowboy froze in the air. He turned, and the cold twin eyes of the shotgun stared back at him. It was a powerful argument, and the big cowboy went pale. "Din't mean no trouble, Gus."

"Take a walk, Jethro. Cool yer head."

Jethro sauntered toward the door, and Duane turned his vision toward the bartender, a real-life hero who'd just stood up for justice and the American Way of Life. The bartender noticed Duane, scowled, and waddled toward him. "This ain't no playground, boy. You don't drink, you can't stay here."

Duane flashed his friendliest smile, but the shotgun was aimed directly at him. "I'm looking for a job, sir."

"We don't need nobody."

Duane hitched up his pants, strode toward the front door, and his stomach felt like a cavern. The stench of tobacco, sweat, and ladies' perfume hung heavy in the air. He turned toward the bar, and noticed a huge painting hanging above it of rosy-skinned naked ladies cavorting around a bathtub in a vaguely Turkish palace. His eyes widened at rosebud nipples, the curve of haunches, and previously hidden spots revealed to his curious eyes. The painting seemed like a window into a caliph's harem, so vivid were fleshtones and lines.

He pushed through the bat-wing doors, and cool night air cleared his head. John of the Cross lived years on a few crusts of bread, so what'm I worried about it? I'll be all right, as long as I have faith in God, he told himself.

The row of horses at the rail looked at him forlornly, waiting patiently for their respective riders. They wanted to go to the barn for uninterrupted sleep, because men were hollering, throwing bottles, and shooting guns constantly.

Duane cupped his hands, and carried water from the trough to his lips. He gulped it down, and recalled Lester Boggs inviting him for dinner at the Crystal Palace. A smile broke over Duane's youthful face, but then he realized that he didn't know where the Crystal Palace was. I'll have to search for it, he thought.

He poked his hands into his pockets, and strolled along the planked sidewalk, passing men seated on benches, sipping bottles of whiskey. In the street, other groups held conversations, with more whiskey bottles traveling from hand to hand. They're all drunk, and they're all carrying guns. No wonder there's so much shooting.

He walked by a hardware store, a butcher shop, and a store named Miss Fifi's, a ladies' dress shop, that were closed for the night. He came to the Black Cat Saloon, the Red Rose Saloon, the Line Shack Saloon, and ahead was darkness at the edge of town.

He looked both ways, and no horses or carriages were in sight. He ran across the street. His left foot sank into a pile of muck halfway to his knee, and when he tried to extricate it, the suction wouldn't release him.

Two white horses pulling the ornate black shellacked carriage turned the corner, heading straight for him. Duane angled his leg from side to side, yanked again, heard a *slurp* sound, and his leg came loose at last. He stepped back, as the carriage passed by, a lantern glowing on either side of the driver, room for only two or three people inside. Duane gazed at the strange conveyance, and a ray of moonlight fell on the face of a woman inside, her eyes scintillating in the darkness.

She looked like the Madonna of La Salette, her golden hair covered by a black shawl. Her gaze fell on him, their eyes met, and then the prancing horses pulled her off into the night. He moved toward the far side of the street, and stared in amazement at the carriage. The window in back showed only one head, so she was alone. She must be a rich man's wife, or on her way to a late Mass. A wave of dizziness came over him, and he reached toward a post for support. I've got to get something to eat, before I fall down, he thought worriedly. He took a deep breath, and advanced slowly over the sidewalk. The carriage rolled toward the bright lights at the center of town, the driver hunched on his seat atop the cab. Duane remembered the rich lady's face—oval, sad, contemplative. She's an angel, he thought. Her husband is a lucky man.

Duane wondered what it would be like to actually *live* with a beautiful woman, and sleep with her every night, performing all the delicious acts he'd dreamed about alone in the monastery. In his mind, life with a woman appeared more desirable than the Kingdom of Heaven itself. He felt a deep compelling need for feminine companionship, and knew he'd never be able to keep his hands off them. That's why he could never be a priest or brother. Women made him feel sweet inside, like the Christmas Midnight Mass.

Ahead was a sign that said:

CRYSTAL PALACE

Duane contemplated a steak dinner with all the trimmings, as he barged through the doors. Before him appeared another huge drinking and gambling establishment, with a long bar on the left, another on the right, tables in the middle, and a big black stove in back, spewing black smoke into the air.

The fragrance made Duane weak in the knees. Please Lord, let me find Boggs before I starve to death. He roamed among the tables, hoping to find the gnarled, weatherbeaten visage of his benefactor, but his heart sank with every passing moment. He saw a vast sea of cowboys, soldiers, freighters, gamblers, businessmen, and whores, but no Lester Boggs, cowboy at large.

Maybe he was here and left, Duane thought unhappily. Or maybe he had a few drinks, and doesn't even remember his own name, never mind mine. Duane's features sagged with the realization that he was hungry, as food was gobbled noisily all around him, but none for him.

His legs gave out, and he dropped onto a chair at a table with an empty glass beside a rusty tin can overflowing with cigarette butts. He wanted to be positive, but it wasn't easy with the miss-meal cramps. A few feet away, a man with a beard and an enormous gut slept next to a plate containing a half-eaten steak and a pile of oleaginous fried potatoes. Duane's mouth watered at the sight of the food. They'll throw it out with the garbage, but it could be a meal for me. I wonder if anybody'd notice if I . . . ? He glanced around, and everyone in his vicinity appeared busy with card games, arguments, and their own meals. One man rose unsteadily to his feet and hollered, "To Bobby Lee!"

A roar went up from everyone in the saloon, as glasses were hoisted in the air, while others sprawled in drunken stupors, and wouldn't stir if a horse came crashing through the ceiling. His eyes focused on the half-gnawed steak beckoning to him from the plate. Duane had the peculiar sensation that his stomach was glued to his backbone, as he fretted on the chair, pondering the consequences of sin. It's better to starve than burn forever in the fires of hell, but does God really care about that piece of meat over there?

He looked to the left and right, and everyone appeared preoccupied with card games, newspapers, great debates, or glasses of whiskey. Slowly, casually, Duane rose to his feet, whistled a tune, looked at the ceiling, sniffed the air, and then lunged for the piece of meat on the plate. He thrust it beneath his left armpit, and headed for the door.

Oh God, thank you for the blessings of this meal, he said silently. If ever I get any money, I'll give half to the poor, I promise. He made his way among boisterous throngs, heading for the planked sidewalk outside, when a figure loomed out of the smoke before him. A hefty man in a fancy red shirt, wearing a gun, pointed his big sausage finger at Duane. "I saw that."

Duane wanted to flee in the opposite direction, but the man grabbed his lapel, reached under his armpit, and pulled out the guilty steak. "We don't like scavengers in here." He tossed the steak into the nearest filth-encrusted spittoon, and putrid substances splashed onto the floor. "This ain't no charity ward. Get the fuck out've here."

The bouncer pushed him toward the door, Duane stumbled over his feet, received a solid kick in the posterior, and went flying through the air. He landed in the street next to a palomino gelding munching hay. The horse turned his great head and looked reproachfully at Duane, as if to say, If you hang out in saloons, what do you expect.

Duane picked himself up from the muck and manure of the street. The bouncer's response seemed morally inadequate in the former acolyte's theological mind, and he felt like going back and giving him a piece of his mind. He may be bigger than I, but so was Jasper Jakes, he thought angrily.

He pulled a pebble from beneath his toes, as deep hunger radiated from his stomach. He knew he had to find a job quickly, otherwise he was going to starve to death. He heard the faint sound of a woman singing across the street in the Round-Up Saloon. Duane was sensitive to the timber of the human voice, for he'd sung religious songs practically since he could walk. He found himself captivated by the purity of her tone, not to mention her delicate phrasing. Distracted from his concave stomach, he wondered what she looked like.

He waited for five cowboys on horseback to pass, then crossed the street. He couldn't discern the words of the song, but she sounded as if she'd lost something valuable. The window was covered with grime, and Duane rubbed a clean spot with the palm of his hand, then leaned forward and peered into the saloon.

It was similar to the previous ones he'd seen, with one important difference. Instead of a chop counter in back, it had a stage, and on it, standing beside a man plunking a piano, stood a woman with a familiar and haunting face.

It was the Madonna of La Salette whom he'd seen earlier in the carriage, her face framed by long blond hair. She gesticulated gracefully with dovelike hands, wore a long green and white dress with flounces and tassels, and sang the sad tale of a soldier who died gloriously in the war.

Duane forgot his hunger, as he stared at the golden goddess with the dulcet voice. It was as though she were revealing the innermost secrets of her heart, her voice flowing like ambrosia out the doors of the Round-Up Saloon. "She's so beautiful," Duane whispered.

"Ain't that the truth," said a voice next to him.

Duane turned to a short cowboy with a long black

beard, wearing a tattered hat, the inevitable flask of whiskey in his hand.

"Who is she?" Duane asked, returning his eyes to the vision of heaven warbling on the brightly lit stage.

The cowboy spat something brown and grisly onto the sidewalk. "That's Vanessa Fontaine, and you ain't got 'nough money to smell her underwears, so fergit it. She's the girlfriend of the richest man in town."

"Is she a prostitute?" Duane asked, surprised.

"Ain't they all?" The man raised the bottle in the air. "Care fer a snort?"

"I don't drink."

"Whydahellnot?"

"They say it's bad for you."

The man pounded his hairy fist against his chest, and it sounded like a bass drum. "I been a-drinkin' since I was borned, an' I can still whup my weight in Commanches. Here!"

He held out the bottle, and Duane didn't want to insult the cowboy, but neither did he want to drink the devil's potion. A few drops can't kill me, he rationalized, curious to know why men craved whiskey.

He reached for the bottle, and let a small amount roll over his tongue. It tasted odd, not bad at all, but then suddenly a hidden match set it aflame. His eyes watered, he coughed, and the cowboy snatched the bottle from his hand, lest he spill a drop. Blinded with tears, Duane collided with someone walking swiftly from the opposite direction.

"Git out'n my way!"

Duane was pushed hard, and felt himself flailing through the air. He crashed into the hitching rail, somersaulted over it, and landed in the water trough. The horses shied back, jolted from their night torpor, as Duane's head bobbed to the surface. He spit out a stream of water, looked at the man who'd tossed him aside like a pile of old rags, and wasn't surprised to note that it was Jethro, the same brute who'd thrown him against the wall of the Longhorn Saloon about an hour ago. Jethro pushed open the doors of the Black Cat Saloon, and disappeared.

Duane sloshed water onto the planked sidewalk, as he climbed out of the trough. It reminded him of when Jasper Jakes had insulted him before everyone in the dining hall. If somebody stood up to this cowboy, the way I stood up to Jasper Jakes, he thought heatedly, maybe he'd stop pushing people around. Duane felt the temperature rise beneath his soaking clothes. I'm not going to let him, or anybody else, push me around ever again, and I don't care how big they are, he vowed.

Duane hated to be treated like garbage, because it confirmed his worst doubts about himself. He wasn't afraid of bigger opponents, because he'd learned that they move slowly, with much wide-open territory, but if they landed a solid shot, you're out like a light. Duane shoved open the doors of the Black Cat Saloon, and stepped out of the light from the back. It had no stage, and Jethro stood at the bar, quaffing a mug of beer. If he thinks he can push me around, he's got another think coming, he hissed silently. He'll regret the day he ever set eyes on me. Duane didn't feel like a poor little orphan boy anymore, but a young stud looking to kick ass.

Duane was infuriated by the insult, and his rational thought processes clicked off. He headed for the bar, passing poker players, newspaper readers, and men selling horses and cows. Resentment oozed out his pores, as his eyes fixed on the big cowboy at the bar. I'll smack that mug of beer down his throat, Duane thought, prodding himself onward. Nobody tosses me into a horse trough and gets away with it. By the time he reached the bar, he was ready to roll. He grabbed Jethro's shoulder, spun him around, and whacked the mug out of his hand.

Cold bubbling liquid flew through the air, spraying over nearby customers, who fled out of the way. Jethro took two steps backward, blinking, wiping stinging beer out of his eyes. The Black Cat went silent, as every eye turned toward the bar.

They saw a big, broad-shouldered cowboy and a slim, disheveled young man soaking wet and dripping onto the floor, although it hadn't rained for a week. The spectators stood for a better view, because it looked as though the main attraction was about to begin.

Jethro had been drinking since noon, and didn't believe he'd ever seen Duane before. He raised his paws, an expression of malevolent evil coming over his face, and then he lunged toward Duane, but Duane dodged quickly to the side.

Jethro tried to follow Duane, cocked his left hand, and prepared to throw a jab, but simultaneously lowered his right hand slightly. Duane spotted the opening, and shot a straight right over the top, with all of his one hundred and fifty-three pounds behind it. His fist streaked forward, landed on Jethro's nose, as cartilage crunched, and blood spurted beneath Duane's knuckles.

The crowd roared, Jethro reeled backward, and Duane was astonished by the effectiveness of the blow. He stared at Jethro, who appeared confused, wiping blood off his nose with the back of his hand. Duane happened to notice the immensity of Jethro's shoulders, his barrel chest, and hamlike fists. What a punch I must have, Duane pondered.

Meanwhile, Jethro's face flashed deep, insatiable vengeance. Duane realized, with mounting concern, that his opponent was no overgrown schoolboy, but a gigantic fully matured beast with mayhem in his heart. For the first time since landing in the water trough, Duane put himself into perspective.

Jethro launched a right toward Duane's head. Duane raised his arm to block the blow, and it felt like a sledgehammer. His brains rattled in his head as he tried to dance away, his shoulder feeling dislocated. Jethro stalked him, a determined expression on his countenance, and blood dripping from his nose. He feinted a left jab, as Duane tried to dodge out of the way, and walked into a right cross like the freight train from St. Louis.

Everything went black. Duane heard bells and birds, and when he opened his eyes, he was lying on his back in a puddle of bilious substances spilled from the nearby spittoon. The immense gnarled face of Jethro appeared above him, and Duane felt himself being lifted into the air by the front of his shirt.

Jethro raised him slowly, while drawing his right fist back for the final blow. The crowd watched in morbid fascination at the cowboy giant and the limp young man in his grasp. Duane knew what was coming, but was paralyzed by the earlier blows.

"You little fuck," Jethro snarled. "I'll teach you to mess with me."

The fist zoomed forward, and grew larger in Duane's eyes. It landed on Duane's cheek, and Duane's lights went out once more. He soared through the air, crashed against the bat-wing doors, and landed with his face in a pile of muck at the curb, where he lay still for a long time.

CHAPTER 2

"YOU ALL RIGHT, KID?"

Duane opened his eyes. He lay in the street, and it felt as if a balloon had take up residence underneath his left cheek. "Where am I?"

"You just got the shit kicked out of you."

Duane tried to focus on a skull-like face with a cheroot stuck between the teeth. It looked familiar, but it definitely wasn't the face of Brother Paolo. Duane glanced around, expecting to see familiar monastery buildings, but instead saw the main street of Titusville. His ribs felt broken, and his head throbbed with pain.

"You're not going to die on me, are you?" the face asked. "Don't you remember me? I'm Clyde Butterfield, and I told you to buy a gun. You'd better get out of the street before a wagon runs you over."

The dapper gentleman helped Duane to his feet, and maneuvered him toward the sidewalk. Duane's legs were uncoordinated, he felt sick to his stomach, and an elf pounded a chisel into his brain. He dropped heavily onto the bench in front of the Black Cat Saloon. Butterfield withdrew a flask from inside his frock coat and held it out to Duane.

"I don't drink," Duane said, as he located new agony in his neck.

"Wake you right up."

Duane's head was full of fog, and the sidewalk undulated before his eyes. He took the flask, tipped it back, and swallowed a small amount. For the first three seconds, it was mellow and smooth, and then became liquid flames down his throat. He coughed, hacked, and spit up blood.

"To tell you the truth," Butterfield said, "I'm surprised he didn't kill you. He hit you so hard, I thought your skull would bust apart."

Duane touched his nose to make sure it still was there. His jaw felt loose on its hinges, and he was certain that his rib cage had been caved in. "Naw, he didn't kill me," Duane replied, trying to be brave, but he winced, and his voice came out in squeaks. It hurt when he breathed.

"You had him, but you let him off the hook. If you'd stayed after him, you would've beat him, instead of the other way around."

Duane recalled the initial stage of the fight, when he'd bloodied Jethro's nose, then stopped to assess the damage.

"If you ever hurt your man," Butterfield confided, "finish him off, and think it over afterward. Want a smoke?"

"Don't smoke."

Butterfield puffed his long, thin cheroot, gazing askance at Duane. Then he reached into his pocket and pulled out a handful of coins. "Get yourself a good meal, then find a bath and a hotel room. I'll meet you tomorrow night at the Crystal Palace, and we'll discuss your future."

Duane looked at the coins, and thought he heard pity, or was it disdain, in Butterfield's voice. A flush of bad temper came over Duane, and he slapped Butterfield's hand. The coins went flying in the air, and Butterfield made a motion toward his gun.

Duane limped away, bending slightly to favor his aching ribs. He came to an alley, and absentmindedly turned into it. A group of cowboys threw dice at the side of the building, and everybody held a bottle. Duane sidestepped around them, and made his way toward the backyard. The shame of defeat hurt worse than the pain in his head and chest, and he ground his teeth angrily.

Butterfield was right, he admitted. I should've stayed after him, but I had to admire my handiwork, like an idiot. He came to the backyard, and saw sheds, privies, and piles of trash. No one was around, and he slipped into the shadows at the side of a building, sat on the ground, and wondered what to do next.

I've been in Titusville approximately four hours, and so far I've been robbed, beaten, insulted, and humiliated, he thought dejectedly. I'm supposed to be looking for a job, but instead I got into a fight with a man twice my size, and I could be the hero of the Black Cat Saloon right now, except I didn't have the guts to finish him off.

He recalled the moment he'd smashed Jethro in the nose. A few more solid punches to the head—that's all it'd require. I've been out of the monastery a week, and already I'm thinking of beating people, Duane thought ruefully. I can't be a very intelligent person, if this is the direction my mind takes.

For all I know, Jethro's an orphan, too, and something's hurting him inside, just like me. If I were a true Christian, I would've turned the other cheek. Maybe I should go back to the monastery, apologize profusely, take the vows, and become a brother, he speculated.

He recalled the serenity of the monastery in the clouds, where few people ever visited, and mountain winds whistled through the steeple of their little chapel. His life had been orderly, and he'd studied hard. That's where I belong, not this filthy hellhole, he said to himself.

He recalled the impression of Jethro's boot squashing his hindquarters, not to mention Jethro's fist crashing into his cranium. What about justice and free will? Duane wondered. Does he have the right to kick me in the ass, just because I'm in his way? I don't kick people in the ass. Somebody had to stop him, and it happened to be me!

He dropped to the next level of reflection. But he's so much bigger than I, and fighting is wrong in the first place. I've already broken countless commandments, and if I had a few dollars in my pocket, I'd probably wallow in prostitutes like the pig that I am.

I'm a sinner, he admitted. Just like every other poor fool in the world. I've just had the stuffing beat out of me, and I'm starving to death. I should've had a job by now, but I've been doing everything wrong.

He heard the sound of a wagon, and became still in the shadows. The conveyance approached through a far alley, and he could perceive lamplights flickering on its sides. In the moonlight, he saw the same fancy carriage he'd noticed easier, the one belonging to the singer, Vanessa Fontaine. The carriage appeared headed toward the rear of the Round-Up Saloon.

I guess he's going to drive her home, Duane thought. Maybe I can see her close up. He advanced across the yard, and dropped behind the first trash barrel. The driver appeared to be dozing, but the two horses' ears perked up at the sound of Duane's muffled footsteps. Their huge luminescent eyes followed his progress around the perimeter of the buildings, until finally he came to a stop behind a stack of firewood near the rear door of the saloon.

She might not come out for another three hours, Duane told himself, and I'm supposed to be looking for a job. Just as he was about to head for the nearest saloon, he heard a peal of woman's laughter erupt from the depths of the establishment.

The sound sent a chill up his back, and he wished he had a clean, sweet-smelling woman to kiss. He recalled Vanessa Fontaine on the stage of the saloon, trilling her tale of love. He felt woozy. He rested his head against the firewood, and he took a few deep breaths to clear his mind.

His eyes fell on a trash barrel, and he thought, I'll bet it's full of steaks that the customers were too drunk to eat. I'll just wash one off in the horse trough and have me a meal. But then his eyes caught movement near the barrel, and his hair stood on end. Creatures with bright little eyes, plump furry bodies, and long skinny tails, scurried about, nibbling tidbits. Duane lost his appetite immediately.

The back door of the saloon opened. Duane raised his head above the firewood, and saw a man in a vest step outside, gun in hand, looking both ways. Another man appeared, holding the arm of Vanessa Fontaine. The men led her toward the carriage, as the driver jumped to the ground.

Duane realized that Vanessa Fontaine was tall for a woman, built on the slim side, just as he. Moonlight silhouetted her profile, revealing a gently curved nose and blond hair beneath the hood of her black cape. Duane had never seen anything like her among the girls who came to the monastery. They'd been farmers' daughters in plain homespun dresses, but Vanessa Fontaine looked like a celestial creature from another realm.

She entered the cab, and the driver climbed onto his seat. He snapped his whip, and the matched white horses headed toward the street. Duane found himself moving toward the alley, following the carriage. He saw the outline of her head through the back window, and wondered what kind of person she was.

He drank water from the trough in front of the hitching rail, and felt stronger. I'll see where she lives, just for the fun of it, and then I'll come back and look for a job. Or maybe I'll go out on the sage and trap a rabbit.

He felt revived, as he moved along the sidewalk, passing men sleeping on benches, in alleys. One stalwart fellow was out cold in the middle of the sidewalk. Duane stepped over him, as the coach turned left at the next corner, and Duane followed like a lean hungry wolf of the night.

Lanterns on the carriage vied with the moon for lighting the way, but all other lamps were out in the increasingly residential street. They came to a neighborhood of larger homes and more spacious yards, with wagons and carriages parked outside. Some houses were neatly painted, with white picket fences, while others were in varied states of construction. This is a growing town, Duane realized. Lots of potential here for a man like me.

Duane slipped through the shadows, as cool night wind blew in from the sage. The carriage turned right, and Duane followed it to a narrow road with only a few houses. The driver pulled his reins back, steering toward a two-story, boxlike structure sleeping in the night. Duane hopped the fence, landed behind a bush, and a dog barked across the street. The driver climbed down and opened the door.

The wraith in black shawl emerged from the carriage, and moonlight glinted on her golden hair. She fairly flew to the front door, opened it, and was gone. A lamp was lit inside the residence, sending pale yellow rays through the windows. Duane heard something crash, as the singer rattled a string of outrageous curses in a strange lilting drawl.

A door slammed, and it seemed as if the whole house shook. Duane was fascinated by her behavior, for he'd grown up without women, and they were strange alien beings to him. The women who'd visited the monastery had been devout Catholics, whereas this woman evidently was Jezebel herself!

Duane felt nauseated, and weakness came over

him. I've got to get something to eat, he reminded himself. The lamp went out in the house just as he was about to rise. He lowered himself as she burst onto the porch and ran toward the carriage, holding her skirts in the air.

The driver opened the door for her, and she said: "Hurry, because I'm late."

She stepped into the backseat, the driver lashed the horses, and the sleek animals pulled the carriage away from the curb. Galloping hoofbeats could be heard, as the contrivance rumbled toward the center of town.

Duane's vision blurred, and only the rapid deployment of his hands prevented his face from crashing into the dirt. Black curtains fluttered before his eyes, and the tinkling of bells came to his ears. He tried to rise, but fell on his butt. I'm liable to die on her lawn, if I don't get something to eat soon.

His system weakened by inadequate nutrition, a vicious beating, and a few swallows of rotgut whiskey, he tried to stand, but his knees were wobbly. I'll never make it to town, and I'll bet her kitchen is stocked full of food. His mouth watered as he imagined sliced beef, roast chickens, fried potatoes, sliced tomatoes, mounds of rice, and pies bursting with apples and cinnamon. I wonder if her back door is locked?

Duane glanced around, and all was still. The nearest house was fifty yards away, completely darkened. Duane crept over the scraggly lawn, heading toward the rear of the house. He drooled uncontrollably, and felt like fainting. I'll only take food, and I'm sure she can afford it, he rationalized. You don't want me to die, do you, God?

Prodded by hunger, he arrived at the back door,

twisted the knob, but it was locked from the inside. He tried to open a window, but it, too, was latched. Duane peeled off his tattered frock coat, wrapped it around a rock, and pushed it firmly against the window.

The glass broke, shards fell to the floor inside, and a dog barked across the way. Duane vowed to run if he saw a lantern, but the dog stopped barking, and passed to his whining phase. No lanterns could be seen. Duane returned to his broken window, reached inside, and flipped the latch. Then, slowly, he raised the window. He jumped into the air, bellied over the sill, and landed on the floor inside, next to the kitchen table.

A bowl of fruit was positioned on a doily in the middle of the table, and Duane grabbed an apple. He stuffed it into his mouth hungrily, chewing even the seeds. A tin breadbox on the counter became his next objective. He pried the top off, and saw a half loaf of bread with several corn muffins. He grabbed a muffin in his fist and mashed it whole into his mouth, chewing like a fanatic.

The doughy substance thickened in his throat, and he nearly gagged. He opened the front door of the wood icebox, groped inside, and his hand fell on half a chicken. He pulled it out and dug his fangs into the moist white breast. Chewing frantically, he darted around the kitchen, searching for liquid to wash it all down.

A sliver of light flickered on something in the hallway. Gnawing on the chicken, Duane proceeded down the hall to the next room, which had upholstered chairs, a sofa, and a fireplace. The twinkle came from the top of a cabinet crafted from dark wood.

He bent before it, and was amazed to see tiny statues of unicorns made from gold, silver, and crystal, with Vanessa Fontaine's necklaces and bracelets draped over their horns, while earrings sprawled among their hooves.

It looked like fairyland, and Duane stopped chewing for the first time since breaking into the house. He wondered what kind of mind would concoct such a show. She's a little girl underneath it all, he realized. For the first time, it occurred to him that she might have a mind. He took a step backward, to see what else the room held.

His eyes widened on a painting four feet square hanging above the dresser. He leaned forward and feasted his eyes upon the image of Vanessa Fontaine, wearing a blue gown, standing against a backdrop of red roses. The likeness was almost real, and her big blue eyes seemed to be saying, Please don't rob me. Her reproachful eyes drilled into him, and he felt guilty for breaking into her home.

He heard a key in the front door, and his hair stood on end. He froze before the painting of Vanessa Fontaine, as a dainty foot made contact with the vestibule. Duane dove behind the sofa, as her footsteps approached. She headed for her jewelry, muttered something dark and incomprehensible, and began clawing among the unicorns. "Where the hell's that necklace?" she murmured.

Duane peered around the end of the sofa, as she fussed and puffed at the cabinet, knocking over unicorns, opening drawers. He hoped she wouldn't look down, where he'd dropped a spare chicken bone. His heart beat like a tom-tom, and he broke into a cold sweat at the mere thought of jail.

Suddenly she went stiff, and he realized that she'd spotted the chicken bone, only a few feet from an apple core that he'd also lost track of. He pulled his head back swiftly as she spun around, eyes ablaze with fear. She pulled up her dress, whipped out a derringer, cocked the hammer, and said, "Who the hell's here?"

She's caught me, Duane thought, as his lungs emptied of air. Oh my God, if you get me out of this one, I'll go back to the monastery and sing your praise for the rest of my stupid existence. He heard her footsteps approach, and knew he was finished. "I didn't mean any harm," he said weakly.

"Show me your hands, or I'll put a bullet into you—so help me, Jesus."

He thrust his arms into the air, and she blinked in disbelief, her jaw agape. But she kept the derringer aimed with both hands at the center of his chest.

"Come out of there, and don't make any funny moves."

He gazed into the over-and-under barrels of the derringer. "I wasn't going to take anything valuable. I haven't eaten since morning, and I was getting hungry. It was just some chicken, a few apples, and all your corn muffins. As soon as I get a job, I'll pay you back."

All my corn muffins? Her forehead wrinkled with mystification. She glanced at the top of the dresser, where she kept her jewelry, and knew each piece intimately; they were her favorite possessions, but nothing was missing, not even a unicorn. She turned toward the young man, and he was pale, cadaverous, raw-boned, with long black sideburns and velvet eyes almost as beautiful as a woman's. Her eyes roved down his filthy garments, and his filthy feet dwelled in crude leather sandals. She glanced back at his face, and it looked as though someone had beaten the hell out of him recently. How old are you?" she asked.

"Nearly eighteen."

"Where are your folks?"

Duane turned his eyes away. "Killed in a Commanche raid."

He looks like a lost little kid, she considered, and those clothes are pathetic. She lowered her derringer. "All right—I won't call the deputy this time."

Duane's hands fell to his side, and his face became contrite. "When I looked at your picture over there, I knew I shouldn't have come here. It was as if you were talking to me."

"I was robbed in another town once," she replied dourly, "and that's why I had the painting done. If anybody wants to take what's mine, I want him to look me in the eye."

She still didn't know what to do with the burglar. He looked like a lost puppy dog. With a sigh of defeat, she raised the side of her dress, then dropped the derringer into its holster.

"You don't have any money at all?" she asked.

"Some boys robbed me."

"Where were you going to sleep tonight?"

"The Sagebrush Hotel."

He speaks well, she figured, and obviously has an education. "Where does your family live?"

"Everybody's dead," he admitted.

"How do you exist?"

"I was raised in a monastery, and left a couple of weeks ago."

A *monastery*? she wondered.

"I'll be on my way," he said. "I'll also pay you for the window that I broke. Do you know of any jobs?"

"What can you do?"

"I thought I'd become a cowboy, but I don't know how to ride a horse."

She smiled in spite of herself. No humbug could come up with a line like that, she figured. He appears innocent, untouched, special, and he was raised in a monastery? She couldn't help being curious about him. Dress him in decent clothes, he'd turn the heads of women old enough to know better, she concluded.

"You don't have to sleep outdoors," she said. "I've got a guest room, and you can stay here."

"Here?" he asked, wondering if he'd heard correctly. "With you?"

"Do you expect me to move out of my own home? But you'll have to take a bath first, because I can smell you all the way over here. Don't touch anything—I'll be right back."

She swooped toward the door, the ends of her black silk shawl trailing behind her. I hope this isn't another mistake, she thought, but somebody's got to help a young person in distress. She approached the carriage, and her driver, Jed Wilson, opened the door.

"My plans have changed," she said. "Tell Mister Petigru that I'm not feeling well."

Jed nodded sullenly, then hoisted himself atop the cab. Vanessa returned to her parlor, where the young man stood with his hands behind his back, staring at her painting. He blushed, and his fluttering eyelashes devastated her. "Don't you have shoes?"

He shook his head, embarrassed by insufficient footwear and ripped raiment.

"You're a mess," she said. "Come with me." She led him to the kitchen, where the floor was littered with corn muffin crumbs, broken glass, and more chicken bones. "I've got some wood out back. Do you know how to light a fire?"

He was out the door before she could ask another question. She sat near the window, and said to herself: I hope this isn't going to be another mistake.

Meanwhile, in the backyard, Duane wondered if he should make a run for it. He was afraid she'd call the deputy, and he didn't want to end up in jail. Firewood was stacked neatly in a shed, and he loaded up his arms. He recalled her finely chiseled profile, rosebud lips, and long legs. How can I spend the night under the same roof with that woman, and not go berserk? he questioned.

He returned to the kitchen, where she sat on the rocking chair in the corner, smoking a cigarette nervously. He dropped to his knee beside the stove, stuffed in paper and kindling, added firewood, and lit a match.

Crackling sounds could be heard. Duane set the drafts expertly, then worked the pump at the sink, filling pails with water. She watched beneath heavy-lidded eyes, and saw muscles straining against his clothes. He's an undernourished Adonis, she considered. "When'd you get out of the monastery?"

"About two weeks ago. Got tired of the life."

"Why'd you go to a monastery in the first place?"

"My folks were killed by Commanches when I was a baby, and that's where I ended up."

I can't believe that some voracious woman hasn't grabbed him by now, she mused. He carried the pails to the stove and arranged them over the flames, as perspiration glistened on his tanned features.

"Washtub's in the closet," she said.

He opened the door, pulled out the big tin tub, and set it on the floor near the stove. "You don't talk like the people around here," he told her. "Where are you from?"

"South Carolina," she replied, "but that was long ago—before the rebellion."

Duane knew about the rebellion, although there'd been no fighting near the monastery in the clouds.

"Why'd you pick *my* house to rob" she asked, "out of all the others in this neighborhood?"

"I saw you sing earlier, and followed you home. I didn't intend to rob you, but then I got hungry, and figured you could afford it." He forced himself to look at her face, and not hide his eyes in an obscure corner of the kitchen. "I thought you looked like the Madonna of La Salette."

"A lot of people in this town consider me a fallen woman, if you know what that is."

"I saw you at the Round-Up, and a feller told me that you're the girlfriend of the richest man in town."

"What else did he say about me?" she asked crossly.

"We were too busy listening to you. You have a beautiful voice, and perfect pitch."

"You can't put on those dirty clothes after you take a bath. I'll get you a sheet to wrap yourself in."

She left the kitchen in a swirl of perfume, and he felt dismayed. *She belongs to the richest man in town, and could never care for somebody like me.*

The black carriage stopped in front of the Carrington Arms, and Jed Wilson jumped to the ground. He tied the horses' reins to the hitching post, ducked underneath it, and landed on the sidewalk before the wide veranda.

It was mostly deserted now, along with surrounding sidewalks and alleys. Jed pulled out his pocket watch: nearly one in the morning. *Mister Petigru'll jump all over my ass,* he thought, *but it's not my fault.*

Jed was an ex-cowboy and former blacksmith now earning more money than ever as Vanessa Fontaine's stagecoach driver, bodyguard, and all-around errand boy. It was humiliating to take orders from a woman, but less demanding physically than roping and branding steers. Jed tended toward laziness and overindulgence in drink. He was pushing forty; time to settle down.

In the lobby, a drunkard sprawled on a chair, fast asleep, and another bedecked a sofa, his mouth open and his tongue hanging out, snoring loudly. Jed walked past the desk, and the clerk nodded to him. The carriage driver climbed to the third floor, and knocked on a door.

"About time you got here." Edgar Petigru, richest man in town, stood in his dimly lit suite of rooms, wearing a black satin smoking jacket. He was average height, nearing fifty, with short salt-and-pepper hair parted on the side. "Where's Miss Fontaine?"

"She said she's sick, and can't come tonight."

"Come on in."

Jed entered the suite, and saw a bottle of champagne in a brass bucket full of ice, while candlelight illuminated little sandwiches and delicacies atop the dresser.

"Care for a drink?" Petigru asked.

"Don't mind if I do."

Petigru indicated the bottles lined on a cabinet, and Jed poured three fingers of whiskey into a glass. Petigru reached into his pocket, took out a ten-dollar coin, and flipped it toward Jed, who caught it.

"Is she really sick?" Petigru asked.

"She looked fine to me."

"Keep an eye on her, and report back in the morning."

After Jed departed, Petigru wanted to throw the specially prepared food out the window. "Women," he muttered. "Drive a man out of his mind." He absentmindedly munched a chicken sandwich, as he wondered what Vanessa was up to this time.

Edgar Petigru had come West from New York City after the war, to make his fortune in cattle, land, and anything else he could turn into an honest or dishonest dollar. His grubstake came from his mother, who lived on Fifth Avenue.

It took him six months to reach Kansas, where he'd heard tales of vast wealth in Texas. Cattle herds had multiplied incredibly during the war, while the rest of the country was hungry for fresh meat. A steer that cost a few dollars in Texas could fetch twenty-four dollars at the railhead in Kansas.

It sounded like a hot proposition to Edgar, so

he'd journeyed to Texas, discovered Titusville, and began buying land. The first thing he built was a saloon, and he'd slept in back with the kegs of beer. His second and third buildings also were saloons, and soon he was running girls in addition to selling whiskey. Money began pouring it, and he invested in the hotel. One deal led to another, and then he bought the Lazy Y Ranch from an old reprobate who'd never married, and wanted to return East, where his folks lived.

In New York City, Petigru would be considered well-off, but in Titusville, he was the leading citizen, with the mayor and deputy sheriff in his pocket, along with nearly everyone else in town. I can have anything I want, except the one thing I need most, he thought wistfully. He gazed at the daguerreotype on the table beside him, and it showed Vanessa Fontaine posing on a chair, legs crossed, a smile on her face. Before she'd arrived, with her old rebel ball gowns and broken-down luggage, Edgar had slept with a succession of dance hall girls, and had come to enjoy their company. But Vanessa could play the piano and sing, and wanted to know if he could use an entertainer. He asked if she'd mind taking her clothes off for the boys, and she'd slapped his face royally.

At the moment of contact, he'd realized that she was an exceptional woman. Gradually he drew the story out of her. She'd been the daughter of a wealthy South Carolina planter, and they'd lost everything in the war. Her father committed suicide, her brother was killed at the front, so was her fiancé, while her mother died shortly thereafter. The spoiled belle was forced to earn her living in the cruel postwar South during

Reconstruction, where a former slave could become lieutenant governor.

She'd told Edgar that prior to the war, she'd taken piano lessons from a German professor who'd known Franz Liszt, and had sung in church choirs since she was little. All her life, people had been telling her that she had musical talent, and when the war ended, it was all that she had to sell. So she'd drifted West, singing old Confederate war songs in taverns, hotel drawing rooms, and saloons.

Petigru considered himself a connoisseur of women, and was surprised by such rare beauty on the frontier, where women aged quickly due to hard work and blistering sunlight. Back in New York, he'd seen actresses and heiresses from all over the world, and even had the pleasure of witnessing one of Jenny Lind's historic performances at the Castle Garden. He considered Vanessa Fontaine the equal of any woman he'd ever admired.

Their relationship had begun as employer and employee, but it wasn't long before he was madly and hopelessly in love with her. He paid her far more than the going rate, provided the coach, and even signed over the house to her, so she wouldn't have to feel insecure about having a roof over her head.

Everyone in town thought she was his women, but no one knew the truth. He loved her, but she didn't love him. He felt certain that one day she'd appreciate him, for he was a cultured person from the upper classes, like her. What else was there for her to choose? A rowdy, drunken cowboy?

*　　*　　*

Duane lay in the tub, warm water washing over him. He felt soothed, his belly full, and a gorgeous woman sat in the next room.

Her voice came to him. "Have you fallen asleep?"

He dried himself and wrapped the sheet around him. Holding it like a robe, he walked barefooted to the dining room. She sat at the table, with slices of cold meat, cheese, a loaf of bread, and a bottle of wine. "Have something to eat," she said.

He proceeded to consume sandwiches hungrily, as she observed him through guarded eyes. Not fully grown, probably a six-footer in another year or two. His skin is smoother than mine, his nose straighter, and his face is flawless, except for the bruises, she observe.

"You've been in a fight?" she asked.

He nodded, chewing a mouthful of food. "I lost, but a fellow said I could've won if I stayed after my man."

"What'd you fight about?"

"Somebody pushed me."

She reached under her skirt, pulled out the derringer, and dropped it onto the table. "You should carry one of these."

He picked it up, and it was warm with her body heat, exuding her flowery fragrance. "I've never smelled ladies' perfume before."

"Get used to it, because I wear it all the time."

This toy can kill a man, he mused. The over-and-under barrels were gold-plated, and the grip inlaid with dark wood. He aimed it at a blue and white porcelain vase full of flowers.

"Don't pull the trigger," she warned.

He tested its weight in his hand, as she continued to observe him carefully. A typical man, they all
love guns, and give them half a chance, they'll start
a war on you, she thought. She leaned forward,
took the gun out of his hand, raised the side of her
dress, and deposited the weapon into its black
leather holster.

I can't have a boy like this around here, she realized. Sooner or later we'll end in bed, and God only
knows where that'll lead. He needs a momma, so I
guess that's what I'll have to be for a while. "If you're
going to find a job," she said, "you've got to start
early in the morning.

He stood at attention, thrust out his chest, and
intoned, "I'd like to thank you, Miss Fontaine, for
helping me out, and not calling the deputy. You can be
sure that I'll—"

She interrupted him. "If there's anything I can't
stand, it's a lecture. Go to bed, because I've got things
to think about."

Like a mummy in a white sheet, Duane moved
down the dark corridor, came to the guest room, lit
the lamp, and saw a bed four times as wide as his
cot in the monastery, covered with a striped Indian
blanket. He puffed up the pillow, turned off the
lamp, dropped to his knees, and clasped his hands
together.

"Dear Jesus, please shower your blessings upon
that woman out there, and please help me keep my
hands off her, so that I won't violate any of your commandments. And thank you for sending such a wonderful person into my life, to save me from
starvation." Then he mumbled an Our Father, Hail

Mary, and Glory Be, crossed himself, and crawled into the bed.

It was filled with the heady aroma of her perfume, almost as though she were under the covers with him, but when he reached for her, he was alone. The bed was softer than his straw cot at the monastery, as though he were floating on air. The guest bedroom seemed incredibly luxurious, unlike his plain cell, his only adornment a crucifix nailed to the wall.

I thought I was going to sleep outdoors, but now I'm living like a rich person. In the secular world, you can be robbed, see a killing, get the hell beat out you, and end up living with the most beautiful woman in the world, all in the same day, he told himself.

In the living room, Vanessa sat in her rocking chair, a glass of wine in her hand. It was silent down the hall, and she supposed that her guest had fallen asleep. I wonder what he'd do if I took off my clothes and crawled into bed with him?

He'd probably jump three feet into the air, she thought, and her lips creased in a smile. He wants to be a man, but looks like he's uncomfortable in his skin. She shook her head ruefully, because she knew that she couldn't seduce a mere boy. I've done some bad things in my day, but not that, she mused.

She turned toward the stand, and looked at a daguerreotype in a silver frame. It showed a young man with the twin bars of a captain on his shoulder, a faint blond mustache, and deep-set burning eyes. They'd been engaged to marry, but he'd died at Gettysburg, in the biggest cavalry battle of the war.

And now I'm living on the charity of a Yankee businessman. I've fallen a long way, she thought sadly.

Often, in the dark of night, she recalled the old family plantation, gala balls, hunts, dashing young men on their splendid horses. Now most of those laughing cavaliers were reposing beneath the soil of Virginia, while she was a high-class prostitute in the eyes of the world.

She'd slept with a man here or there, to fill her belly and move onto the next rung of the ladder. It was either that or put a bullet through her brain, and many times she'd given that special consideration, because the price of life had seemed awfully high.

She'd slept with a gambler, a banker twice her age, and a man who claimed to own a railroad, but she found out three days later that he'd lied. Once, out of loneliness, she'd slept with a piano player who was more friend than lover, and it wasn't something that she was proud of.

She'd shown up in Titusville on her last legs, but fortunately Edgar Petigru had helped her, and thus far she'd been able to keep him at bay. But he'd fallen in love with her, had asked her to marry him, and she was planning to go ahead with it. It was better than worrying about what would happen when she lost her looks and voice.

Vanessa fully intended to submit to Petigru, so that she'd never have to worry about money again. He was a smart businessman, and shared her love for music and art. She felt nothing for him, but had decided long ago, after Beauregard had been killed, that she could never love another man.

Although she'd slept with others, it hadn't been

like Beau. That was love, and Edgar Petigru something else entirely. She hadn't been with a man for pure fun since 1863, but now toyed lazily with the idea. I guess I'm not dead inside after all, she reflected. I should never've let that boy stay here, but it's too late now.

She felt sleepy from so much worry and concern. Leaving the dirty glasses for the maid, she picked up the lantern, headed down the corridor, as rays of moonlight fell like spears all around her. She slowed as she approached the guest room, blew out the lantern, tiptoed to the door, and opened it silently.

The room was dark, but she could perceive Duane's outline against the white sheets, sprawled on his back, his arms like Jesus on the cross. The covers had fallen off him, and she felt a mad urge to bury her teeth in his shoulder. A shiver passed through her, and she stepped back quickly. I don't need this complication, on top of my other complications, she chided herself.

Vanessa entered her bedroom, closed the door, and drew the drapes together. A town like this, a face like that—everyone'll be talking about him spending the night here. She relit the lamp, undressed in front of the mirror, and viewed herself critically. Every night she noticed a new wrinkle, sag, or bulge. If I don't get married soon, I may never be able to attract a man, she reminded herself.

She blew out the candle, crawled into bed, and hugged her pillow, thinking of the young man in the guest room. *Somebody's* got to look out for him, she tried to tell herself. Southern hospitality didn't end the night they burned Old Dixie down. I'm not Petigru's slave, or anybody else's. If I can't help a young man in need, what kind of world is this?

But she knew that she was lying. If he were a hunchback or midget she would've sent him away with a loaf of bread and a few dollars. I've got to stop thinking about him, she said silently, as she wrapped her long legs around her bedclothes. I'm going to get myself into deep trouble, if I don't settle down.

CHAPTER 3

DUANE OPENED HIS EYES, AND DIDN'T know whether he was in his cell at the monastery, a stagecoach stop, or a hotel room? French perfume arose from the pillow, and he visualized Vanessa Fontaine sipping wine in the darkness of her parlor. He felt electrified, as he contemplated her long, lean body, and breasts that could fill a man's hands.

Sunlight leaked through the drapes of the guest room. He had no idea of the time, but was mildly hungry. Somehow he couldn't get out of the warm comfortable bed. He bounced languidly a few times, and smiled at the continuing motion.

Now he understood thin straw mattresses in the monastery. A soft feather bed tempted a man to indolence and sins of the flesh. He thought of Vanessa sleeping beneath the same roof, entwined in her night-gown and Civil War dreams. I've got to move out of here, he prompted himself, otherwise I'm liable to do something unbelievably bad.

He exerted his remaining willpower, and sat up. Unfamiliar clothing was draped over the chair beside him. Black jeans, red shirt, yellow bandanna, and black leather belt with big brass buckle. Quickly, he dressed before the mirror, anxious to see how he looked. Everything fit too big, but he gave the general appearance of a cowboy, except he'd never seen a cowboy wearing sandals.

The house was filled with the aroma of fresh coffee. In the kitchen, a large-busted, middle-aged Negro woman worked at the stove.

"I guess you're the new house guest," she said. "Have a seat in the dining room. Are the clothes all right?"

"Best clothes I ever had," he admitted.

"I picked them out myself. My name's Annabelle."

"Duane Braddock."

"You're so pretty, you should've been born a girl."

Duane pondered her remark, as he padded toward the dining room. I should've been born a girl? He found *The Titusville Tribune* on the kitchen table, and the headline said:

SOUTHERN PACIFIC RAILROAD
SELECTS TITUSVILLE FOR NEW TERMINAL

Duane read the story with mounting interest. According to unnamed authoritative sources, a major railroad would be coming to Titusville soon, bringing prosperity to everyone in the region. Potential investors were advised to buy land and build businesses without delay, before prices soared. There were statements from the mayor, president of the town council, and numerous civic leaders. This sounds like a city on the move, Duane thought. I'm in the right place at the right time. If only I had money to invest.

He turned the page, and his eyes fell on a headline:

IMMENSE CONFLAGRATION!

A fire had killed several hundred people in Chicago, rendered ninety thousand homeless, and consumed two hundred million dollars in property. My God, thought Duane, reading forward as rapidly as his brain cells could assimilate information. The numbers staggered him. It was widely believed that the tragedy had begun in a barn.

He continued eagerly to peruse the paper, gleaning facts about shipwrecks, wars, plagues, and injustice in every corner of the globe. It shocked him, for he'd been sheltered from the vagaries of the secular world. Maybe I should become a priest after all, he speculated. A straw mattress isn't so bad, and I can live without women, can't I?

"Good morning, Duane."

Titusville's foremost celebrity walked stiffly into the dining room, smoking her first cigarette of the day, wearing an ankle-length pale violet gown, her long blond hair pulled back and tied with a ribbon. She was sleepy-eyed, pale, and carrying a pot of coffee. Annabelle followed with a platter of ham, eggs, grits, and freshly made corn muffins. Annabelle placed the food on the table, and Vanessa sat opposite Duane, crossing her legs.

Duane scrutinized the woman of his dreams after she got up in the morning, and she was glorious with her pale, almost translucent skin.

"It's not polite to stare at a woman in the morning," she said. "Have some coffee."

She poured black steaming liquid into his cup, and he noticed the fine bone structure of her hand. She appeared even slimmer and more fragile in the light, and then she coughed, touching her hand to her breast.

Duane brought his eyes to that portion of her anatomy. She wasn't large-bosomed like some of the Mexican girls who'd come to the monastery, but she wasn't deprived by any means, and Duane wondered what it would be like to rest his head between those delicious fruits.

Meanwhile, she glanced at him while he sipped his coffee, and was surprised by how mature he appeared in his new clothing. In the bright daylight, he didn't appear quite so cherubic. This is more man than boy, she realized. She perceived a trace of cruelty around his eyes, and maybe a glint of madness, too.

"Thanks for the duds," he said. "I shouldn't have any trouble getting a job dressed like this."

"Annabelle didn't buy boots or a hat, because we don't know your size. When you finish breakfast, you can go to town and pick them out yourself. Just tell the man to put them on my account."

Duane was stunned. "You mean I can buy a real cowboy hat, and real cowboy boots?"

"That's what you'll need if you're going to be a cowboy.

"But I don't know how to ride a horse!"

"Then we'll have to arrange lessons, won't we?"

"I can't afford riding lessons. First I'll have to get a job."

"You can pay me back later. I don't want you emptying cuspidors in one of those filthy damned saloons. Somebody's liable to shoot you for the fun of it."

She handed him a platter with four eggs, a slab of ham, and a stack of grits. It appeared a princely feast to one who'd eaten mainly tortillas and beans for the past seventeen years. Without a word, he dug into the food, trying to maintain basic table manners, but failing miserably.

She watched him eat, and he became the hungry little orphan boy who never got enough in his belly. You're here to help him, not take advantage of him, she told herself. His face will look like a saddlebag after a few years in the sun.

His big brown eyes looked up at her. "We're not kin, and you don't even know me. Why are you doing all this?"

"Somebody'd got to take care of lost kids."

So that's the way she sees me, he realized with consternation. I should go over there and grab her, then she'd know I'm not a kid. But somehow his legs wouldn't move. He thought the ceiling would fall if he tried to kiss her. Disconsolately, he resumed eating.

I've hurt his feelings, she realized. He scowled, with brows knit together, and looking like a gloomy schoolboy. She placed her hand on his. "I'm sorry."

"Don't like people feeling sorry for me," he muttered darkly.

The wildcats of the world will tear him to pieces, she thought, but I can't hold his hand every step of the way, and he has to learn for himself.

After breakfast, in her office, she wrote a note:

Dear Mr. Sullivan,
Please provide the bearer of this message
with anything he requires, and put it on my bill.

She handed the note to Duane, then opened a drawer in her desk, selected a twenty-dollar double eagle, and held it out to him. "You'll need pocket money, so take this."

Duane stared at the coin, unwilling to accept it, so she pressed it into his palm. "Get out of here—I've got work to do. Just make sure I don't have to look at those horrible sandals anymore, understand?"

Duane passed the kitchen on his way out, and found Annabelle washing dishes in the sink. "I want to talk with you," she said, a stern tone in her voice. She dried her hands on a towel, then turned toward him and pointed her dark brown forefinger at his face. "Now you be careful when you're in town today, hear? There's lots of bad men here, so don't get into no more fights. And you'd better leave by the back door, 'cause we don't want neighbors' tongues to wag more than they do already."

Duane departed through the kitchen door, and raised his hand to shield his eyes from the sun. Across the way, a middle-aged woman was hanging wet bloomers on a clothesline, and Duane hoped she didn't see him. He veered around the house and headed for the street, hands in his pockets, whistling a Gregorian chant. This is going to be a great day, he thought. I can feel it in my bones.

The woman across the way was Mrs. Florence MacGillicuddy, wife of a lawyer. Why that low hussy, she thought, placing her fists on her hips. And in broad daylight, too. She thought that she'd better tell Mrs. Washington, her next-door neighbor, of the new dimension of sin that had descended upon the neighborhood.

Meanwhile, in the small barn behind Vanessa's home, Jed Wilson sat on his cot, looking out the window at the young man in black jeans heading toward the street. Did that whippersnapper spend the night with Miss Vanessa? he wondered. I'll bet old Petigru will hit the ceiling when he finds out. He tossed his coffee cup into the wash basin, put on his cowboy hat, and headed for the door.

Duane walked toward the commercial district, and thought about Vanessa Fontaine. Women were alien beings to him, and it was difficult to divine what transpired in their inscrutable minds. A hot flash came over him at the mere thought of touching her naked body. I've got to view her as the Madonna of La Salette, he admonished himself. And I must move out of her house as quickly as possible. He thought of her narrow waist, surging breasts, and long, lissome legs. I guess I'm crazy about her, like everybody else in this town, he concluded.

He wasn't sure about his feelings, because all he knew of love was what he'd read in books at the scriptorium by Sir Walter Scott, Robert Burns, and Charles Dickens, among others. From them he'd learned that men and women sometimes developed overpowering feelings of desire that even drove them to murder!

His eyes fell on a sign that said:

SULLIVAN'S HABERDASHERY

He crossed the street, dodged a wagon piled high with stench-ridden buffalo hides, and on the other side, a few drunkards were passed out on a bench, adding their own special aroma to the atmosphere. He opened the door of the haberdashery, a large, cool room smelling of leather and wool, with clothing hanging from pegs on the walls, boots displayed on a rack, and hatboxes stacked on shelves. A man with white hair parted down the middle stood behind the counter, adding a row of numbers. "Can I help you?"

"Are you Mister Sullivan?"

"As far as I know."

Duane handed him the note, which Mr. Sullivan scanned quickly. Then the entrepreneur smiled genially. "What would you like?"

"Hat and pair of boots."

Mr. Sullivan led him to a corner of the store, wrapped a tape measure around his head, and took down a box. "I think this would suit you just fine."

The hat was black, with a flat brim, black leather neck strap, and a hatband of silver conchos tied together with a black leather thong. "I don't think so," Duane replied. "I might be in Indian territory some day, and those conchos could be seen for a hundred miles."

"When yer in Injun territory, just take 'em off." Mr. Sullivan untied the leather thong and removed the silver disks from the crown. "Drop 'em into your saddlebags, and when you come to the next town, tie em on again. Let me tell ya—this is the kind of hat the girls notice. That hatband was made by an Apache princess, and it's one of a kind. Put it on—see if you like it."

"I'd wanted a white cowboy hat."

"I'll get one down, but in the meantime, try that fer size."

The black hat appeared well made, the brim wide enough to keep sun and rain off him. He put it on, tilted it rakishly to the side, positioned the strap beneath his chin, and walked to the full-length mirror.

A desperado stood before him, light shining off the silver hatband, and he smiled in recognition of himself. Maybe people'll leave me alone, when they see me in this hat.

"Here's a white one," said Sullivan, proffering a ten-gallon sombrero similar to the one Duane had seen in the window the night before.

Duane dropped it square on his head, and saw an awkward farm boy, the kind of bumpkin that cardsharps cheated, and whores swindled. "Let me try on the black one again."

They swapped hats, and Duane positioned the black one low over his eyes. If I saw myself walking down the street, I'd run for my life, he thought. "I'll take it," he drawled, trying to sound like an old, experienced cowpuncher. "Now I'll need me a pair of boots."

"Have a seat, and take off them things yer wearin'."

Duane glanced at himself again in the mirror. The hat went with his black jeans, and now all he needed were black boots to complete the picture. Mr. Sullivan brought two rectangular sheets of paper and a pencil, and bowed before Duane like an choirboy at Mass. He placed Duane's left foot on one sheet of paper, traced around it, then repeated the process with Duane's other foot.

"Takes about two weeks," Mr. Sullivan said. "What color you want."

"Black, but do I have to wait that long? I need a pair of boots now."

The storekeeper raised his eyebrows in disdain. "We only sell custom-made boots here. Ready-mades ain't worth a damn anyway. How can a man in Austin know yer feet?"

"But I can't wear these sandals anymore," Duane replied. "They're no good for anything."

Sullivan snapped his fingers. "Just a minute!" He studied the outlines he'd just made of Duane's feet. "Hmmm. Well, I might have something, but how do you feel about wearing a dead man's boots?"

"Dead man's boots?" Duane asked. "What'd he die of?"

"He's the feller what got shot last night by Saul Klevins. He ordered the boots, but ain't never worn 'em. Put on a thick pair of wool socks, and they might fit fine."

The storekeeper propelled himself toward his vast array of boxes, and Duane asked himself: Do I want to wear a dead man's boots? He recalled the shooting in front of the Longhorn Saloon. A man died before his very eyes, and the killer got free drinks.

Mr. Sullivan appeared with wool stockings and a pair of plain brown work boots with high cowboy heels and round tops.

"I wanted black," Duane explained.

"You work in 'em for a while, they'll turn black—don't worry. The main thing is the fit. Put on the stockings."

Duane pulled them on, and then tried one of the boots. It slid over his heel easily, then he tucked in his new pants cavalry style, and wiggled his toes. "Feels loose."

"You'll be glad after a day's work, and your feet swell up. Put on the other one and take a few steps, because you really can't tell sitting down."

Duane thrust his foot into the other boot, headed toward the mirror, and nearly pitched onto his face. He'd never walked in raised heels, but they gave him the special cowboy swagger that he so admired. He hooked his thumbs in the front pockets of his jeans and looked at himself in the mirror. "Isn't it bad luck to wear the boots of a dead man?"

"I'll give 'em to you fer half price, since the original owner ain't never gonna claim 'em, poor son of a bitch. He should never've gone outside with Saul Klevins, because Saul Klevins is a cold-blooded killer, and he does it fer a living."

"Do you sell guns?"

"Gunsmith's down the street."

Duane pulled his hat lower over his eyes, and changed position in front of the mirror. "Do you know where I could get horse-riding lessons?"

"How come you don't know how to ride a horse?"

Duane didn't want to retail the old monastery story again. "I'm from the East," he lied.

Sullivan screwed up an eye. "You don't sound like yer from the East, but you want to ride horses, you should git a job in a stable, or on a ranch. We don't have no schools for horseback riders in Titusville."

Duane ambled out of the store, leaning from side to side like a real cowboy. Down the street, he spotted a sign that said:

GUNSMITH

Hoofbeats clattered, the odor of manure was in the air. Duane promenaded toward the front window of the gunsmith's shop, and saw pistols, rifles, derringers, gun belts, rifles, and shotguns. When I get some money, I'll ask somebody to help me pick one out, he told himself.

A head crowned with a shock of red hair craned around the door. "Lookin fer a gun, cowboy?" The gunsmith wore chin whiskers, white collar, and a string tie.

Duane felt flattered that someone had called him a cowboy. He thrust out his chest and said in a deep voice, "As a matter of fact, I was."

"Then come on in, and I'll show you the latest advances in the modern pistol, plus I have a fine collection of Sharps buffalo guns, and you know that there's fortunes in buffalo skins just north of here." He ushered Duane into the store, and inclined him toward a case full of guns with shiny grips of wood and ivory, carved in designs of horses, eagles, sunbursts, and the lone star insignia of the great state of Texas. "What you say yer name was, cowboy?"

"Braddock."

"I'm Cal Saunders. Braddock? Seems I heard that name before. Your family in the storekeeper business?"

"Not that I know of."

"Seen the new Remingtons?" He reached into the case and pulled out an unadorned six-shooter with bright metal barrel and plain wooden grips. "Some say that the Colt is the best gun made, but for my money, I'll take a Remington any day. You see that strap of metal on top? It makes it strong, whereas the Colt is held together by two little wedges at the bottom. The Remington is a much finer weapon, and I think you'll like the balance."

Saunders held out the Remington, and Duane took it in his fist. A pleasurable sensation passed up his arm, and he felt as if he'd become, for a second, a man in a black mustache.

"How does it feel?"

Duane raised the Remington, closed one eye, and lined up the V of the rear sight with the nub in front.

"What does it cost?"

"Fifteen dollars."

"And a holster?"

"Depends on which one you pick. I got all kinds."

Guns seemed a complicated science, and Duane

decided not to buy until he learned more. "Haven't made up my mind," he said. "Maybe I'll come back later."

"I can take a deposit, and hold the gun for you. These Remington's go like hotcakes after a shooting, like the one we had last night. You see it?"

Duane nodded, as he placed the gun on the counter.

"Braddock? Seems I know that name."

Duane leaned against the counter, scratched his cheek casually, and drawled, "There was an outlaw named Braddock once, but he was no relation of mine. Ever heard of him?"

The gunsmith wrinkled his brow. "Was he from Missouri?"

"Don't recall," Duane replied. "Got shot by a sheriff, I believe."

"Ain't that what happens to all of 'em?"

Duane waited, hoping for more information, but the merchant held up the Remington instead. "I'll give you the gun and a plain leather holster for eighteen dollars, and you'll never get a better deal than that. What do you say?"

Duane wanted to ask more questions about the outlaw named Braddock, but didn't want to appear obvious. "I'm not ready yet," Duane replied. "See you later."

"Anytime," the gunsmith said, a twinkle in his eye.

Duane walked out of the store, feeling strangely exhilarated. He'd liked the weight of the gun in his hand—solid chunk of machined metal. *I wonder if anybody in town gives shooting lessons?*

His eyes fell on a sign hanging over the sidewalk a few doors down:

LONGHORN SALOON

Maybe I should go in and strike up a conversation with a cowboy. Possibly I can hire somebody to give me riding lessons, he speculated. He elbowed through the swinging doors, stepped out of the light, and surveyed the scene before him, which was not much different from the crowd last night, except for fewer patrons. Above the bar, harem girls cavorted in their gigantic tub, waited on by Negro eunuchs in turbans. Duane found a space at the bar, placed his foot on the rail, and opened his mouth, but didn't know what to say to the bartender a few feet away. I can't drink whiskey, Duane cogitated, because whiskey will kill me, but they'll laugh if I order sarsaparilla. If I'm going to be a cowboy, I'd better start living like one.

"What's yer pleasure?" asked the bartender impatiently. He wore a dirty white apron and a black patch over one eye.

"Whiskey," Duane replied.

The bartender plucked a small glass from beneath the bar, dropped it before Duane, and filled it half full of murky brown fluid. Duane reached into his pocket, and flipped the twenty-dollar double eagle at the bartender, who bit the coin, to make sure it was real.

Duane pocketed his change, and carried his glass of whiskey to an empty table against the wall. He sat, pushed his hat back on his head, and gazed into the glass of iridescent fluid. The voice of Brother Paolo came to him from the monastery in the clouds.

Whiskey is the one thing, outside of women, that can utterly destroy a man.

But Brother Paolo was far away, and the Longhorn Saloon wasn't the monastery in the clouds. I'm going to be a cowboy, and I don't care if it kills me. He grabbed the glass, raised it to his lips, drained half of it away, and swallowed fast. Mellow at first, just like last time, it became the Chicago Fire in a matter of seconds. His eyes bulged; he coughed, and his hat fell off. It hung down his back, suspended from his throat by the black leather neck strap.

A few tables away, a group of gamblers snickered. "Somebody ought to teach that boy how to drink."

Duane covered his mouth with his hand, as he hacked uncontrollably.

A few blocks away, Edgar Petigru sat in his office, studying his ledgers. His saloons were making piles of money, but real-estate sales had been almost nonexistent for the past few months. People didn't want to invest in Titusville until it was confirmed that the railroad would come through.

Edgar had heard many tales of Texas towns that started strong, and then withered away as army posts moved, mines petered out, or the railroad chose another direction for its rails. Guess right, you could be rich as Joe McCoy in Abilene, but you could lose your shirt and even your life if you bet on the wrong town. How can I convince the Union Pacific to build a trunk line to Titusville? he asked himself.

There was a knock on the door. "Who is it?"

The door opened, and Jed appeared. "I seen a man

leavin' Miss Vanessa's house shortly before noon today. Whoever he was, he stayed all night."

Petigru stared at him. "Does he have a name?"

"Nobody's never see'd him before. He looked like a cowboy, but din't have no boots."

"He was barefoot?"

"Looked that way."

Petigru leaned back in his chair. "Probably a beggar, and he slept beneath the front porch."

"I see'd 'im leave by the back door. He was young . . ." Jed tossed the last word out casually, but it struck Petigru like a flying chunk of iron.

"I'm sure there's an innocent explanation," Petigru said. "See what you can find out about him, and let me know if he shows up there again."

"I'm a little short of money . . ."

Petigru tossed him a coin. "Keep your eyes open, and your mouth shut."

Duane sat at the table against the far wall of the Longhorn Saloon, studying denizens around him. Alcohol dispersed through the tissues of his body, and he felt mildly to moderately happy. The saloon was the strangest place he'd seen. Now that he examined his fellow Texans close up, he saw a variety of discreet little scenes.

The gamblers were as devout and concentrated as the abbot on a High Holy Day. If these men turned their energies in the direction of God, what a force for good they could be in the world, he reflected. Some games were for mere pennies, played by shifty-eyed, sorrowful cowboys, while coins were piled high on other tables, where fancy ruffled shirts bumped the stakes higher. Duane's sharp eyes caught one of the dudes dealing a card off the bottom of the deck.

At another table, a group of bleary-eyed cowboys mumbled to each other, dragging coins around the table, and trying to read their cards. They appeared in a stupor, or like mechanical men, their brains pickled by whiskey.

Several tables were beds for men who'd already passed out, and it wasn't even three o'clock in the afternoon. Duane heard political discussions, a lecture on the merits of a horse named Tony, a paean of praise to the sexual stamina of a whore named Sally, and a detailed account of a recent noteworthy barroom brawl in Santa Fe.

Meanwhile, a few tables away, a fiftyish man in a suit, with gray mustache and goatee, read a book through wire-rimmed eyeglasses, while steadily sipping a glass of whiskey. He looked out of place, like a scholar or professor, but he was a part of the saloon's eclectic ambiance, too.

"Don't I know you?"

The voice startled Duane, and he turned toward a familiar lantern-jawed face beneath a wide-brimmed cowboy hat. It was Lester Boggs, the cowboy from the stagecoach trip, peering intensely at Duane.

"You were supposed to buy me a steak last night," Duane said, "but you never showed up."

Boggs sat on the chair opposite Duane, and looked him over carefully. "Where'd you steal the clothes?"

"A friend of mine bought them for me."

Boggs fingered the material of Duane's shirt. "Not

bad at all. You look like you're doin' all right fer yer-self. Who's yer friend?"

Duane didn't want to describe his night with Vanessa Fontaine, so he replied: "How come you didn't show up at the Crystal Palace Saloon?"

Boggs spat disgustedly into the nearest cuspidor, missed by three inches, applying another horrendous stain to an already disgusting floor. "Had me a run of bad luck," he confessed. "I went a-lookin' fer that galoot what owed me ten dollars, but when I found 'im, he denied that he owed me anything. Well, one thing led to another—and to make a long story short, I spent the night in jail. You got any money?"

"Damn right," Duane replied proudly. "I'll buy you a steak."

Boggs slapped him on the shoulder, and Duane nearly fell off his chair. "I always knowed you was a good boy," Boggs said. "When I was in that stage-coach, I kept a-lookin' at you and a-sayin' to myself: that young feller's a-gonna be somethin' some day. Where'd you steal the money?"

"My friend lent it to me. I'm going to become a cowboy, as soon as I learn to ride a horse. Do you think you could teach me?"

"I was born on a goddamn horse. Ain't nawthin' to it. But first, let's git them goddamned grits."

They headed toward the chop counter, and Duane felt like a lord of the sagebrush in his new clothes, with his authentic cowboy friend. At the counter, Boggs held up two fingers, and the Negro cook flipped two enormous steaks onto tin plates, smothered them with potatoes fried in beef fat, and ladled on the gravy. Duane paid, and then Boggs led him to the bar. Two mugs of beer were poured. Duane dropped the necessary coins in the bartender's palm, and they returned to their table beneath a moth-eaten Commanche blanket nailed to the wall.

Boggs didn't say a word, as he wolfed down the food. He'd eaten one stale biscuit in jail, and had dreamed about a steak dinner with fried potatoes. He looked at Duane, and thought that the kid appeared somehow bigger and older than he remembered. Boggs cleaned every morsel off his plate, and then gnawed the bone like a dog.

The Carrington Arms was the largest and most luxurious hotel in Titusville, but it looked like a three-story shack to Edgar Petigru, as he crossed the street in late afternoon. There were no coppers directing traffic, and he was nearly run down by two drunken cowboys racing each other through the main street of town.

Petrigru reached the far sidewalk with a splatter of mud on his pants. Titusville was a long step down for the sophisticated New Yorker, but it offered solid opportunities for rapid capital expansion. Someday I'll go back to New York, and thumb my nose at old Cornelius Vanderbilt. Edgar imagined himself riding up Broadway in an open carriage, waving to the throngs like the Prince of Wales during the latter's visit to the great metropolis in 1860.

Petigru entered the lobby, full of men talking horses, women, and business. Some of the men looked like bummers, but could own thousands of head of cattle on a vast almost unimaginable range. He made his way to the dining room, where Titusville's leading citizens gathered at the end of each day. Whiskey prices were the highest in town, to guarantee the overall auspicious tone of the room, which was laughable to a man who'd been a member of the Union Club on Fifth Avenue. He remembered a line attributed to Julius Caesar:

I'd rather be first in a small Iberian village
than second in Rome.

Two unlit crystal chandeliers were suspended from the ceiling, as light radiated through tall windows overlooking Main Street. Above the fireplace hung a huge oil painting of a herd of cattle galloping through a thunderstorm. Portly Mayor Lonsdale noticed Edgar's approach, and muttered to the others. The town's leading citizens laughed heartily, as they turned toward Edgar Petigru.

Are they making fun of me again? he wondered, as he drew closer. Banker Holcomb, whose girth nearly matched his height, pulled out a chair. "Have a seat, Ed."

Edgar sat on the proffered chair, then removed his mauve calfskin gloves. A bow-tied waiter approached from Petigru's left. "The same?"

Petigru nodded, and the waiter launched himself toward the bar. Councilman Finney, a short, red-haired man, grinned like a monkey on the far side of the table. "Yer one cool son of a bitch, Petigru—I've got to say that fer you."

"In what way?"

Finney looked at Judge Jenks, another citizen who appeared never to've missed a meal, and both giggled like little girls. Petigru creased his forehead. "What's going on, gentleman? I'm afraid I don't get it."

Finney leaned toward him and said confidentially: "If my woman spent the night with a certain young stranger, I would've shot him by now, but there you are, orderin' the usual whiskey like nothin' happened. You Yankees are like ice, and maybe that's why you won the war."

Edgar, like most members of New York's high society, was expert at hiding his true feelings, but it took all his willpower to keep himself placid before such provocation. People gossiped in New York, but no one would dare say such a thing to another man's face. Maybe I should remain silent, and let it pass, he thought.

Mayor Lonsdale winked at Edgar. "I guess we'll be a-gittin' a new singer at the Round-Up, eh?"

The table exploded with mirth, and Edgar once more pushed down his discomfort. But on the surface he raised an eyebrow and asked innocently, "Whatever can you be talking about?"

Judge Jenks leaned forward, his lips wet. "You mean you ain't gonna kick her ass out've town?"

"Who?"

"Miss Vanessa—who else?"

Edgar smiled, and showed the palms of his hands. "Gentleman, I think you're letting your imaginations run away with you. I understand that a beggar visited her home this morning, but you're making it sound like a cheap bedroom comedy."

Banker Holcomb snorted. "Visited? Is that what they call it these days?"

The foremost citizens roared, and Petigru's ears

became warm. They've never accepted me, and never will, he realized. But I don't care, because I'm going home once I've made my bundle in this filthy little corner of the world.

Lester Boggs chewed the steak bone until it was whiter than an ivory key of a piano. He chucked the bone over his shoulder, and it sailed through the air, but before it touched the floor, a fat, black mongrel dog scuttled from beneath a table and clamped it in his jaws. Then the animal retreated to the murky depths of the saloon, to suck out the marrow.

Boggs polished off his mug of beer, burped, wiped his mouth with the back of his hand, and asked: "How much money we got left?"

"About thirteen dollars," Duane replied.

"Why don't we go to the cribs?"

Duane stared at him. "Well . . . I . . . I've never been to the cribs before."

"How come?"

"There's a lot you don't know about me, Boggs. I was raised by Catholic priests until two weeks ago."

"You mean you never been greased? So *that's* what's wrong with you. Listen, kid—you can't be a real cowboy till you been to the cribs. It's practically a rule in this part of Texas."

Duane shook his head stubbornly. "I don't want to go to bed with a woman I don't even know, and have to *pay* for love."

"Every man pays for love, one way or t'other. Let's git movin', 'cause Saturday night's a-comin on, and we want to beat the crowd."

"What's so great about the cribs? Why don't you get married and settle down like a normal person, Boggs?"

"I'd rather buy the milk, than buy the cow. Listen, kid, no ranch'll have anythin' to do with you, when the word gets around that you won't go to the cribs. What the hell're you afraid of? Fer only a dollar, both of us can have a good time, and some of them gals're real pretty."

"Pretty?" Duane asked, perking up his ears. "Really?"

"Blonde, brunette, fat, skinny—anything you want." Boggs spat in the cuspidor, then leaned forward and gazed into Duane's eyes. "If you want to be an angel—go back to the priests, but if you want to be a real man, it ain't good to go without a woman fer long. You'll get a little loco, and if you ask me, I think you're at that point 'bout now."

Maybe that's what's wrong with me, Duane thought. I need a woman. "Do you think they might have a tall, slim blonde?"

Boggs smiled, held out both his hands, and whispered: "Anything you want, kid."

He'll tell any lie, to get me to take him to the cribs, Duane realized, but for fifty cents I could get naked with a pretty girl? "Are you sure it's just a dollar for both of us?" Duane asked.

Boggs leaned back, tilted his hat low over his eyes, and rolled a cigarette with quick, sure movements. "You can't get greased any cheaper'n the cribs. What's it gonna be?"

"Will you teach me how to roll a cigarette like that?"

"I'll teach you how to roll a cigarette, ride a horse, drink whiskey—anything you want."

They headed for the door, and Duane tried to imitate the insolent roll of Boggs's shoulders. He knows what this world's about, Duane thought. Everything happens for a reason, and maybe this cowpoke is my new spiritual advisor.

They walked down the planked sidewalk, and Duane puffed out his chest proudly. If anybody looked at us right now, they'd think I was a cowboy, too, he thought proudly. He felt as though he were fulfilling himself for the first time, but something was missing, as if he were trying to climb on a horse, but the saddle kept slipping.

Boggs slapped the back of his hand against Duane's leg. "You see this galoot a-comin'? They say he was one of the meanest gunfighters that ever was."

Duane perceived Clyde Butterfield, the fancy gentleman who'd advised him to buy a gun after he had been robbed by street urchins. Butterfield appeared not to notice Duane as he strolled along with thumbs hooked in his suspenders, hat slanted low over his eyes, cheroot sticking out of his teeth.

"Howdy, Mister Butterfield," Duane called out.

The tall man with the ruffled shirt slowed his pace, his eyes widened in surprise, and then he smiled warmly. "Well, I'll be goddamned. Didn't recognize you for a moment, in your new clothes. Looks like you're doing okay. Where you headed?"

"The cribs."

Butterfield touched his forefinger to the brim of his hat. "Give 'er one fer me."

The ex-gunfighter stepped out, chin high, hat brim

low, spurs jangling every time his heels came down, as he made his way toward the Black Cat Saloon. Duane watched him in wonderment and admiration. "He was a real gunfighter?"

"That's what they say, but now he plays cards fer his supper."

Duane thought of his father lying somewhere beneath six feet of Texas, probably without a decent tombstone. I should ask Butterfield if he ever heard of my father, he thought. Boggs grabbed Duane's sleeve, and pulled him toward the outskirts of town. "Let me tell you about the cribs, so you won't act like a greenhorn onc't we git thar. Now, the cribs ain't fancy, so don't go expecting no palace. And there ain't a hell of a lot of privacy. As fer the gals theirselves, well—some of 'em ain't so young. In fact, to tell you the God's honest truth, the gals in the cribs are usually the bottom of the barrel. But it's the cheapest place to get greased."

"I thought you said the girls were young and pretty."

"Kid, I been lookin' at cows so long, anything in skirts looks young and pretty to me."

There was a knock on the door, and Vanessa stirred on her pillow. She lay on her bedspread, attired in a pale purple silk dressing gown gathered at the waist with a matching belt. "What is it?"

The bedroom door opened, and Annabelle stood there, a distraught expression on her moon-shaped face. "Miss Vanessa, there's . . ."

She was pushed out of the way, and Edgar Petigru

stood in the doorway, wide-brimmed hat in hand. Vanessa shot to a sitting position, her heart racing wildly. "What are you doing here!"

Edgar closed the door behind him, then bowed mockingly low. "I thought I'd thank you personally for making me the laughingstock of the town, Vanessa. It's not every day that such an honor is bestowed upon me."

She rubbed her eyes with the backs of her fingers. "What in the world are you talking about?"

"Don't play innocent with me, young lady. This is Edgar, remember? Who was the young man you spent the night with?"

"Is this your idea of a jealous rage?" she asked, smiling haughtily. "I don't believe I've ever seen you in such a state. Would you like some of my smelling salts?"

"Who was he?"

"You're being absurd, and this isn't funny anymore. First of all, he spent the night in the guest room. He's a poor, pathetic, homeless boy. I fed him, gave him a roof for the night, and sent him on his way."

"Where did you meet this poor, pathetic boy?"

"In the living room of my home. He'd broken in to steal some food, but he just needed a helping hand, so I gave it to him in the spirit of Christian charity."

"Is he here now?"

"He left for town early this morning, and I haven't seen him since. Why don't you give him a job on your ranch?"

Edgar was taken aback, his self-assurance shaken by her careless jocular manner. "How old is this so-called boy?"

"Nearly eighteen."

"That's not a boy!"

"He's an orphan, and was raised by Catholic brothers. He has nobody in the world, Edgar, and it would be wonderful if you found him a position at your ranch. I heard you say the other day that you were looking for more good cowboys."

"Are you sure you didn't go to bed with him?"

"Regardless of what you think of me, Edgar, I'm not insane, and I wouldn't gamble everything I have for a few hours with a boy that age."

Edgar walked to the liquor cabinet, poured whiskey, and splashed some water to take the edge off the incendiary local product. Then he sipped slowly and considered her last statement. She was many things, but not a fool. "I apologize for my bad manners, but the whole town is talking about it. Evidently some people saw him leave around noon today. What did you say his name is?"

"Duane Braddock. You can dispense with the whole problem by giving him a job at your ranch. Then he'll have someplace to sleep, and the gossip will end. He appears strong and healthy, especially if he gets a few more decent meals in him, and I'm sure he'll be able to pull his own weight."

The more the businessman thought of it, the more reasonable the solution became. "Tell him to report to my foreman first thing Monday morning."

Vanessa kissed his cheek. "Thank you, but there's just one minor problem. You see . . . well . . . through no fault of his own—he doesn't know how to ride a horse."

Edgar threw up his hands in despair. "I'm going to

hire a cowboy who doesn't know how to ride a horse? It looks like I'm going to be the laughingstock of this town for a second day in a row."

"But he can learn, and you'll save him from starvation or even worse, because he's probably more sensitive than most young men his age. I mean, he was raised in a monastery, and doesn't know much about the real world. Don't ranches have apprentice cowboys?"

Edgar sighed in defeat. "I'll tell my foreman to hire him regardless of his lack of experience."

She placed her hands on his waist, and rested her cheek on his breast. "Thank you, Edgar. You won't regret it, I promise."

A jumble of squat, flat-roofed huts could be seen at the edge of town, with dim lights burning in windows. It was on the far side of a stream, and Duane and Boggs had to cross a crude log bridge, as the sage echoed with auditions of a million insects. Light danced on swirling waters, and a few cowboys sat with bottles at the bank, having slurred conversations while waiting for friends to return from the twinkling region of sin and degeneracy stretched before them. Two cowboys approached on the path, and one of them said: "I remember a whore I screwed once in Dodge. She had a face like a moose, but . . ."

Duane strained to hear the rest of the story, but the bubbling stream swallowed it up. Someone fired a gun, then a woman yelped with laughter. A hodgepodge of rough-hewn planked shacks with crooked roofs and leaning walls was affixed like a pustule to the side of the incline, and looked like the nether regions of hell.

"The cribs closest to the stream is usually the busiest," Boggs said. "We'll go on a ways, to get the fresher meat, if you knows what I mean."

Duane realized that Boggs was teaching him arcane facts about the real world, and was, in fact, a tenured professor of crib lore. At least I'm in good hands, Duane thought, trying to see the educational side of his painful predicament. He was terrified of being embarrassed with a woman, yet couldn't imagine how he could perform with one he didn't love. Duane was becoming increasingly skeptical of the great romantic experience looming before him.

"This looks like a good one," Boggs replied, angling his head toward a nondescript hut jammed among the others.

Duane wondered which warped plank of wood or crooked nail caught the experienced cowboy's eye, as they headed toward the door. A cry of pain, or was it joy, pierced the night, and someone stroked an off-key fiddle. Boggs knocked on the door, two eyes appeared through a square opening, and moments later the door opened. Boggs stepped forward confidently, and Duane followed him into a small, boxy room with whitewashed walls and several heavily painted women in all sizes, colors, and shapes, dressed in short revealing dresses. A wave of cheap perfume mixed with sweat struck Duane's sensitive ecclesiastical nostrils, and he felt sick to his stomach.

He turned, and saw two heavily armed men at the door. They looked at him with grins, and he couldn't simply run away like a frightened child. This is going to be an extremely difficult night, he realized.

Boggs pulled Duane's sleeve, dragging him farther into the room. "Which one you like?"

Duane shuffled his feet nervously. "Don't know yet."

"It ain't like buyin' a horse, kid, so relax. Ah . . . by the way, pard, you'll have to give me fifty cents."

Duane dropped coins onto Boggs's hand, and the cowboy sped toward the most corpulent woman in the room, with thighs like watermelons beneath her short pink skirt. She appeared demure, as she arose to take his hand. Like lovers, they headed toward the canvas flap that covered the doorway at the edge of the room.

The remaining whores grinned at Duane, pushing out their bosoms, spreading their legs lewdly. Duane felt like fleeing, but knew that his future as a cowboy lay on the line. He had to go through with it somehow, but there were no pretty girls in the room. I'll just pick one of them, he thought. What difference does it make? One prostitute grasped her breasts and showed him her tongue. Another lifted a leg and performed an act so horrific that Duane had to turn his eyes away.

"*Un niño*," murmured one of the women.

They laughed, and Duane blushed. He spoke Spanish fluently, and he'd just been called a baby. I'll pick one of them, and to hell with it, he decided. Just as he was about to point, the back door flap opened, and a younger woman with the hefty build of a farmer's daughter limped into the room. Her left leg twisted outward strangely, and her arm perched in the air like the broken wing of a bird. She was a cripple, but considerably better-looking than the others.

He pointed toward her in desperation. "I want you."

He took her by surprise, and she regarded him warily. "What's yer name?"

"Duane. How about you?"

"Sally Mae." Then she smiled sweetly. "I'll show you a real good time, Duane."

She hooked her arm in his, and hobbled toward the door. He followed her into a labyrinth of small rooms covered with canvas doors, and heard beds creaking, sighs, moans, curses, grunts, oaths, and other peculiar semihuman and quasi-animal sounds. "Oooohhhhh," a man cried in the darkness, as though dying from a wonderful new disease.

She entered one of the rooms, lit the oil lamp, and beckoned for him to follow. She had a narrow cot, a dresser covered with tiny bottles, and a wooden chair. This is where she lives, like an animal in a stall, he thought sadly.

"You all right?" she asked.

Duane nodded nervously, wishing he could run out the door, but they'd laugh him out of Titusville.

"Yer first time, huh?"

"No," he lied, "I did it lots of times before."

She held out her hand. "Fifty cents."

He reached into his pocket, handed her a dollar. "That's okay," he said embarrassedly.

"Take yer clothes off, and I'll be right back."

She limped into the corridor, but Duane didn't feel like removing his new clothes. He was afraid someone would steal them, and he'd never been naked with a woman before. I can't go through with this, but what'll I say when she comes back? he asked himself.

Honesty is the best policy, Brother Paolo had told him. Duane sat on the edge of the bed, pushed his hat on the back of his head, and waited for Sally Mae to return. He'd always dreamed that his first love would be a beautiful, passionate sacrament, but instead he was in the cribs with a poor cripple whom he didn't even know.

The curtain was pushed to the side, and she returned to the small enclosed area. He placed one finger in front of his lips, then moved toward her. "I lied before," he whispered in her ear. "I've never done this before. Please don't be mad at me, and I don't want my money back, but could I just walk out of here, and nobody has to know?"

Her eyes went soft on him. "If you leave so soon, everyone will know what happened. Why don't you lie down for a few minutes, and we can talk."

Duane sighed in gratitude. "You're very kind."

He placed another dollar in her palm, she dropped it into her bosom, and then kicked off her shoes. She lay down sideways with her back to the wall, and made room for him. "C'mon."

He took off his hat, pulled off his boots, and stretched beside her in the darkness. Their bodies touched, and somehow, despite embarrassing circumstances, he was forced to conclude that she felt rather nice, and didn't seem crippled when lying down. Her perfume was harsher than Vanessa's, but the effect was the same. He realized that she was probably no older than Vanessa.

"You really never done it afore?" she whispered into his ear, as her warm breath wafted through him, weakening his fortifications. "Yer just funnin' me, ain't you?"

She kissed his lips, and she tasted like ambrosia in the darkness. Meanwhile, the man in the next stall, only inches away, bellowed like a buffalo in heat. She touched her cheek to Duane's, and more fortresses crumbled inside him. He felt her breasts against his shirt, the first breasts of his life, and his final reserves were devastated. He placed his hand on her silk gown, and discovered that she was wearing nothing beneath it, producing a sensation unlike anything he'd ever known. A strange new artery pounded insistently in his throat, as she breathed into his ear: "It's warm here. I think I'll take me clothes off."

She arose beside him, pulled the sash of her gown, and it opened like curtains, revealing a landscape of breasts and stomach. In an instant, she was back on the bed, wrapping her arms around him, licking his lips.

He thought the top of his head would blow off, as he clutched her toward him. It was his first flesh-and-blood encounter with feminine energy, and felt like she were swallowing him alive.

"Yer awful good-looking," she murmured. "When I saw you out there in the parlor, I hoped you'd pick me."

His male vanity rocketed through the roof, but then he reminded himself that he was in the cribs, and she probably said it to every cowboy who walked through that door. His hands roved up her naked back, as she unbuttoned his shirt.

She pressed her lips against his chest. "You take them clothes off," she murmured, "and I'll make a man of you."

Duane's blood thundered, and he felt on fire. Far

be it from me to violate this fine old cowboy tradition, he admitted to himself. He rolled out of bed, untied his bandanna, hung it over the chair, and wondered how many other articles of male clothing had lain on that rickety wreck of furniture. He pulled off his shirt, jumped out of his pants, and dove on top of her.

"You're a wild horse," she whispered, and then her lips became covered with his hungry mouth, as he clasped her in his strong arms. It was his first time naked with a woman, and the reality exceeded even his most lurid dreams.

"Are you all right?" she asked.

She touched him in a certain delicate spot, and he had to admit that this woman, whom he'd never seen before, had made him more excited than he'd ever thought possible. He wrapped his arms around her, and rolled her onto her back. Duane felt strong enough to run all the way to San Francisco, when something new and entirely unexpected happened, as if he'd been struck by lightning. My God, he realized jubilantly. *I'm doing it!*

The bed squeaked noisily, joining the vast chorus of other abused and overworked mattresses in the area, augmented by hushed whispers, godawful moans, whimpers, sighs, and burps. What was I so worried about? Duane wondered, as he undulated frenziedly in the dark. This is the best goddamned thing I ever did!

CHAPTER 4

DUANE DRESSED IN THE FLICKERING LAMP-light, as mattresses twisted and tossed all around him. Sally Mae touched her lips to his, then pushed him toward the door. "Time's up."

She led him down the corridor, and somehow he felt taller, stronger, and brand new. Now he understood why men came to the cribs, and expected to return on his own someday. At least I'll have something interesting to confess next time I see a priest, he thought jokingly. They came to the parlor, where a new group of burly cowboys were engrossed in the selection process.

Duane leaned toward Sally Mae. "How's about one last kiss?"

Even as the words left his mouth, Duane knew

he'd said something ridiculous. The room became still, and everyone was looking at him. But it was too late to take it back.

"Ain't that sweet!" ridiculed a voice nearby. "He thinks the whore's in love with 'im! Hey, kid—you give me fifty cents, I'll never fergit you. I'll even kiss yer pointy little head fer a dollar."

The cowboys chuckled derisively, and Duane could see that they were in advanced states of inebriation. The cowboy who'd spoken wore a black bandanna, was Duane's height, but weighed thirty pounds more. The cowboy elevated his voice a few octaves. "How's about one last kiss, Sally Mae," he mimicked, rolling his eyes with mock delight.

The cowboys laughed, and a few whores chimed in. Sally Mae looked Duane in the eye. "He can say what he wants, but I had a real good time with you, Duane, and you know it."

"Sure she did," hollered the obnoxious cowboy who had a blunt nose with a scar on his chin. "She has a real good time with *every* waddie who walks in here. Hell, I'll give her fifty cents, she can say it to me, too." The cowboy pulled coins from his pocket, and he held the change to Sally Mae, and said: "Tell me you love me, darlin'. Say how much you care."

Duane glanced at Sally Mae, who appeared embarrassed by the attention she was attracting.

"Wouldn't you gimme a kiss fer five cents?"

An expression of hurt came over her face, and Duane caught a glimpse of the crippled girl who was unable to fend for herself, couldn't get a husband, and wound up in the cribs. Only a fiend could take pleasure in humiliating such a creature, Duane thought.

"Whore—come here! I got somethin' fer you!"

The cowboy gripped his groin, and Duane felt rage come on like a tornado. "Leave her alone!"

Black Bandanna angled to one side, then the other, as he regarded Duane. "Mind yer business, Sonny Jim. I've squashed gnats bigger'n you." The cowboy lunged forward, grabbed Sally Mae's arm, and pulled her abruptly toward the canvas door. She lost her balance, and was on her way to the floor, when Duane steadied her. Black Bandanna stepped backward, to see what had happened, and before he could get set, something crashed into his forehead. The room went black for a moment, and then he took a step backward, the tints brightened.

Duane stood in the middle of the floor, legs spread, cowboy hat low over his eyes. Black Bandanna touched his fingers to his mouth. A trickle of blood appeared.

"Go git him, Dave," said one of the cowboys.

"Kick his ass," added another.

The Mexican madam waved her frail arms. "If you want to fight—go outside!"

Two cowboys lifted her off her feet and carried her out of the way as though she were a tadpole. She responded with an ear-splitting screech, kicked her matchstick legs, and another cowboy covered her mouth with his hand, as Dave spat a gob of blood into the nearby cuspidor. Dave's eyes went mean as he glared at Duane. "Boy, I'm a-gonna beat the piss out of you."

He lowered his head and charged, hurling a left jab to Duane's face, but Duane danced out of the way at the last moment, and put all his weight behind a right cross to Dave's temple. The blow landed solidly, and Dave staggered to the side, his eyes closing.

Dave's shoulder bounced off the wall, and Duane followed with a left hook to the ear. Dave's head spun around, and a fist was rammed into his stomach, doubling him up. Duane took one step to the side, and threw an uppercut. It landed underneath Dave's chin, snapped his head, and sent him sprawling across the room. Dave sat on the floor for a few moments, blinking in astonishment, trying to figure out which horse had run into him.

Duane had reacted in a sudden flash of anger, without thinking, but now realized that three other cowboys were eyeing him with increasing hostility, and each carried a gun in a holster. They advanced toward him, and he raised his fists for the final round.

"Don't nobody move, or I'll shoot yer durned head off." The voice came from the door, where the two guards stood, guns in their hands. "You want to fight—go outside."

Sally Mae whispered into Duane's ear. "Let the others go, but you stay here for a while. Otherwise they'll kill you."

Duane appreciated the logic of her suggestion, but felt jumpy and wild. Dave picked himself up off the floor, and touched his fingers to his pulped lips. "I'd like to get a piece of you outside, Sonny Jim. How's about it?"

"After you."

The cowboy strolled toward the door, throwing punches into the air. "Gimme some room, and I'll clean the town with that li'l son of a bitch."

Dave stepped outside, and Duane moved to follow

him, but Sally Mae grabbed his sleeve. "Come back to my room for a while. Please?"

My father died in a fight, Duane thought, and maybe I will, too, but if you don't stand up to them, how can you call yourself a man? He recalled Sally Mae cringing beneath Dave's heedless remark, and removed her hand from his shoulder. He followed the cowboys out the door, and the cowboys waited in the alley.

"I think we orter shoot him," one said.

"Naw," replied Dave. "I'll take care of 'im myself."

He raised his fists and advanced toward Duane, while another bunch of cowboys emerged from a near-by hut. "Looks like a fracas over thar."

Dave smiled confidently as he decreased the distance between him and Duane, but Duane kept shifting position, dancing lightly on his feet, bobbing his head. Brother Paolo had been a pugilist during brief vacations from his undistinguished career as a *bandito*, and had taught Duane that you defeat a bigger man by constantly moving, making him miss, and making him pay.

"Just stay still fer one second," Dave said, "and I'll knock yer block off."

Duane stopped dancing, and made himself a stationary target. Dave wound up and threw a hard left jab to Duane's nose, but Duane darted to the side, firing a jab into the pit of Dave's stomach. Dave was wide open, and Duane's fist buried to the wrist into soft belly flesh. It was the identical spot that Duane had hammered before, and all the wind expelled from Dave's orifices. The cowboy keeled over, and Duane caught him with a left hook to the head. Dave dropped to his knees, trying to clear his brainpan, and Duane flashed on Sally Mae reviled like Mary Magdalene. Before Duane could stop himself, he kicked Dave squarely in the face, and the cowboy flew onto his back.

Duane heard shuffling behind him, and spun around. Dave's three cowboy friends were coming for him. With a wild, inarticulate cry, Duane charged. They were surprised to see him coming, and that was all the time he needed to bash the face of the cowboy on the right, but the other cowboys crowded around, throwing punches. Duane was whacked in the mouth, clubbed on the ear, and sent reeling. He tripped over his high boot heels, and fell on his side.

They came after him angrily, trying to kick his head off. Duane grabbed one boot, twisted, and that cowboy teetered into the muck.

"Whip his ass!" somebody shouted.

All four cowboys surrounded Duane, who struggled to fend off blows from all directions. A spur ripped his new pants, a silver ring cracked him in the mouth, and another fist collided with his ear, causing him to hear bells pealing in the monastery in the clouds.

Duane recalled the words of Saint Paul: *Even if you are angry, you must not sin,* but it didn't have much relevance to the situation. He knew that he had to achieve something spectacular, otherwise they'd murder him. All the frustrations and muffled longings of his orphan's predicament detonated inside him, and he went berserk.

Plunging into their midst, his arms flailed and

boots winged through the air. Duane took a punch to the eye and another to the mouth, as he stood toe to toe with four men and slugged it out. He was in a frenzy and felt no pain, as cowboy spectators cheered him on. Duane smacked somebody in the nose, broke another cowboy's front tooth, and kicked Dave in his most tender spot. Dave went down like a ship in the night, gripping his groin and howling, as one of his cohorts caught Duane with a solid right to the temple.

Duane saw fireflies, and his legs wobbled. The next punch lifted him off his feet and sent him flying through the darkness. He landed on his back, and tried to rise, but a boot zoomed out of nowhere, and clipped the top of his head.

Everything went black, as Duane rolled onto his side. He lay on the incline toward the stream, the crowd of cowboys circling around.

"Stomp 'im, Dave," one of the cowboys said.

"Stomp 'im, hell," replied Dave, yanking a gun out of his holster. "I'm a-gonna put a bullet in his head." He thumbed back the hammer and aimed at Duane's forehead.

"Don't move," said a voice to his left.

Dave turned and saw a bow-legged cowboy aiming a Colt at him. "You better mind yer own business," Dave growled. "This ain't yer fight."

"Ain't no cause to kill 'im," said Lester Boggs. "Holster yer iron, or I'll put one 'twixt yer eyes."

Dave thought for a few moments, then dropped his gun into his holster and spat at the ground. "If I ever see that kid again, I'll kill 'im."

"Let's git greased," replied one of his cohorts,

wiping blood from his ear. "This is a-gittin' to be a pain in the ass."

The battered warriors placed their arms around each other's shoulders, and headed toward the nearest crib, while the crowd stared at the figure lying with his face on the ground.

"Feisty little son of a bitch," somebody uttered.

"He sure gave 'em a run fer their money."

"Looks like he's daid."

The new cowboys huddled around, as Boggs rolled Duane onto his back. Duane's face was streaked with blood, and the whites of his eyes showed.

"Anybody know who he is?" someone asked.

"He's my pard," Boggs replied, pressing his ear against Duane's heart. "He's still alive. Maybe one of you fellers should git the sawbones."

They raised Duane by his hands and legs, and carried him toward the stream. Lamplights reflected on tiny wavelets, and a cool breeze blew in from the sage. They laid him at the water's edge, filled their hats with water, and spilled it over Duane's face, but he didn't move a muscle.

"You sure he's alive?" somebody asked Boggs.

"He was a few minutes ago. Give 'im more water."

The cowboys refilled their hats, then poured cold water over Duane, washing blood from his pallid features. Duane groaned, and moved his head a half inch to the side.

"He's coming back," announced Boggs, dipping his hat into the stream.

He dropped more water over Duane's face, and Duane opened his eyes slowly. His first thought was that he was drowning, and he sputtered frantically, trying to rise. Another hatful of water struck him in the face, and he gasped, coughed, and spit.

He blinked, and saw himself in the center of a ring of cowboys, all gazing intently at him. His ribs felt broken, his ham bone ached, and his face felt like raw meat. He didn't even know his name, or where he was.

He gazed past the legs of the men, and saw the cribs in the distance, lights shimmering behind dirt-caked windows. He recalled the loss of his virginity, and before he could relish his elevation to manhood, he'd got into a brawl with four cowboys.

"Yer lucky to be alive," said a heavyset man with a white mustache. "One of 'em kicked you in the head so hard, I thought yer brains fell out."

"Maybe they did," Duane replied, spitting something foul and bloody from his mouth, and he hoped it wasn't his tongue.

"You're one crazy son of a bitch. What's yer name?"

Duane perched on his knees at the side of the stream, and splashed his face with water. It appeared that one of his teeth was chipped, and his left eye was so puffed, he could barely see out of it. He worked his jaw, and it felt somewhat out of line. He was woozy, and wondered if he'd ever be normal again.

"Here," said a voice beside him.

Duane saw a bottle of whiskey in the hand of the man with the white mustache. Without hesitating, Duane accepted it, pulled the cork, and took a swig. It went down like molten lava, and the sudden shock jolted him toward a more comprehensive awareness of his situation. Slowly, laboriously, he rose to his feet, drank another swallow, and handed the bottle back. "Much obliged."

"You look like you might make it, after all. What you say yer name was?"

Boggs stepped forward, a big smile on his face, as his eyes focused on the bottle in the man's hand. "His name's Duane Braddock, and we come here together. I was a-mindin' my business, a-waitin' fer him, when it sounded like all hell broke loose, and you boys know the rest. Mind if I have a drink?" Boggs deftly plucked it out of the man's hand and leaned back. His Adam's apple bobbed twice, and the quantity in the bottle diminished considerably.

The crowd dispersed, as cowboys drifted back to the cribs. It was just another incident in their violent lives, and the time had come to return to the business that had brought them to Titusville in the first place. They laughed, slapped each other on the shoulders. Duane realized that all cowboys weren't bad, but they all weren't good, either.

He felt strangely euphoric, as if he were older and more wise. "Boggs, do you think we can rent a horse this time of night, so you can give me some riding lessons?"

"I think you took too many shots to the head, kid. Besides, the first lessons on ridin' a horse should be got afore you ever sit on one, so yer prepared. How's about a saloon?"

Vanessa Fontaine sat before her mirror, applying cosmetics to her cheeks. *Every year it takes a little longer,* she mused. She didn't slather herself with grease and powder like the saloon girls, but merely heightened the color of her natural features, outlining her eyes, so that cowboys in the farthest reaches of the saloon could see her dramatic expressions. She knew that they worked hard, and the only fun they had was on Saturday nights, when they came to town. Most were Confederate Army veterans, and she felt special affection for them, despite their constant drinking and brawling.

Unfortunately, she was utterly miserable. She knew now that she could never be happy with Edgar, no matter how many houses he bought her. Eventually they'd live in New York City, and go to the opera every night, but something always would be lacking.

Her encounter with Duane had convinced her that she could never be content with a man for whom she didn't feel at least a modicum of passion. I'm not sleeping with Duane Braddock, she told herself. It's not good for me, it's not good for him, and it's wrong from every conceivable point of view. She grit her teeth and forced the thought out of her mind.

Duane and Boggs sat at a table in the middle of a small smelly room known as the Blind Pig Saloon. Located off the main street, it featured the cheapest rotgut whiskey in town, and the oldest, most broken-down prostitutes that Duane had ever imagined in his wildest nightmares.

"They got a shack out back," Boggs explained. "Fer a quarter, these gals'll do anything, and when I say anything, I mean *anything*."

Duane pressed the cold wet bandanna against the knot on his head. His hat hung down his back, his shirt was torn, and several teeth felt loose in his mouth, but somehow Duane felt a strange contentment. So this is why men drink, he mused. In the scriptorium, Duane had seen the reproduction of a painting by Hieronymus Bosch, and it reminded him of the grotesque scene in the Blind Pig Saloon: men and women with red faces pawing each other shamelessly, quaffing alcohol, and squealing with delight.

Boggs hung his hat on a peg, leaned back, and propped his long, skinny legs atop the table. "This is probably as good a time as any to give you yer first lecture on horses. First of all, you got to take care of yer horse like he's yer child, make sure he gets enough to eat, brush 'im down onc't in a while, and you got to show 'im that you care about him, otherwise he'll git mad at you, and a horse can keep a grudge just like a man."

"How come all those horses are saddled out there in the noise all night, where they can't get any sleep?"

"How do you know they can't sleep?"

"How much sleep would you get if you were tied to a hitching rail next to saloons full of men hollering constantly, getting into fights, and throwing bottles around."

"A horse—he don't give a damn."

"If I had a horse, I'd put him in a stable where he'd be dry, with good food to eat and clean water to drink, not like those troughs full of cigarette butts and whiskey bottles."

"Horses like cigarette butts, and as for whiskey, I

once knew a horse . . . but you won't believe me, so fergit it."

"Are you going to tell me that you knew a horse that drank whisky?"

"Well, I did. I'm not sayin' that he went into a saloon and ordered a bottle, but you put some in a bowl, he'd lap up every drop. And it didn't seem to bother 'im at all."

What kind of man would give whiskey to a horse? Duane wondered. "Is there anything else that I have to know before I actually climb on a horse?"

"You know what reins are?"

"You pull them in the direction that you want to go, or pull back when you want to stop."

"Yer way ahead of the game, I can see that. The only other important item is spurs. If you ever see a horse with a lot of scars, you know he's been ridden by a low-down dirty skunk. A man uses his spurs sparingly, sort of as a nudge more'n anything else. Horses're smart, they know what you want, and it's just a matter of gittin' 'em to do it. Don't be afraid of 'im, 'cause they'll see it right away. Make sure you smooth out the blanket afore you put the saddle on, and don't tighten the cinch too much, or too little."

"What if the horse tries to throw me?"

"All you can do is hang on with yer heels, and sooner or later he'll settle down. You might get throwed a few times, but don't let that stop you. Hell, even 'sperienced cowboys like me get throwed from time to time. Hold the reins tight with one hand, and let yer other hand hang loose, fer balance. It's a test of will between you and the horse, and you got to outlast 'im. There's an old sayin':

Ain't never been a horse what couldn't be rode
Ain't never been a cowboy, what couldn't be
throwed."

Boggs is so logical, Duane thought, and he's got an answer for everything. How fortunate I am to have such an experienced man to lead me through life. Why, I'd still be a virgin, if it weren't for him.

"The Spaniards brought the first horses to Texas," Boggs continued, "and nearly every horse you see is descended from them mangy critters."

He even knows the *history* of horses, Duane considered, scratching his jaw in deep thought. Maybe he never studied Saint Thomas Aquinas, but he sure as hell knows the cowboy business.

"When you shoe a horse, you turn yer back to 'im, hold his foot 'twixt yer legs, and hammer in the nails. But first you got to trim his hooves with yer knife. It's a hard job, and if you slip, you can cripple 'im fer life. We get a job on a ranch, I'll show you how it's done."

Somebody shouted on the far side of the saloon. "You son of a bitch! Put yer hand in me pocket again, I'll shoot yer ass!"

At the bar, two men faced each other a few feet apart. They were dirty, desperate-looking drunkards with red noses and long, tangled beards.

"What the hell're you sayin'!" the other one bawled. "You better take that back!"

"You better kiss my ass!"

Both men went for the guns, and everyone in the vicinity ran for the door, while the rest hit the floor. Duane was on his way down, when he heard a shot ring out, and the saloon filled with gunsmoke. Women screeched, and two more shots were fired in rapid succession.

"I'm hit!" someone yelled.

Boggs grabbed Duane's shirt. "Let's git out of here."

Duane felt himself being dragged toward the back door in a wave of squirming, grunting bodies. Somebody threw a chair through a window, and then jumped through.

"Call the deputy!" screamed the bartender.

But nobody wanted a confrontation with that gentleman, and the cowboys stampeded like a herd of cattle, hurling Duane outside.

"This way," said Boggs, pulling Duane across the backyard. "Don't stop fer nawthin'."

The voice of the bartender came from inside the saloon. "He's daid!"

A man can die in a second, Duane realized, as he followed Boggs across the courtyard. Duane recalled Brother Paolo warning him about the secular world, and now he understood his spiritual advisor's urgency. He found himself yearning for monastic tranquillity, where a man's dreams and prayers couldn't be eliminated by the pull of somebody's trigger.

They came to Main Street, ablaze with lights from saloons. The competing melodies of pianos, fiddles, and accordions could be heard from a variety of directions, and all the hitching rails were occupied by long rows of horses. It was Saturday night in Titusville, and the roof was about to blow off the town.

"We got any money left?" Boggs asked, narrowing his eyes on Duane's pocket.

"I think we should turn in, and look for jobs first thing in the morning."

Boggs leaned from side to side, thumbs hooked in his belt, knees pointed outward. "Tomorrow's Sunday. Cain't we have one last slug afore we goes to bed?"

This man wants to corrupt me, and maybe the devil has sent him for that purpose. Duane prepared to say no, when he heard a lilting voice emanate from the Round-Up Saloon.

"You all right, boy?" Boggs asked.

"Let's have a drink at the Round-Up," Duane replied.

A crowd gathered in front of the saloon, pushing and elbowing through the door. Vanessa's voice floated over their heads, and Duane felt enchanted by the dancing melodies.

"We're filled up!" hollered a voice inside. "You cowboys come back some other time, hear?" He wondered how to get in.

Duane dropped to his knees, then crawled among men's legs, trying to reach the door.

"What the hell's goin' on down there?"

Somebody kicked him in the ass, but he continued to scurry along like a lovesick hound dog, and then dove through the opening at the bottom of the batwing doors, nearly colliding with the leg of a table.

He arose behind the table, and saw *her* standing in the lamplight, singing about a wounded Confederate soldier dying amid cannon fire on the banks of Bull Run. Duane was struck by the sorrow in her voice, but that didn't stop him from undressing her shamelessly in his imagination. If I could place my hands on that woman, it would be the pinnacle of my life, he thought wickedly.

His mind filled with salacious images of himself and Vanessa Fontaine in a big feather bed. He imagined himself kissing her most secret places, and having her wrap her long, sinuous legs around him. Temperature rose inside his clothing, and he loosened his bandanna. Why should I sleep in the Sagebrush Hotel, when I can spend another night in her guest room, and maybe . . .

The best seats at the Round-Up were occupied by local notables, and among them perched Edgar Petigru, attired in a black suit with black bow tie, as if attending the Academy of Music in Manhattan. He even carried a black cane concealing a sword, designed to protect gentlemen against New York street urchins, but also useful against the Titusville variety.

Edgar was accustomed to the world's foremost singers, dancers, and musicians, all of whom traveled to New York City in the course of their illustrious careers. He'd seen Lester Wallack in *She Stoops to Conquer*, Edwin Booth, King of the Tragic Actors, as *Hamlet*, and the celebrated Carlotta Carozzi-Zucchi as Leonora in *Il Trovatore*. He prided himself an expert on the performing arts, and it was from that lofty height that he considered Vanessa's performance at the Round-Up Saloon.

The stage was ludicrously small, compared to the Academy of Music, but the standard Titusville audience didn't require an extravaganza by Verdi or Donizetti. All they wanted was a beautiful woman to drool over, and didn't care how or what she sang. It could be the Portuguese national anthem, for all they cared.

Edgar barely heard the music, he was so concerned about investment prospects. It didn't occur to him that most of the men in the audience were former Confederate Army veterans, and they loved to hear Vanessa sing great songs of their youth. It carried them back to halcyon days before the war, when they were younger, richer, and more idealistic. Edgar couldn't comprehend the subtle interaction and mutual respect between Southern women and Southern men. Indeed, he thought the spectacle a tawdry, tasteless show.

How can such people appreciate music? he wondered. They barely live above the level of animals, and sensitivity is alien to their natures. They grovel and fill their bellies like pigs. If the great Carlotta Carozzi-Zucchi walked into this room right now, one of these cowboys would pinch her ass, he thought disgustedly.

Vanessa came to the end of her song, the saloon became silent for a few moments, then applause broke out like thunderclaps, accompanied by shouts and mad whistles. Cowboys rose to their feet, pounding their hands loudly. Coins rained onto the stage, and Vanessa bowed low, a fifty-cent piece bouncing off her head. She's no diva, Edgar thought cynically, but she's wearing a dress, and that's all they care about.

Coins continued to fall upon the stage, as Vanessa bowed again. Slowly, she arose and held her arms out as if to hug all her cowboy admirers. They, too, had lost everything at the Appomattox Courthouse, and in her estimation, they were kin.

She turned her eyes toward the table where Edgar Petigru sat, and blew him a kiss. He smiled broadly, applauding politely, but she knew what he thought of her singing. She didn't hate Edgar, but neither did she love him. She appreciated what he'd done for her, regardless of his ulterior motives.

She turned toward the door, where the largest and surliest segment of the crowd usually congregated— robust, sunburned faces shouting her praises. She was about to accord them a special bow, when her eyes fell on a former youthful guest in a fantastical cowboy hat.

He appeared older in the murky saloon light, squeezed among other cowboys, beating his hands together eagerly, silver conchos throwing sprays of sparkles at the ceiling. There was something wrong with his face, as if he'd been in a fight.

She wanted to bask in adulation all night, but her essential self never forgot that she was an entertainer, and if you gave them too much, they'd get tired of you. Smiling, blowing kisses, she backed toward the wings, as they chanted: "More—more—more—more . . ."

She slipped into the backstage corridor, where Annabelle draped a shawl over Vanessa's bare shoulders, then escorted the perspiring singer down the narrow, crooked corridor to her dressing room. Vanessa dropped onto the couch, and felt as if she'd given an essential part of her substance away.

"Have a cup of coffee, Miss Vanessa," Annabelle said, fussing at the small wood stove in the corner.

"Pour some brandy in it, would you, dear?"

"It used to be a bottle a month—now it's a bottle every week."

"There's something I'd like you to do for me," Vanessa replied, ignoring common sense yet again. "In the saloon, near the door, you'll see Duane Braddock. Tell him that I want to speak with him, would you?"

Annabelle raised her eyebrows. "You know that Mister Edgar is in the audience, and he don't like it when you talks to *any* man, never mind a *young* man like Mister Duane."

"I have a right to friends, regardless of what Mister Petigru thinks. Get going."

Annabelle departed. Vanessa waited until she could hear no more footsteps, then bounded up, washed perspiration and cosmetics from her face, patted her skin dry, and sat before the mirror. She applied a new layer of coloring with a practiced hand. A woman wants to look her best, especially when she greets a *young* man.

The door continued to engorge more cowboys into the saloon, and a sea of bodies stretched to the back. Duane tried to move, as other cowboys searched for drinking and cigarette-smoking room. Duane received a shoulder in the back, pitched forward, and crashed into a short, bow-legged cowboy with his hat low over his eyes. "Watch yer step," the cowboy growled.

"Sorry," mumbled Duane, trying to catch his balance. His eye fell on a lamp hanging from the wall, flame flickering mischievously. What if there's a fire? Duane wondered. He imagined sheets of flame covering the walls, as men battled each other to escape. This place would go up like a pile of straw, Duane realized.

He was startled to see Vanessa's Negro maid pushing her way through the throngs. She drew close to Duane, and said: "Miss Vanessa wants to palaver with you. Foller me."

She plowed into the crowd, and cowboys made way for the plump, determined woman. Duane followed her toward the stage, and heard a voice nearby: "Ain't that the kid what got beat up in the cribs?"

On the other side of the room, through wreaths of smoke, Edgar Petigru had observed Annabelle appear from the wings, exchange a few words with a cowboy, and then escort him backstage. What the hell's going on here? he questioned.

Mayor Lonsdale turned toward Edgar. "That's the feller what spent the night with Miss Vanessa, and now he's a-headin' backstage? What's goin' on there, Mister New Yorker?"

Edgar's face grew sternly judgmental. "Her guests are none of your business, and please keep your snide remarks to yourself, you goddamned buffoon!"

"What was 'at?" the mayor asked, whipping out his Colt, and pointing it toward Edgar, who suddenly found himself looking into the mouth of a gun barrel. He tried to say something, went pale, and everyone at the table erupted into laughter. Mayor Lonsdale stuffed his Colt back into his belt, and Judge Jenks slapped Edgar on the back. "Relax," the judge advised, his face creased with glee. "Have another drink. You'll never put a bridle on that gal, so fergit it."

Annabelle opened the door. "H'yar he is," she said in a worried voice.

Vanessa lay resplendent on the couch, her wrist behind her golden curls. Duane was tempted to dive on top of her, but instead stepped politely to her side.

"Find something to do," Vanessa said to Annabelle.

Annabelle mumbled something incomprehensible as she closed the door, leaving Duane alone with the most notorious woman in Titusville. He cleared his throat and said, "You don't look well, Vanessa. Can I get you something to drink?"

"I'm perfectly fine, Duane, but have you been in another fight?"

"I fell down," he said in a low voice.

"I don't think you can get hurt that badly by simply falling down, but won't you have a seat? I've got good news."

Duane lowered himself to the chair, noticing rows of tiny bottles and pots in front of the mirror, just like Sally Mae in the cribs. The fabric of her robe lay against her long legs, and Duane could perceive their flexuous outlines. He coughed, crossed his legs, uncrossed them, and wondered where to put his hands.

She noted his discomfort, as her pride soared through the ceiling. "Guess what, Duane? A friend of mine owns a ranch, and he said that he'd give you a job."

"Did you tell him I don't know how to ride a horse?

"Somebody will teach you—it's all taken care of. Go to the Lazy Y first thing Monday morning, and report to the foreman. I'll hire a wagon to take you, and now that that's settled, you can tell me what you were fighting about." She examined him more closely, because it appeared that his left eye was nearly closed. "Why do you fight so much? Is something bothering you?"

He looked glumly at his boots. "If I tell you, you'll get angry."

"I promise that I won't." She raised her right hand solemnly.

"Now you're making fun of me."

She became exasperated. "I'm not making fun of you. You're so easily insulted, and I'll bet that's why you keep getting into fights. If we can't be honest with each other, I don't think we can be friends, Duane. You'll have to leave my dressing room, if you won't tell me."

Duane didn't want to leave, but neither could he tell her the truth. He was afraid the sky would fall, if he exposed his heart to her. "Guess I'll have to leave," he said. "Thanks for getting me the job."

He arose from the chair, but she placed her hands on his shoulders and forced him back down. "What you're saying is you don't trust me. Well, I guess you don't understand me very well. I believe in friendship, and you can always rely on me, but if you don't trust me—what can I say?"

She reclined on the sofa, an expression of chagrin on her face, and Duane was immobilized by her feigned unhappiness. "It's not that I don't trust you, Vanessa. But it'll make a mess between us, and you'll probably throw me out of your dressing room anyway."

"I promise that I won't throw you out of my dressing room. What more do I have to say?"

"It's not easy to put into words."

"I've never noticed any deficiencies in your speech before. You're a very articulate young man, but you're afraid of something, despite my assurances."

"You want to know what's bothering me?" he blurted angrily. "All right—here it is. I'm in love with you, but you treat me as if I were a kid."

The dressing room went silent. She'd expected a revelation of no great importance, but instead a declaration of love from an appealing *young* man prodded her conceit to even greater heights.

He raised his hand fearfully. "Don't get mad."

She found her voice somewhere around her toes. "I'm not mad." She coughed a few times. "If friends can't bare their hearts to each other, it's . . ." She had no idea of what to say.

"You asked me to be honest," he told her, "and I was. What should we do now?"

"You're going to the Lazy Y on Monday, to start your new job."

"What about us?"

"There is no *us*."

"But you said yourself that we should be honest with each other, and tell the truth, but now you're clamming up. I know what you think of me—another young idiot."

She examined him in his oversized cowboy clothes, and the black hat set off his ruddy features. "No, you're not a young idiot, but I'm engaged to Edgar

Petigru, and I'm afraid that's immutable."

"If things were different, do you think you and I might . . . ?"

"But things aren't different."

They stared into each other's eyes, and he wanted to touch the pale alabaster of her cheek. Her eyes filled with fear, and then, just when his fingers were inches from her satin skin, the door flew open.

"What's going on here!" demanded Edgar Petigru.

Duane drew his hand back quickly, as if caught picking someone's pocket. Vanessa recovered professionally, and swept toward Edgar, kissing him on the cheek. "Darling, I'm so glad you're here. This is the boy I told you about, who wants to be a cowboy. Edgar, meet Duane Braddock."

Edgar took a step backward and measured his rival carefully. He realized immediately that a boy wasn't standing before him, but a man at least two inches taller than he, with a trim, rangy build. If Edgar didn't know any better, he'd think the young man was a seasoned rider of the sage.

Duane took his cue, and tried to grin convincingly, but it came out false. "Thanks for giving me the job, Mister Petigru. I'll work hard—you can count on me."

Duane held out his hand for a friendly shake, while Edgar eyed it suspiciously. The entrepreneur realized that he was in grave danger of appearing foolish, so he smiled fraudulently, and gripped Duane's hand.

"Vanessa told me all about you. Report to my foreman, and tell him I said to hire you."

"Sir, I've got a friend who's an experienced cowboy, and I wonder if you'd have a spot for him, too?"

Edgar shrugged, and tried to speak in a deep rancher voice, but it came out oddly off-key. "We're a growing operation, and we can use all the *experienced* men we can find. Sure—take him along with you— why not?"

Duane muttered his gratitude as he fled out the door, leaving Edgar and Vanessa alone. "What a strange young man," remarked Edgar.

"You'd be strange, too, if you were having a normal conversation, and somebody charged into the room without knocking. You know, Edgar—you don't own me, just because you've bought me a house!"

She slammed her fist on the dressing table, and little bottles performed a lopsided dance. Edgar was mortified, because the walls were thin and her volume substantially higher than usual. He held his finger in front of his lips. "Now, dear," he began, "try to see my side. There I was with my business associates, and it's common knowledge that you and I are . . . having a romance of a certain kind, but then you invite *him* backstage, in full view of everyone, but not me."

"I did invite him backstage," she replied coolly, "to tell him about the job, because he's very poor. He would've left in a few moments, and I had intended to spend the rest of my time with you, but you have so destroyed the atmosphere between us with your thoughtless and inconsiderate actions, that I've changed my mind. If you'll excuse me, I must prepare for my next show."

"But . . . but . . ." Edgar sputtered, as she pushed him toward the door. He wanted to explain that it was his saloon, and she was working for him, but before he knew it he was in the hallway, her door latching behind him. He scuffled to the main room of the saloon, and realized that everybody was looking at him; sniggers reached his ears. She's making a fool out of me, he told himself, and if I let her get away with it, I'll be laughed out of town.

The street was filled with cowboys talking loudly, drinking whiskey from bottles, and no women were in sight. It's a man's world, Duane reflected, just like the monastery in the clouds, but Vanessa Fontaine has got the richest man in town jumping though hoops, and me, too.

He thought of her sitting insouciantly in her chair, chiding Edgar. What is it about her that makes me loco? Duane wondered. A lifetime in a monastery has done me no good, because I'm bad to the bone.

His hatband gleamed in the moonlight, as he searched for Boggs in every congregation of drinkers, cardplayers, and crapshooters. Titusville had twenty saloons, and Duane was resolved to search them all, especially since Boggs was going to teach him to ride a horse.

He veered into the Longhorn, another dirty, dingy little corner of hell, redolent with whiskey, tobacco, sweat, and cheap perfume. A black-tressed prostitute in her midthirties swung her hips toward Duane as he stood in the doorway, black leather thongs hanging down his tanned cheeks.

"Howdy, cowboy," she said, flashing her best smile, and she had two teeth missing on top, and one gone from the bottom.

"I'm looking for a fellow named Boggs," Duane replied.

"What're you want a feller fer, when you can have a gal." She pressed her body against him and touched her tongue to his neck. If a man has enough money, he can screw himself into the grave, he realized.

"Let's go in back," she whispered, biting his earlobe.

"I've got things to do."

He eluded her grasp, and scanned the sea of heads and hats before him, but couldn't spot Boggs. Saul Klevins sat at the bar, and Duane moved into the shadows, so he could observe the famous gunfighter at leisure. Klevins wore his black leather vest, black hat, and white shirt, his six-shooter low on his hip. He looked like a weasel, with his round nose and sinister grin, and was the major local celebrity, except for Vanessa Fontaine. Everyone deferred to him like vassals in the days of chivalry.

Duane heard a rough voice in his ear. "Hey, kid—buy a drink, or get the fuck out." It was the bouncer, a bearlike man wearing pants low on his hips, crotch down to his knees.

"I was about to order," Duane lied.

"What's yer pleasure?"

"Whiskey."

The bear waddled toward the bar, and Duane spotted a lone table in the middle of the floor. He sat, while continuing to observe Saul Klevins. Is it a skill that he acquired, or do you have be born with it? he questioned. Saul Klevins perused the saloon back and forth, although he appeared to be relaxing with friends. Some men herded cattle, others worked in general stores, but a gunfighter killed for money, like a mercenary soldier. Duane's father had been one of them, and he knew that the poison swam in his blood, too.

The bear returned with the glass of whiskey, and set it before Duane. Boggs wasn't in the saloon, and it was time to move on, but a cowboy doesn't walk away from whiskey. Duane leaned his head back, poured the whiskey down his throat, and swallowed furiously. The glass emptied, and Duane slammed it down on the table.

He suddenly became disoriented, as alcohol dumped into his bloodstream. His eyes protruded from his head, he sucked wind, and felt as though a firestorm had broken out in his chest. A wave of dizziness came over him; he desperately needed water. He arose from the table, and broke into a paroxysm of coughing.

Somebody slammed him on the back. "You all right, kid?" A mug of beer appeared before Duane. "Have a drink."

Duane swallowed twice, as cool foamy liquid bubbled down his throat and put out the fire. Duane handed the mug back to the bearded, grinning cowboy, then made for the door, but it felt as though he'd wandered onto the deck of a ship in stormy seas. The room pitched and tossed, and he walked into one of the wooden posts that held up the ceiling.

"You okay, kid?"

The voice came from a grotesquely painted prostitute in a red polka dot dress. She reached out and pinched his cheek. "Come lie down with me. I'll make you feel real fine."

"Got to find somebody," Duane replied, lurching toward the door.

He stepped outside, and the cool night hair steadied him. I can't drink a glass of whiskey in every saloon, Duane realized. They'll find me in the gutter with all the other drunkards. He moved through the noisy night, arrived at the Cattlemen, pushed open the doors, and headed toward the bar. Without a hitch in his movement, he scouted the back of the saloon, cut through the tables, and was out the front door again.

He searched three more saloons, still no Lester Boggs. A substantial crowd gathered in front of the Round-Up, as cowboys tried to squeeze inside for the next show. Boggs won't be in there, Duane thought. He'll be in the most filthy and disgusting saloon available. Duane remembered the Blind Pig off Main Street. Of course.

Bodies became too numerous on the sidewalk, so he cut into the muddy street, walking behind horses' tails. He made a few turns, and came to the dark alley where the Blind Pig was located, its lights twinkling through dirty windows. A decent person wouldn't dream of going to such a place, and that's why Boggs is probably there.

He entered, stood in the shadows, and examined the small, crowded establishment, about one-quarter the size of the Round-Up, with no dance floor, no chop counter, nothing but whiskey and whores. One of the latter creatures sidled up to him, and he turned to her garish cosmetics. She was sixty if she was a day, had no teeth in her mouth, and grinned merrily. "You look like you could use a good screw."

"I'm looking for a friend of mine," Duane replied,

extricating himself from her claws. He plunged deeper into the Blind Pig Saloon, and it looked like the lower depths of hell, with grimy, sweaty cowboys squeezing against painted harlots. His eyes fell on Lester Boggs sitting in a corner, with a whore on his lap, both lapping whiskey. Duane pulled up a chair opposite them. "Figured this is where you'd be, pardner. Where'd you steal the money?"

Boggs replied without batting an eyelash: "You remember that feller I was supposed to meet—the one what owed me ten dollars? I ran into him in the pisshouse behind the Cattlemen Saloon. He was sober fer a change, said he remembered that he owed me, and paid up. This here bundle of beauty a-sittin' on my lap is Maggie. Say hello to Duane Braddock, Maggie."

"Hiya Duane," she said with a wry grin, and she, too, didn't have a tooth in her head. "Yer kind've cute."

Duane leaned toward Boggs. "You'll never guess what happened. I've found the both of us cowboy jobs at the Lazy Y. A friend of mine introduced me to Edgar Petigru, who owns the spread. He hired me even though he knows that I can't ride a horse."

Boggs looked seriously inebriated, his eyes half closed, face flushed with rotgut whiskey. "You got some pretty good friends in this town. Who is he?"

"He's a she." Duane didn't want to mention Vanessa's name, so he told another lie. "Old friend of the family."

"Back in the stagecoach, to tell you the truth, I thought you was a little simple, but it ain't even Monday yet, and you got *both* of us a job? I guess you ain't as dumb as you look." Boggs spat toward the cuspidor, but the cargo landed on the boot of a cowboy passed out at the next table.

Maggie unwound her tongue into Boggs's ear. "Let's go in back, cowboy. I'll give you the ride of yer life."

Boggs winked at Duane and said: "See you in a little bit."

Boggs drained his glass of whiskey, took Maggie's hand, and they walked like bride and groom down the aisle, heading toward the rooms in back.

Duane felt dispirited by lonely men willing to descend to any depths for a few fleeting moments of women's love. He couldn't help comparing the Blind Pig to the monastery in the clouds. This is exactly what the Gospels tell you to avoid, Duane realized, and here I am in the middle of it, a glass of rotgut whiskey in my hand.

He drained off half the glass, and infernos licked his throat. You can't really understand sin unless you wallow in it, he decided. I won't come to town for another month, so I might as well enjoy it while I'm here.

A familiar voice came to him from the direction of the bar. "Isn't that the little son of a bitch over thar?"

Duane was shocked to see the four cowboys whom he'd fought earlier at the cribs. They peered in his direction, and didn't appear willing to let bygones be bygones. Dave wore a white bandage on his nose, and his face was puffed like Duane's. "I orter shoot 'im like a fuckin' dog!" Dave said.

It was difficult for Duane to believe that they were actually discussing the termination of his existence. Casually, he arose and headed toward the door, leaving his half-glass of whiskey behind.

"Hold on!" Dave sidestepped among tables, moving to cut off Duane's retreat, and he felt a rise of panic. He wanted to run for the back door, but could get a bullet in the back. He slowed his pace, as Dave blocked his path.

"Where d'ya think yer goin', Sonny Jim?" asked Dave.

"What's it to you?" Duane replied.

Lightning flashed out of Dave's eyes, and his broken nose still hurt despite several shots of whiskey. Dave thought he had a score to settle with Duane, and the time had come to submit the bill. "Yer a mean little son of a bitch," Dave said, "but I'm a-gonna kill you."

Duane knew that whatever he said, it'd only make matters worse. Please, God—don't let him shoot me. Dave reached down, pulled out his Colt, drew back the hammer, and aimed the barrel at Duane. "You done fucked with the wrong cowboy."

Duane closed his eyes. Hail Mary, full of grace, the Lord is with thee, blessed is . . .

His prayer was interrupted by a sound from the bar. "If yer a-gonna shoot 'im, do it in the alley. I ain't got time to clean up the mess, and the deputy ain't wuth a fiddler's fuck."

The bartender was an old, white-haired man with a tobacco-stained mustache, wearing a dirty white apron and holding something that looked like a blunderbuss.

Dave motioned with his gun to the back door. "Git movin'."

Duane realized that he was headed for his summary execution, and wished somebody would step forward to save him. Then a shot rang out, and Duane felt a stab in his heart. He was certain he'd been hit, but out of the corner of his eye, he saw the bartender stagger to the side. One of Dave's cowboy pals had taken a side shot at him. The bartender fell to the floor, the blunderbuss fell out of his hands, and the Blind Pig became very silent.

Cowboys and whores drifted toward the doors, while others ducked behind the bar, or dropped to the floor. Dave lined up his sights on Duane's shirt, and Duane realized that his only hope was to buy time. "I'll go outside with you," he said.

He headed toward the back door, expecting a bullet in his skull, but instead heard footsteps behind him, and realized that Dave and the others were following. He pushed open the back door, and stepped into a yard with a foul-smelling privy ten yards away, next to the woodpile.

Duane wanted to run for his life, but he couldn't run faster than a bullet. Men poured out the back door of the Blind Pig, while others streamed in through alleys, for word was spreading through town that a shootout was imminent behind the Blind Pig Saloon.

Duane faced the battered cowboy across the backyard, and tried to understand. I should never have left the monastery, he chided himself. Brother Paolo warned me, I didn't listen, and now I'm going to pay the price.

Dave raised his gun and aimed down the barrel at Duane. "Say yer prayers—you little shit."

Duane stared at the gun barrel and tried to steady himself. Hail Mary, full of grace . . .

Dave's finger tightened around the trigger, the flames of hell danced before Duane's eyes. "Give 'im a fightin' chance," somebody said. "Otherwise, it's murder."

Another voice chimed in: "You can't kill an unarmed man, cowboy. Why, tain't fair."

Dave nodded toward one of his friends. "Hardy—lend 'im yer gun."

"Aw shit," Hardy replied. "Why don't you just shoot 'im and git it over with?"

Another voice came from the crowd. "You got to give 'im a play," he said. "We're all witnesses here."

Dave spoke again. "I said give 'im yer gun, Hardy."

Hardy stepped forward, cursing beneath his breath. He unbuckled his brown leather gun belt, and passed it to Duane. Duane weighed it in his hand thoughtfully for a moment, then fastened it low around his waist. He tied the leather thong at the bottom of the holster around his leg, just like the other men in the crowd, but he knew it was all futile, and he didn't have a prayer.

The gun felt heavy and strange against his leg, but he was armed for the first time in his life, and maybe his last. He eased the gun out of the holster, wrapped his long fingers around the grips, and inserted his forefinger into the trigger guard. "I've never fired one of these things before," he admitted.

"Yer a-gonna larn fast," Dave said, "otherwise I'll shoot ya where ya stand."

"How does it work?" Duane asked, trying to remember what the gunsmith had taught him, something about cocking a hammer.

The crowd was stunned into silence. The kid didn't even know how to fire a gun? It looked like slaughter was about to commence. Duane chewed his lower lip, and wondered how he could discern whether the gun was loaded. For all he knew, Hardy had given him an empty weapon. He angled it toward the ground, and looked into the cylinder.

"Does anyone mind if I show him how to use it?" asked a voice in the crowd.

Duane was surprised to see Clyde Butterfield, hat tilted rakishly over his eyes, cheroot in his teeth, thumbs hooked in his gun belt. The ex-gunfighter sauntered out of the crowd and into the line of fire. "The kid doesn't even get a chance?" he asked, a disapproving note in his voice.

"Git out'n my road, or you might get shot, too, you old fart."

Butterfield tensed, but Dave's cowboy friends aimed their guns at him. "Hold it right there, mister," one of them said. "Unless yer ready fer lead."

"I only want to show the kid how to use the gun. You boys aren't afraid of him, are you?"

"Hell no," Dave replied. "I'll shoot him, and then I'll shoot you."

Butterfield walked lazily toward Duane, and came to a stop a few feet away. His jocular manner vanished, his face became solemn, and he peered intensely into Duane's eyes. "Listen to me, boy," he said. "This cowboy has been drinking all night, and he's nearly out on his feet. You can live if you do as I say. Now draw your gun like so." Butterfield gave him a side view, and demonstrated the classic draw. "The goal isn't to fire the first shot, but the first *accurate* shot.

When the barrel of your gun clears your holster, snap it up, and fire at the center of his chest. You can't take forever to aim, but you can't shoot wild, either. It's got to be one smooth motion. Draw, snap, thumb back the hammer, aim, and trigger. I'll show you again."

"Let's speed it up over there," said Dave. "I ain't got all night." Dave reached into his shirt pocket and took out a plug of tobacco, as Butterfield performed the draw once again.

"You don't have to be a genius to do this," Butterfield explained. "It's got to feel right, that's all."

Duane smiled bitterly. "I don't have a chance, and you know it. It's kind of you to help, but that man's fired his gun before, and I've never fired mine. Experience has to count for something in this game, doesn't it?"

"I know that you're a beginner, but he's half in the bag. Look at him—he's practically reeling. I'm telling you straight, boy, you've got a chance to live here. It's up to you, but don't give up before you even pull the trigger."

Duane turned his gaze across the backyard, where his adversary eyed him with open contempt. How'd I get into this? Duane wondered.

"What's the hold-up?" Dave asked.

Butterfield smiled, his cheroot still clamped between his teeth. "Just showing him how to pull the trigger, that's all. You wouldn't want to gunfight a man who didn't know how to pull the trigger, would you?"

"Keep it up," Dave replied. "I got a bullet fer you, too."

Butterfield turned toward Duane. "Listen close,

because it might be the last lesson you ever get. A gun-fight is more than just fast hands. It's also what you got inside you, that makes you tick. What is it that you want more than anything in the world?"

Duane saw Vanessa Fontaine seated at her dressing table, her silk robe clinging to her long, graceful limbs. "It's a woman," Duane admitted.

"You'll never kiss her again, if you don't shoot that son of a bitch over there." Butterfield took a step backward, then turned toward Dave again. "You don't mind if he makes a few practice draws, do you?"

"Yer gittin' to be a pain in the ass, you know that, old man?"

"Are you looking for an easy win?"

Dave spat some tobacco juice at the ground. "I'll let 'im practice, just as long as he don't point that gun in my direction."

Duane turned toward the crowd, which moved out of his line of fire. He moved his legs apart and went into the gunfighter's crouch that Clyde had just demonstrated. He poised his hand, then reached down, grabbed the gun, drew, and aimed.

"Very good," Butterfield replied dryly, "except you forgot a very important point—you didn't thumb back the hammer. And when you snapped up, you went too high, and then you had to bring the gun barrel down, which wastes time. You're never going to see that gal again, unless you wake up."

Duane went into his crouch again, and it felt like a familiar posture. He reached for the gun, and caught a glimpse of a strange phantom in a black mustache standing at the edge of the crowd. The Colt flew into Duane's hand, but didn't rise so far this time, and he didn't forget to thumb back the hammer.

"Much better," Butterfield said. "Once more."

Duane focused his mind, went into the crouch, slapped his hand down, yanked iron, snapped, thumbed, and pulled the trigger. *Click.*

Dave's voice came to them from the far side of the yard. "I'm a-gittin' tired of this horseshit. Let's git started, kid."

Butterfield turned toward Duane. "Even if he gets off the first shot, don't get flustered. Your gun's going to kick hard, so be prepared. If he hits you, keep on going. You aren't scared, are you?"

"You're damned right I am!"

"You can always get down on your knees and beg for mercy. He might let you go, but on the other hand, he might not."

"I'm not getting on my knees for anybody."

Butterfield loaded Duane's gun, then handed it to him butt first. He placed his hand on Duane's shoulder and looked into his eyes. "Go ahead and shoot this fucker down."

Butterfield winked, then stepped backward toward the crowd, holding his hands in the air. Duane holstered his gun, and turned toward his opponent. "I'm ready."

"'Bout time," Dave replied, irritation in his voice. He faced Duane and spread his legs apart. "Go ahead and draw," he said. "Ladies first."

Duane blushed at the insult, and for the first since the encounter began, felt a rise of anger. I hate him, he thought, and if I don't shoot him, I'll never kiss Vanessa Fontaine.

Duane worked his shoulders, loosened his fingers,

and went into his gunfighter's crouch. He had the eerie feeling that the man with the black mustache was behind him, guiding his movements. This is it, he thought. Kill or be killed, down and dirty to the bitter end. His life passed before his eyes, as he recalled coming to consciousness in the monastery in the clouds, living under the Rule of Saint Benedict, singing Gregorian chant in the chapel, and ending up in Titusville, Texas. How strange is the trajectory of a man's life, he reflected.

"You better git a move on, boy. Yer pissin' me off."

Duane brought his right hand to rest above the walnut grip of the Colt. He leaned forward, due to the high heels of his boots, then his hand darted downward, and he saw Dave go into motion before him. A hush fell over the crowd as the barrel of Duane's Colt cleared the top of the holster. He raised the barrel up Dave's body, thumbed back the hammer, but he was nervous, and raised too high again!

Dave fired the first shot, and Duane felt hot lead pass his cheek. Gritting his teeth, he brought his gun barrel in line with Dave's chest, and pulled the trigger. The report of the gun startled Duane. It kicked into the air, smoke billowed around him, and gunpowder filled his nostrils. He peered through black clouds, and saw Dave staggering at the far side of the yard, both hands gripping his stomach, his head bowed as if in prayer. Dave's hat fell off, and then he followed it to the ground, where he landed in a clump.

Silence filled the backyard, and Duane's mouth hung open. He was still in the shooter's position, arm extended before him, a wisp of smoke arising from the barrel of the Colt. I just shot a man. My God! he yelled silently.

Across the yard, Dave's cowboy pals kneeled around him, and one listened to his heart. "Somebody better git the sawbones."

Duane felt as though he were looking down at himself with the gun in his hand. I was headed for the priesthood, he thought. *Thou shalt not kill.* A crowd gathered around him, gazing in awe, and he couldn't believe that he still was alive. *Glory be to the Father, the Son, and the Holy Ghost.* In jerky movements, he dropped the Colt in its holster. Clyde Butterfield approached, smiling proudly at the success of his novice. "You did it, just as I said, but the best is yet to come. You won't have to pay for another drink for the rest of the night, and you'll probably even get laid!"

CHAPTER 5

BUTTERFIELD LED DUANE INTO THE Longhorn Saloon. "If his aim had been three inches to the left, he would've cleaned your clock."

They headed for a round table at the back, where a cowboy was passed out. Butterfield picked him up, then deposited him in the aisle. "Have a seat," Butterfield said. "I'll get us a bottle."

Butterfield stepped over the drunken cowboy, as Duane sat at the table. He leaned back his head, closed his eyes, and saw himself standing in the backyard of the Blind Pig, the smoking gun in his hand, Dave crashing to the ground before him. And Duane didn't even know who Dave was, or where he came from. If I hadn't left the monastery, this never would've happened, Duane realized.

I killed him, but he wouldn't let me off the hook, he reasoned. The incident behind the Blind Pig seemed a dream, but everyone in the saloon was looking at him with fear, admiration, curiosity, and other expressions he couldn't fathom. Something told him that his life would never be the same.

Butterfield returned to the table, carrying a bottle and two glasses. "On the house." He sat opposite Duane, filled the glasses with whiskey, and pushed one toward Duane. "Happy days."

Duane touched his glass to Butterfield's, then took a sip of smooth, silky whiskey. He and Butterfield sat in silence for several minutes, then Butterfield grabbed Duane's shoulder. "Don't let it git you down, kid. I know how you feel. My opinion, for what it's worth—it's better to die clean, than be a coward."

Duane pondered that philosophy, and admitted that it made a certain sense. It would be humiliating to back down, and wherever you went, somebody might know who you were, point the finger, and make remarks.

"For a kid who says he's never fired a gun before," Butterfield said confidentially, "you sure had a fast hand. Are you sure you haven't been bullshitting me?"

"If I'm bullshitting you, then I'm bullshitting myself as well. And I don't even know who that cowboy was, or anything about him." Duane narrowed his eyes as he scrutinized Butterfield more carefully. "I can't help wondering why you stepped into the line of fire. You could've been killed, and you don't hardly know me."

Butterfield grunted. "Life's too short fer questions,

kid. Just keep this in mind: no matter how fast you are, there's always somebody a little faster." He tossed down the remainder of his glass.

"They say that *you* used to be a gunfighter, Mister Butterfield."

Butterfield paused, becoming more serious. "Long time ago," he replied in an almost inaudible voice.

"Ever hear of an outlaw named Joe Braddock?"

"Met a lot've people in my day, kid. Can't remember them all."

"He was my father, and I'm trying to find out who he was."

"Why?"

"I never met him."

"There are probably a hundred Joe Braddocks in Texas, who were outlaws. Now, if you'll excuse me, I'll see about getting us laid."

Butterfield arose from the table, and Duane realized that he'd pushed the ex-gunfighter too hard. Duane's mind was a jumble of images mixed together and folded over, as he watched Butterfield head for the door. It was difficult for him to believe that he'd actually *killed* a man, although the gun on his hip was proof that it truly happened. He drew the Colt and held it in the candlelight, so he could see it better.

It was the first time he'd really looked at its plain wooden grips and smoothly machined iron, a utility model with no designs or special flourishes, but it did the job. He raised it to his nose, and could smell the faint aroma of gunpowder.

The whiff brought the scene back in all its awful splendor. If the cowboy had aimed three inches to the right, Duane would be on his way to boot hill. Duane saw the cowboy stagger, clutching his stomach. A powerful, brutish man had become a hurt creature, without a will of his own, in the time it takes to draw and fire.

I beat him, Duane thought. He felt proud and guilty at the same time. I'm the son of an outlaw and a whore—the bad seed. And then he was forced to admit something that he'd been hiding ever since he'd left the monastery in the clouds.

The fight with Jasper Jakes wasn't the cut-and-dried affair that he liked to believe. It was true that Jakes had goaded him, but Duane could've walked away easily. The monastery wasn't a saloon, where you were expected to defend your honor, whatever that meant, with fists, guns, knives, broken bottles, or anything else you could lay your hands on.

He'd lacked the will to depart the monastery on his own, so laid into Jasper Jakes one afternoon, and then the abbot made the decision for him. I'm a schemer, he thought, and now I'm a killer. That cowboy might've had kids, and I made them orphans. He recalled a line from the Bible: *How filthy and abominable is man, who drinketh iniquity like water.*

A bartender carried a bottle of whiskey to the table, and said, "Mister Klevins sent this one over, sir."

Duane turned toward the bar, and saw the fastest hand in the county raise a glass in the air in a silent toast to the newest gun in town. Duane lifted his own glass, swallowed a small amount, and noticed eyes turned in his direction; they were talking about him. Two days ago, when I first came to this town, nobody knew my name, he mused. Now I've killed a man, and who can say where it'll end?

In the dressing room of the Round-Up Saloon, Vanessa wiped perspiration off her face. She'd just completed another performance, and felt worn out. What did I do to deserve this miserable grinding life? she pondered.

She recalled happy days at the old plantation, a never-ending round of delightful activities, instead of the Round-Up Saloon. She reminisced about gala parties that lasted for days, with gentlemen and ladies arriving from all across the South, and even Governor Hammond would attend, not to mention Wade Hampton, wealthiest planter in South Carolina. Now it all had disappeared into the dustbin of history. There was a knock at the door.

"Come in?"

The door opened, and Edgar Petigru entered. "Have you heard the news?" he asked gaily.

"How could I hear any news?" she responded, a note of irritation in her voice. "I spend my life in this room."

"It seems as though your little friend has just shot somebody."

"Duane?"

He smirked. "I didn't know that you had more than one little friend. Of course it was Duane, poor, innocent orphan that he is, whose anguished story you related so movingly earlier in the day. Evidently he's a killer, and he flimflammed the other fellow into a gunfight that he couldn't lose."

"If this is your idea of a joke, Edgar, it's not funny."

"No, it's your boy Duane, all right—gaudy cowboy hat and all. They say it was quite exciting. He behaved as though he'd never fired a gun before, then shot his man down. Even Saul Klevins was impressed."

Vanessa looked at herself in the mirror. It can't be, he thought.

"What's wrong, Vanessa? You're not looking well. Can I get you something to drink?"

Duane sat alone in the corner of the Longhorn Saloon, pondering his conversation with Butterfield. The old ex-gunfighter was playing a peculiar game, and Duane wondered what it was.

He recalled how Butterfield had looked at him funny, after Duane had first arrived in town. And Butterfield stepped into the line of fire, risking his life to give Duane the benefit of his knowledge. I'll bet he knew my father, Duane thought. But for some reason, he won't talk.

A stout man in a frock coat, wearing a stovepipe hat, approached down the aisle, his face wreathed with a smile. He was midthirties, had a pinkish face, and removed his hat with a graceful sweep. "Howdy—my name's Farnsworth—reporter for the *Titusville Sentinel*. I'm also the typesetter, proofreader, and advertising manager, not to mention editor and publisher. Mind if I sit down?"

Duane opened his mouth to respond, but the reporter lowered himself onto a seat without waiting. "It's been a helluva Saturday night. According to unreliable sources, there've been fourteen saloon brawls and two shootings, including yours. What'd you say your name was?"

"I didn't say."

"I arrived on the scene a little late, and you were already gone. They said that you pretended that you never fired a gun before, then drilled him through the chest with your first shot."

Duane looked at the reporter, who resembled a fat, blond rat in a frock coat with a string tie. "I wasn't pretending."

"I've worked on newspapers all across the frontier, and I brought my press to Titusville on the back of a mule, but I never heard of a man who never fired a gun before, and then takes out his adversary with the first shot. Somebody said you were Jesse James, but I saw Jesse once, and he's old enough to be your daddy. Why won't you tell me your name?"

Duane knew that his name wasn't a secret, and he hadn't done anything wrong, but felt uncooperative. "I want to be alone," Duane said, thinning his lips. "If you don't mind."

"Kid, there's something that you don't understand. The story'll get written whether you talk with me or not, but at least I'm giving you a chance to tell your side."

"The man egged me on," Duane said, "and somehow I beat him. That's all there was."

"Not the way I heard it," wheedled the news hound. "They say he was drunk, and you suckered him into the fight."

"Talk to the witnesses."

"Some say one thing, and some say another. The

rest aren't so sure. Certain rumors are flying, and I was just wondering if they're true. You weren't hired to kill that cowboy, were you?"

The accusation was so preposterous, Duane didn't know what to say. "I think you'd better take a walk, mister. You're making me mad."

"What're you going to do—shoot me? You know what'll happen if you shoot a reporter? You'll decorate the southern end of a rope."

"I said take a walk, mister."

Farnsworth saw a wicked gleam in the kid's eye, and discretion was the better part of valor. "If that's the way you want it, Mister Whatever-Your-Name-Is, that's the way it'll be. Good night to you, and by the way, you'd better start watching your back. Some drunken cowboy might want to make his reputation by shooting the kid with the fast hand."

The reporter meandered toward the bar, and Duane reflected on what he'd said. Somebody might want to make his reputation by shooting me? Duane looked to his left and right suspiciously. Then he sipped his drink, feeling confused by onrushing events. It seemed that only a few days ago he'd been in the monastery, and now he was a news item for sleazy reporters. Will I have to leave town? he wondered. But I don't have any money, and I've got a job at the Lazy Y. I wish I could've walked away from the gunfight, but that drunken cowboy wouldn't let me, he thought sadly.

"So thar you are!"

It was Lester Boggs ambling down the aisle, a quizzical expression on his face, his nose wrinkled incredulously. He sat on the chair opposite Duane and said: "What's this I just heard about you? They say yer a professional killer. You been bullshittin' me, boy?"

"I'm not a professional anything."

"They said you were as fast as Saul Klevins."

"It was a lucky shot," Duane tried to explain. "I never fired a gun before in my life."

Boggs raised his eyes skeptically. "It don't make sense, kid. If you never fired a gun before, you'd be dead."

"That's why I said it was luck." The words spilled out of Duane's mouth before he could stop himself. "It felt as if my father was with me, moving my hand."

Boggs looked at the bottle of whiskey next to the flickering candle. "I think you been drinking too much of that shit, kid. Mind if I have some?"

Without waiting for an answer, or obtaining a glass, Boggs pulled the cork and took a swig. "You sure had me fooled. I bet you know how to ride a horse, too. What kind've game're you playin'?"

"It's no game, and the worst part is somebody might want to shoot me, to make his reputation."

Boggs moved closer, and raised an eyebrow. "What's yer real name?"

"You know what my real name is."

Boggs nodded, then winked conspiratorially. "There's a sheriff a-lookin' fer you, and you don't want to make it easy fer him. I understand, 'cause I've gone by different names, too, and in fact, sometimes I forget which is real."

It's no use, Duane thought. They won't listen to me, and there's nothing I can say to change their warped minds. It's like the reporter said: they believe what they want.

Clyde Butterfield strode jauntily toward him, the

inevitable cheroot in his teeth. "It's all arranged at Miss Ellie's," he said. "You're getting laid on the house, and so'm I. The girls can't wait to meet you."

Boggs raised his forefinger. "What about me?"

"Who the hell're you?"

"I'm his horse-ridin' perfessor."

"We'll see if we can find somebody fer you to ride. Let's get a move on, boys, because we don't want to keep the ladies waiting. And I'll take charge of that bottle, if you don't mind."

Butterfield scooped it off the table, and headed for the door in his long-legged, gangly gait. Duane followed him, curious about what other bounties the night would offer. He glanced at the clock above the bar, and it was nearly midnight. The most incredible day of my life, he thought. They came to the doors, and Butterfield blew them open with a mighty thrust of his hands.

Duane stepped outside, and the sidewalk debaters quieted as they stared at the kid with the fast hand. Duane, Butterfield, and Boggs walked three abreast, and everybody got out of their way. Duane recalled reading about the heroes of ancient Rome, when they returned to the Eternal City after a successful military campaign. In the general's chariot stood a little man paid to say over and over: "Remember, thou art but a man."

But Duane didn't feel like an ordinary man anymore. Here I am with a famous ex-gunfighter and a genuine professional cowboy. If life isn't a joke, then what is it?

"Ho!" cried a voice on the other side of the street. "Wait a minute over thar!"

A long-armed man beckoned, and Duane perceived a tin badge on his rawhide vest.

"It's Deputy Dawson," Butterfield said. "Don't pay him no mind, and maybe he'll go away."

Deputy Dawson ducked beneath the hitching rail, and headed into the street. "Hold on, thar."

Boggs frowned. "The son of a bitch has seen us. If there's anythin' I hate, it's a lawman."

"I'll do the talking," said Butterfield, framing his widest smile as the deputy crossed the turd-befouled street. "Why howdy, Deputy. What can we do for you?"

Deputy Dawson ignored Butterfield, turning instead to Duane. "Your name Braddock?"

"That's right," Duane said.

"I hear you shot a cowboy name of Dave Collins in back of the Blind Pig."

Butterfield grinned, and held out the palms of his hands. "Self-defense all the way," he interjected. "This young man wasn't even armed. He did everything he could to back out of it, but the other cowboy wouldn't let him off the hook."

Boggs decided the time had come to add his testimony, although he'd been in bed with a prostitute at the time. "That's the way I saw it, too. The cowboy din't leave 'im no way out."

Dawson looked harshly at Duane. "They say yer a fast gun from the Pecos country, but I don't care how good yer supposed to be. You better stay out of trouble while yer in Titusville, or I'll clap you in jail. And if I can't handle you myself, I'll send fer the Rangers." Dawson looked first at Butterfield, then at Boggs. "You boys had better stay out of trouble, too."

"On our way to Miss Ellie's," Butterfield explained. "Maybe we'll see you there later?"

Deputy Dawson scowled. "You may see me there later, but I'll be on my rounds—I ain't no customer, like some I could name." He readjusted his ten-gallon hat, and moved into the street.

"Tetchy, ain't he?" asked Boggs. "Walks like he's got a broomstick up his ass."

Butterfield replied, "He's got a townful of drunks on his hands, and somebody'll probably shoot him one of these days. I guess it sticks in his craw that they won't make him sheriff." Butterfield placed his arm around Duane's shoulder, and moved him along the sidewalk, as Boggs kept up on the outside. "I've found out a few things about that feller you killed. Him and his pards weren't local cowboys, because nobody had ever seen them before. They were drifters, maybe owl hoots. You'd best keep your eyes open in Titusville, boy. You never can tell when that bullet might come with your name on it."

The most expensive whorehouse in Titusville looked like any other freshly painted structure on the quiet street, except light glowed behind heavily draped windows, while the other buildings were darkened.

Clyde Butterfield guided Duane toward the front steps, as he continued his monologue. "I've been in whorehouses all over this country, and I was even in Frisco once, but the whores at Miss Ellie's are as fine as you'll see anywhere, and you don't have to worry about some galoot coming out of a closet with a lead pipe in his hands. Miss Ellie only attracts the finer class of clientele, such as lawyers, lawmen, and old bluffers like me." With a dramatic gesture, Butterfield ascended the stairs. "Right this way, boys. Don't be shy."

He knocked on the door, and a small window on the other side opened. Two suspicious eyes looked out, then the window closed. The door opened, and Duane gazed down a corridor covered with a red carpet, while red wallpaper adorned the walls. Duane and Boggs followed Butterfield inside, the door closed behind them, and Duane turned around.

Two men with guns guarded the door, just like in the cribs, but these wore ruffled shirts and string ties. They smiled at Duane, as if recognizing one of their own. I'm finally a real man, he realized. All I had to do was kill somebody.

A woman with long, straight black hair and a black satin dress materialized out of the shadows. "You must be Duane Braddock," she said with a smile, extending her hand to him.

He didn't know whether to kiss her hand, shake it, or what? But she solved the dilemma by taking his fingers and squeezing. "Follow me, please."

She led him down a corridor lined with burning candles, and it smelled like the nave of a church. His guide had substantial breasts, and her perfume swirled through his mind. She opened the door on a little parlor with a bottle of whiskey, a bucket of ice, and several glasses on a low mahogany table.

"Miss Ellie wants to meet you," she said to Duane. "I'll get her."

She departed, and Butterfield poured three glasses of whiskey. Duane pulled back the curtain. The houses across the street were shrouded in darkness, while the sky reflected light from the saloon district in the distance.

"Get away from the window," Butterfield warned. "Somebody might take a random shot at you."

The ex-gunfighter reached out and closed the curtain. Duane stepped back from the window, his precious anonymity gone. The door opened, and a brunette in a tight-fitting gown appeared, followed by a redhead and a little wizened old lady with painted eyes and purple lipstick, attired in a glittering sequined sky-blue gown. "So you're Duane Braddock," the old lady said. "Wa'al, I'm Miss Ellie, and I'm pleased to make yer acquaintance. I heard that you was a handsome boy, and they sure wasn't lyin.'" She turned toward Butterfield. "And it's good to see you again, you horny old goat."

She held out her hand. Butterfield bent over, and kissed the hot crinkly skin, as she looked Duane up and down. "In my 'sperience, the main thing a man needs when he's shot somebody is a good piece of ass. Go git 'im, girls."

Smiles on their faces, they moved around Duane, taking his hands, pushing him toward the corridor.

"I'm Barbara," said the brunette.

"Just call me Joyce," said the redhead, as she snaked her hand into Duane's pocket, and squeezed gently.

Duane's boots floated over the corridor and up the stairs, Joyce fondling his body, as Barbara guided him toward their destination. At the monastery, I'd be fast asleep right now, dreaming about being with beautiful women, and now it's actually happening! he mused.

"You don't look so good," said Barbara. "What's wrong?"

"I'm fine," he said deep in his throat, trying to portray a rough, tough hombre, but he didn't even know these women, so how could be consummate the most intimate act of all? Joyce opened the door on a large, opulently furnished boudoir with a massive bed and the largest bathtub Duane had ever seen, full of bubbly water.

"Take off yer clothes," she said nonchalantly.

He stared in awe as she touched something behind her gown, and the entire garment dropped to the floor. Naked as a jaybird, except for her high-heeled slippers, she stepped toward him, a frozen smile on her face. Duane felt off balance, because too much was happening too quickly. He needed to be alone, so he could think everything through.

"You all right, kid?" asked Joyce, an expression of concern on her face.

Duane nodded dumbly, as Barbara unhooked her gown, and it, too, fell away. "I think he needs to relax," she said to her partner.

"Have a seat," Joyce told him. "We're not going to bite you."

"It's not that," Duane blurted, "but I've had a rather . . . well, to tell you the truth, a very bad night."

"You should celebrate," rejoined Barbara, "'cause yer still alive. Maybe you need some laudanum."

"I guess I'm just . . ." Duane searched for the proper word, but somehow it eluded him.

Barbara removed a brown medicine bottle from a cabinet, while Joyce filled three glasses with water.

Then Barbara dribbled a few drops of laudanum into each glass.

"Drink it all down," Barbara said, her naked breasts jiggling. "It'll make you feel better."

Duane sipped the liquid, which had a faint medicinal taste, and didn't burn like whiskey. Meanwhile, Joyce bent over the tub, and touched her fingers to the water. "We don't want it to get cold, do we?"

They approached his chair, smiles on their faces, and he thought: My God, surely they're not going to undress me. "But . . ." he protested weakly, as Joyce bent down and pulled off his left boot. Meanwhile, Barbara unbuttoned his shirt, placed her hand on his chest, and growled like a cat.

Joyce removed his right boot, as Barbara unbuckled his belt. They pulled him to his feet, stripped him naked, and all he could do was stand stupidly beside the chair, thinking of the monastery far from the cares and temptations of the secular world. Now they were leading him toward the bathtub, and he didn't know anything about them. He examined Barbara's face, and then Joyce's. They were painted dolls, not people, and Duane felt no compelling needs.

He came to the edge of the tub, and the only thing to do was get in. He dipped his toe into warm and soapy water, and Duane suddenly felt very tired. He lowered himself into the water, as it rushed up to his neck, and he leaned back. Bright multicolored lights flickered on the ceiling, as the two women joined him in the tub, making soapy little waves. They slithered against him and ran their hands over his body.

It felt cozy and relaxing, and the sheer sensuality of the experience overcame any doubts or fears that he had. He looked first at Joyce, then at Barbara, and wondered about their backgrounds, hopes, dreams, but then their lips and tongues were all over him, and all he could do was surrender to their tender ministrations.

He closed his eyes, as they washed him with naughty hands. First one touched lips to his mouth, then another. He became confused about who was who, and it seemed as if they comprised one woman with many arms and legs, kissing and fondling him, numerous soft breasts rubbing against him, making that pesky artery in his throat throb.

What do I care who they are? he asked himself dreamily. And what does it matter who I am? If this is what happens when you shoot somebody, I'm surprised that people don't get killed more often, he thought, as he gave in to the moment.

Vanessa Fontaine poured a glass of whiskey, then sat in her favorite chair and wondered how to handle Duane Braddock if she ever saw him again. What do you say to somebody who's lied to you, and the little son of a bitch nearly *seduced* me.

She knew that the world was full of tricksters, and chided herself for being so gullible. He made up the whole story about the monastery, to take advantage of my better nature. Now it turns out he's a gunfighter, and God only knows what else he is. What a dirty, sneaky little varmint he turned out to be. She gazed at the lamp flickering through her glass of whiskey. Maybe I should turn the joke around, and bamboozle *him*, she pondered.

* * *

Duane opened his eyes, and found himself flat on his back in a strange bed, his arms wrapped around naked women, their breasts jutting into him, legs entwined with his. He recalled the events of the past few hours, and felt shame mixed with jaded pleasure. In the bathtub, on the floor, and in the bed, he'd performed acts that he'd never dreamed possible between men and women. Barbara and Joyce were totally depraved human beings, and so was he. Now he understood more clearly why people loved to sin. It was more fun than not sinning.

He was surprised to note that he didn't feel guilty about performing lascivious acts with two women he didn't even know. A man must take pleasure where he finds it, he realized, because he never knows when somebody might shoot him in the back.

His memory roved back to the most troublesome part of the evening. It was as though my father were with me, drawing the gun, pulling the trigger. Daddy's legacy wasn't a ranch or a gold mine, but a fast hand, he thought. He tried to feel compassion for the man he'd killed, but Dave Collins had insulted a cripple and started the mess in the first place. If I hadn't gone to the cribs, the incident never would've happened, he told himself.

Duane was cursed with a mind that saw all sides of an issue, and that's why he often was confused. But wasn't Mary Magdalene a prostitute? he asked himself. Maybe she worked in a whorehouse just like this. He hugged the two women tighter, and one of them whispered an endearing word. Tenderly, he kissed her forehead. I've had more women's love in one night than I've ever had in my life.

But despite everything, he didn't know anything about the prostitutes. They might even have children from men they never married, like my mother. If I hadn't killed Dave Collins, they'd probably spit in my eye. I wonder who they think they're in bed with? He felt satiated, yet perceived a need that hadn't yet been touched.

He was getting a headache, and wanted to pray. He was also hungry, and couldn't remember the last time he'd eaten. It was difficult to cogitate clearly with two buxom women in his arms. He crawled out of their arms, as they sleepily tried to keep him with them.

"Where you goin'" Barbara muttered, as she cuddled with Joyce.

Duane dressed at the foot of the bed, and strapped on his Colt. It felt heavy, familiar, and gave him an illusion of invulnerability. Candles burned in the corridor. The whorehouse was silent, as he descended to the first floor, and found himself in a maze of corridors. He stopped and looked around, wondering how to get out, when the woman with long, straight black hair appeared. "Lost?" she asked.

"Where's the door?"

"Why are you leaving so soon?"

"I'm hungry."

"Right this way, Mister Braddock."

She opened a door, and Duane entered a small dining room with maroon drapes covering the window, and a chandelier hanging from the ceiling, illuminating the remains of a roast beef, some chickens, a variety of vegetables, and two apple pies.

"Help yourself," she said, closing the door behind him.

He filled a plate with slabs of meat, scoops of vegetables, and slices of bread, then sat at the table with his back to the wall and ate hungrily, as a fly buzzed over his head. Gradually he felt stronger, more awake, and more confused. He had the impression that he wasn't normal, and possessed a flaw that would hound him for the rest of his days. Why do I ride off in all directions at the same time? Am I a lunatic? Do I belong in an asylum? he kept questioning himself.

Duane finished his repast, left the whorehouse, and slogged along the road, hands in the pockets of his jeans, shoulders hunched over, looking at the ground. I've got to settle down, save my money, and buy my own ranch. Somehow I've got to make my life normal, after I learn how to ride a horse, he vowed.

He saw the dark outlines of Vanessa's house in the distance. You don't wake up somebody in the middle of the night for a little chat, he prompted himself, but didn't she say that friends were supposed to stand up for each other? He traversed the backyard, and her bedroom window was raised four inches. "Vanessa?"

She stirred, and rolled onto her back. Duane's appreciative eyes verified the pointed mounds of her breasts. A bittersweet longing came over him, because he doubted that he'd ever be lucky enough to actually taste one of them.

Suddenly she spun around, a gun in her hand, and aimed it at his head. "Who's there!"

"Duane. I've got to talk with you. May I come in?

Vanessa had just awakened from a deep slumber,

befuddled by the sight of him at her window. I'll make him sorry that he ever woke me up in the middle of the night, she promised. She rolled out of bed, put on robe and slippers, and clumped toward the back door. He stood in the shadows, hat in had. "I know that this is a bad time to come, but I had to speak with you, Vanessa. I need your advice."

"Are you sure you don't need another meal?" she asked coldly. "Or some new clothes? I hear that you're a famous gunfighter, and you shot somebody tonight."

He couldn't comprehend the hostility in her voice, so he ignored it. "That's what I wanted to talk with you about. I'm confused about what to do, and you said once that friends should say anything to each other, so I thought I'd come by to talk. It'll only take a few minutes. May I come in?"

He thinks he can humbug me *again*, she thought, but I'll give him something to remember me by. "Right this way," she uttered, with a false smile. She held the door for him, and he entered the murky kitchen. "Go ahead," she offered, lighting a candle on the stove. "Tell me what's on your mind?"

"You don't sound very friendly, Vanessa."

"You woke me up in the middle of the night. How am I supposed to sound?"

"But you said that friends could depend on each other."

"What do you want this time?" she asked sharply. "I've bought you clothes, given you money, fed you, and found you a job. You had me so bamboozled I nearly gave my *body* to you. You said that you were a poor orphan boy, and I believed you, but now I find out that you're a professional killer."

"I never fired a gun in my life until tonight," he retorted, "and I was lucky, while the other cowboy was drunk on his feet. Or maybe my daddy came up from hell to help me—I don't know. I thought you'd be the one person who'd believe me."

"Why should I believe you?" she asked. "If everybody's a liar, why shouldn't you be one, too? You took advantage of my good nature once, but you'll never do it again. Start walking."

He wanted to tell her that she was mistaken, but no sound emitted from his mouth. His face turned red, as he made a tentative, thin-lipped smile, and headed for the door. It slammed; pots rattled on the walls, and he was gone.

No one had ever called Duane a liar before. He shambled toward the outskirts of town, and recalled his simple life in the monastery, where such events simply didn't occur. He and the other monks never questioned each other's veracity, but lying evidently was common in the secular world. *Why'd I ever leave?*

The monastery had lacked the luxuries of the outside world, but it possessed other goods far more precious, such as trust, and the effort to lead decent lives in the eyes of God Almighty. *Maybe tomorrow I'll go back, but where'll I get the money for the stagecoach?* Life seemed so complex here, and he was unaccustomed to making decisions. In the monastery, every day was exactly like the last, an endless round of prayer, study, and the Holy Sacrifice of the Mass.

He came to the outskirts of town, and ahead was the endless rolling sage. The wind picked up, and

Duane gazed through heavily lidded eyes at the dim outlines of jagged mountain ranges in the distance. Stumbling, holding out his arms to the moon, he followed the wind into measureless wastes, but then fatigue, whiskey, and remorse hit him at the same moment. He lost his footing, tripped over a rock, and plummeted to the ground. Groaning, rolling over, he landed on his back. The heavens were ablaze, and he picked out the Big Dipper, Orion the Hunter, and Cassiopeia, the Lady in the Chair, who looked like Vanessa Fontaine. He closed his eyes, and she was engraved on his eyelids, glowing into his brain.

Five men huddled around the embers of a campfire approximately ten miles away. Like a nest of vipers on a vacant stretch of sage, they seethed and writhed as they passed around a half-full bottle of whiskey, while two empty bottles lay near the fire pit.

Nearby was a fresh mound of earth topped by a pile of rocks and a crude cross made from the limbs of a cottonwood tree. Six feet beneath the mound lay a rustler and outlaw named Dave Collins in eternal slumber.

The men around the fire had weathered faces and scraggly beards. They wore rough range clothes, and all had been cowboys at some point in their lives, but they couldn't knuckle under to rules and regulations, so they rode the owl-hoot trail, stealing whatever they could, killing whenever they had to, and doing anything necessary to prevail.

They were a brotherhood bound together in bloody deeds, and respected no laws save those concocted by themselves. As for women, they bought them same as they bought beans and tobacco. Although they blended in with other cowboys, they were in the Titusville area for one reason only: to rob the bank. They'd seen a copy of the *Sentinel* and realized that Titusville was a prosperous town in the middle of nowhere, a peach ready to be plucked.

The group had ridden into Titusville like any other bunch of cowboys, and reconnoitered the bank. They'd even gone inside, on spurious business, to see where every teller stood, and where the safe was located. All had been proceeding on schedule, until Dave got into a beef with the young cowboy, but Dave always had a mean streak, and no stopping once he got started. The outlaws weren't bothered so much that Dave had been killed, but felt that the kid had tricked him, so that he could add another notch to his gun.

One of the outlaws was Daltry, and he threw the butt of his cigar into the fire, where it sent up a plume of smoke. "I think we orter go in first thing in the morning, track down the son of a bitch, an' shoot 'im like a dog. We cain't let 'im git away with it."

There was silence for a few moments, as the others considered the proposition. One of them was Hardy, who wore the tattoo of a skull on the back of his left hand. "If we're a-gonna shoot him, we should bushwhack him at night when he's tired, and cain't see us. He's a fast hand, and we cain't afford no more mistakes."

"Fast hand—my ass!" said Domenici, a tall, thin outlaw with a black beard to his chest. "Dave fired first, fer Chrissakes. If he hadn't been drunk, he would've killed the kid. What fast hand?"

He was answered by Singleton, who wore an eagle feather in the band of his hat. "He sure looked plenty fast to me. Don't underestimate that kid, 'cause he'd been drinkin' too. I got near him at the end, and he smelled like a still. He ain't nobody to fuck with."

One man hadn't spoken yet—the leader of the outlaw band. At first glance, one might think he were a fat man, but what appeared fat were really thick slabs of muscle. His most arresting features were his small, intense blue eyes that darted about the group curiously, making little notations.

His name was Smollett, and he'd been a major under Jubal Early during the war. He understood logistics, maneuver, surprise, and retreat. Without his professional skills, they would've been hanged long ago.

"I don't think Duane Braddock is worth our trouble," he said in his deep baritone voice. "Dave was always looking for a fight, and only a matter of time before somebody drilled him. Dave's ruined our whole operation in Titusville. We should move to another town, and forget him. If you cut yourself with a knife, you can't blame the knife."

"Forget hell," replied Domenici. "That little son of a bitch killed a good friend of mine. I say we got to even the score."

"We're wastin' our time," said Daltry, chewing his cigar butt, "He's probably left town."

"We can't afford to lose any more men," Smollett reminded them, "and we're running out of cash."

"Fuck cash," Domenici replied.

Singleton spat in the fire, his face narrow like a

polecat's. "I'll go into town first thing in the morning, and find out where he is. Maybe I can come up behind him and put a bullet through his noggin."

Firelight flickered on Smollett's porcine features, as he realized the direction of their intentions. They were extremely violent men, the type that made good soldiers, but good soldiers didn't rob banks, and that was Smollett's main objective now. He couldn't do it alone, and needed them as much as they needed him.

"If you insist on killing this kid," he replied, "we'll have to plan it carefully, because we simply cannot afford to lose any more men due to erratic gunplay."

They glowered at him in the darkness, and he knew that they resented him, for they were the refuse and flotsam of a defeated lost cause, and he'd been a fancy-pants artillery officer. The demarcation between them remained clearly defined, and Smollett wouldn't be surprised if they shot him in the back someday.

"Let's turn in," he said. "Tomorrow night at this time, if we all do as we're told, the kid'll be dead. Then we can get on with our business, which is robbing that damned bank."

CHAPTER 6

SAUL KLEVINS WAS TWENTY-EIGHT years old, a former thief, fancy man, and bouncer. Like many other dishonest drifters, he tended toward erratic living habits, and during one of those scrapes, had discovered his unusually fast reflexes. Since then, he'd killed nine men.

He hated Sundays, because all the so-called nice people were out with their children, commandeering a town that only a few hours before had been the stomping ground of cowboys, gamblers, and outlaws. The noonday sun seared his eyes, he had a headache, and his mouth tasted foul. He lowered the brim of his hat as he trudged along the sidewalk, worrying about his low money supply.

He'd come to Titusville anticipating that somebody in the up-and-coming region could use a fast hand. But since his arrival, he'd earned nothing at his profession, and spent nearly all of his own money. No one was mad enough to hire a gunfighter—yet. Klevins wished he could stir up trouble, for the sake of his earnings.

He pushed through the doors of the Longhorn Saloon, made his way to the bar, and ordered a shot of whiskey, a bag of tobacco, some cigarette papers, and the latest edition of the *Titusville Sentinel.* He carried them back to the chop counter, ordered his customary steak and eggs, and rolled a cigarette while the food was cooked. Then he carried the platter to a table against the wall, opened the *Titusville Sentinel,* and the headline smacked him between the eyes:

PECOS KID GUNS DOWN RIVAL
BEHIND BLIND PIG SALOON
Fast Hand Has Arrived in Our Town
Citizens Warned
The notorious Pecos Kid claimed his first vic-tim in Titusville last night, when he shot a drifter named Dave Collins in a ruckus behind the Blind Pig Saloon.

The Pecos Kid, whose real name is Duane Braddock, pretended to be inexperienced with guns, as he lured Collins into the showdown that cost the cowboy's life.

Klevins glanced up every few sentences, to make sure of everybody's hands, then returned to his perusal of the newspaper. According to the article, the kid with the lucky shot was really a famous gun-fighter! Klevins guffawed, as he shook his head in disbelief. These rubes'll believe anything.

It was the strangest town Klevins had ever seen, like a huge metropolis in the middle of nowhere. It had no industry, not much commerce, and most of the town's buildings were vacant. Klevins was three months behind his rent, and nobody cared. He'd seen towns come and go, and suspected that Titusville would probably go.

Petigru was the big money man behind the town, and also the most hated man in the county. The locals had sold him their land, lumber, cattle, and skills, and all the while kept telling him what he wanted to hear: the railroad is coming. But the Union Pacific didn't appear interested in Titusville, and Petigru could find himself a target when the bottom fell out. At that point, Klevins was certain that he'd have a lucrative assignment.

But the Pecos Kid was a new, unknown card thrown into the deck. Was he the dumb cluck that he appeared to be, or a clever flimflam man? Klevins had seen the shooting, and estimated that the kid would've been killed if Collins hadn't been drunk.

Klevins suspected that the Pecos Kid was the latest product from the imagination of Len Farnsworth, the shrewd local newspaperman, but many local fools would believe it hook, line, and sinker. Klevins searched the newspaper for his own shooting, but there was nothing at all.

Why them sons of a bitches—they cut me out of the newspaper. Klevins's self-esteem was hurt, and he simmered with indignation. If anybody wants a bodyguard, he'll hire Braddock, not me. That goddamn kid couldn't shoot his way out of a gunnysack, but he's in the limelight, while I'm in the shade. I ought to shoot them conchos off his hat. That'd wake everybody up about who's the real gunfighter in this town.

Duane opened his eyes, and once more didn't know where he was. He'd awakened in so many strange places, he was almost afraid to look around. He raised his head and reached toward his gun.

A prairie dog sat on his hind legs, examining Duane curiously. Their eyes met, animal and man, and each saw total incomprehension. The prairie dog, being the smaller creature, decided to scoot off. He left so suddenly, Duane wasn't sure he'd seen him in the first place. His next sensation was a dry tongue, and he realized that his stomach was an empty, echoing cavern.

The sun shone brightly in a clear blue sky, and the morning pleasantly warm. Time for breakfast, he thought, as he rose to his feet. His hat hung down his back, and had become crushed during his sleep, but he punched out the crown with his fist, straightened the brim, and it was like new again.

He saw the town in the distance, smoke arising from chimneys. Something heavy and unfamiliar hung from his hip, and he looked down at the Colt in the worn brown leather holster. He pulled it out, rested his forefinger against the trigger, and the events of the night came back with stunning clarity. I've killed a man, but it's not as if I shot him in the back. I'm probably headed straight for hell, but nothing I can do about it now, he thought.

He pulled back the hammer, blew out the dirt,

spun the chambers, and looked down the barrel. A clump of something was in there, so he searched for a twig, passed it through the barrel, and the foreign matter fell out. He thumbed bullets into the empty chambers, but left one clear. Butterfield had counseled that precaution, otherwise he was liable to shoot his leg off.

He reached into his pocket, and only had three dollars and change left. He wasn't sure that he still had his job at the Lazy Y, after what transpired last night. He walked toward town, as events of the evening continued to agitate his mind, but he didn't feel awkward and youthful anymore. It was a new day, and he was a new man.

He came to the edge of the settlement, where a scruffy little dog barked at him. Well-dressed ladies and gentlemen strolled on the sidewalks, while children played in yards, running, jumping, yelling.

He continued his quest for breakfast, and became aware that people were looking at him. He squared his shoulders and walked with a steady roll of his shoulders, like his spiritual advisor, Lester Boggs. Duane arrived at the Black Cat Saloon, and a man in an apron swept the floor, while a scattering of bleary-eyed cowboys enjoyed breakfast.

"That's him," somebody said.

Duane trudged to the chop counter, and the Negro cook handed him a platter covered with steak, beans, potatoes, and biscuits. Duane carried the food to an empty table against the left wall, where no one could shoot him from behind, unless they had a cannon on the other side of the wall. He sat, speared a fried potato, placed it in his mouth, and opened the dog-eared newspaper that had been lying on the table.

PECOS KID GUNS DOWN RIVAL
BEHIND BLIND PIG SALOON

He stopped chewing, and his eyes bulged out of their sockets. What the hell is this? He read lie after innuendo after exaggeration with mounting indignation, and knew full well who was at the bottom of it, the heavyset, blond-haired reporter who'd "interviewed" him last night. Isn't it against the law to tell lies like this? Duane wondered. Is this what they call freedom of the press? That reporter's got to print a retraction, or I'll sue for defamation of character, if I live that long, he told himself. Why is it that every time I look around, things get worse?

Clyde Butterfield walked down a side street of Titusville, and he looked like he owned the town. The customary thin black cheroot was stuck in his teeth, and he wore a smile for all the world. It wasn't every day that he came to call on the most beautiful woman in town, and he believed that he still cut a fine figure of a man, considering his age. Although he'd deny it, he truly had killed eighteen men, some out of anger, some for money, and a few for the hell of it. But he'd got shot himself one hot August night in San Antone, and spent two years flat on his ass. It caused him to think of many things he'd never known before, such as the ultimate futility of all human endeavor, and since his recovery, he had gone out of his way to avoid altercations.

He saw Miss Fontaine's house halfway down the block, knew that Edgar Petigru had bought it for her, and figured she was with Edgar for the money, because there wasn't much else that the Yankee had. You know what they say about money, Butterfield told himself. It'll make you act real funny.

He climbed the three stairs to the porch, knocked on the door, and struck a pose, one foot in front of the other, thumbs in his suspenders, cheroot in his teeth. The door opened, revealing a Negro woman in a white bandanna looking at him suspiciously.

Butterfield removed his hat and bowed slightly. "I wonder if I might speak with Mister Braddock."

"Who?"

"Duane Braddock. I understand that he's a . . . friend . . . of Miss Vanessa's."

"He ain't no friend of Miss Vanessa's, and he ain't here nohow."

Butterfield bowed again, replaced his hat on his head, and made for the street. Now where would he be? Butterfield wondered. He knew that Duane had left Miss Ellie's in the middle of the night, and assumed that the kid had returned to Vanessa Fontaine. Maybe's he's passed out in a hotel, or maybe he's dead.

He understood Duane's predicament, for he, too, had been the target for lesser men struggling to rise above the morass of the mob. One lucky shot, and they're famous. Even Duane Braddock, who'd never fired a gun before in his life, had become the *Sentinel*'s headline. The power of the press, Butterfield thought cynically.

The door opened behind him, and the Negro woman reappeared. "Sir?"

He spun around, with the reflexes of an ex-gunfighter.

"Miss Fontaine would like to speak with you, sir."

I knew it, Butterfield thought vainly. She's admired me from afar, and wants to meet the other major celebrity in town. With a new spring to his step, he returned to the house, and was led by the maid to the parlor.

"May I get you something to drink, sir?"

"Whiskey."

Butterfield sank into the plush chair, and noticed dainty curtains, lace doilies, knickknacks on shelves. Footsteps approached, and he rose to his feet and even removed his cheroot from his mouth, as he awaited the arrival of the most entrancing woman in Titusville.

She swept into the room, her eyes ablaze with barely concealed anger. "Mister Butterfield," she said, holding out her hand. "I've heard so much about you, sir."

He bent over and kissed her hand gallantly, for he was of the same class as she, the child of wealthy planters ruined by the rebellion, and he'd served on the staff of General Longstreet. Although he was an aging gambler and ex-gunfighter down on his luck, he'd worn the silver leaf of a lieutenant colonel on his collar, and General Longstreet frequently had asked for his advice. The general usually ignored it, but had asked anyway.

Vanessa sat opposite him, her posture erect, the perfect belle of the ball. Butterfield felt as if he were back in Dixie, and he didn't have to worry about how he was going to pay his hotel bill at the end of the month.

"I hope you haven't been tricked by that nasty little Duane Braddock," she said testily. "He's a very charming liar, and he's talked me out of a suit of clothes. I actually believed that he was a poor orphan who'd just escaped from a monastery, of all things. You wouldn't believe the lies that he told me. How much does he owe you?"

"Not a penny," Butterfield said. "And in point of fact, he is a poor orphan boy who just escaped from a monastery. I know, because I happened to be there when he got off the stage. He didn't know where the hell he was, and before he figured it out, a bunch of brats robbed every penny he had."

She leaned toward him. "Mister Butterfield, I don't think you appreciate how cunning he is. It appears that he's *really* bamboozled you, but I understand—he can be extremely persuasive. But just explain to me one thing: if he just escaped from a monastery, how come he's the Pecos Kid?"

"My dear Miss Fontaine—I was there. Duane Braddock didn't even know how to fire the gun, and I had to show him. He watched, he practiced, and he learned a little, but not much. The cowboy drew first, but fortunately for Duane, the cowboy was nearly blind drunk. Duane's no Pecos Kid, but that doesn't mean somebody won't shoot him one of these days."

She struggled to maintain her composure, but his words slammed into her like battering rams. He came here last night, he wanted my help, and I threw him into the cold. My God! she thought, visibly shaken.

"Are you all right, ma'am?"

She smiled politely, for Charleston belles know how to hide emotions, too. "Thank you for coming here, Mister Butterfield. If you see Duane, I hope you'll tell him about our conversation, and convey to him my apologies for my beastly behavior last night."

A sign hung over the sidewalk:

TITUSVILLE SENTINEL
Len Farnsworth
Publisher

Duane turned the doorknob, but the door was locked. He'd already checked the saloons, and didn't think the reporter would be in church. I want to look that son of a bitch in the eye and tell him what he's done to me. Duane kicked the door, the curtain inside moved an inch, a bloodshot eye peeked outside. The door opened, and the great publisher stood in his barefeet and long underwear. "I'll be goddamned," he said. "Come on in, Pecos. Let's have some coffee."

Duane looked him in the eye and said levelly: "You've made a lot of trouble for me, sir, and I might even get killed because of those lies that you wrote."

"Lies?" asked Farnsworth, ushering Duane into the small office, which also served as his printshop, bedroom, dining room, and kitchen. "I gave you an opportunity to explain yourself, but you refused. However, if you want to make the next special edition, let me get a piece of paper, and I'll write everything verbatim."

The room smelled of ink, molding paper, and stale

ideas. Duane looked at the newfangled Washington printing press nearly big as a man, and marveled at the wonders of the modern world. In only a day, you could flood a town with lies.

"Mister Farnsworth," Duane began, struggling to keep his temper under control. "You said I'm a professional gunfighter, but I'm not. Now somebody's liable to shoot me, because of your dishonesty."

Farnsworth snorted derisively. "Don't blame your troubles on me. You're in a fix because of your refusal to cooperate with the press. But thanks to me, you walk into any saloon in this town—somebody'll buy you a drink."

"Or shoot me in the head. You *lied* about me, Mister Farnsworth. I'm not the Pecos Kid."

"You're from the Pecos country, aren't you?" Farnsworth readied his pen. "What did it feel like, the moment your bullet struck Dave Collins in the chest? Did you experience elation, relief, or merely cold hate and lust for revenge?"

"I was happy to be alive, because it was the first time I ever fired a gun, and—"

Farnsworth pshawed. "Inexperienced shooters don't have hands as fast as yours, young man."

"You've got to print a retraction, and tell the truth."

Farnsworth raised his eyebrows. "Since the dawn of time, philosophers have chewed over what constitutes Truth, and as far as I know, no one's figured it out to this day. Do you claim to know?"

Duane realized that he couldn't prove definitively that he wasn't the Pecos Kid. "But you made it all up!"

"I certainly hope so," Farnsworth said, as he

dropped to one knee before the stove. He stuffed old newspaper inside, added kindling, and scratched a match. Duane had thought that Farnsworth would apologize or beg for his life, but instead the reporter seemed pleased with what he'd done. Flames leapt out of the stove, and Farnsworth closed the door. Then he proceeded to grind coffee beans.

"You may not realize it," Farnsworth said, "but I've done you a favor. Shoot a few more people, and somebody might write a book about you. You could be the next Buffalo Bill."

"I don't want somebody to write a book about me, and to hell with Buffalo Bill. Your newspaper has placed my life in danger! Don't you understand?"

"Nobody lives forever," Farnsworth retorted. "Even I, a humble journalist, could be shot by a disgruntled reader such as yourself. I'll bet, when you were on your way here, you thought about killing me."

"That's true," Duane said darkly.

"What a headline: EDITOR SHOT BY THE PECOS KID. Too bad I wouldn't be alive to write the story."

"I lived in a monastery until two weeks ago. You can write to the abbot."

"For all I know, you bribed him."

"You can't bribe an abbot!"

Farnsworth raised his eyebrows. "Let me tell you, boy, that everybody has his price, even an abbot."

"You didn't care about me at all! I was just another story for you!"

"Nobody understands the special problems of the press. My main goal is to make the *Sentinel* interesting, so that people will buy it, place ads, and increase my wealth."

"And if I get shot, so much the better. THE PECOS KID GUNNED DOWN IN BROAD DAYLIGHT Another great headline, right?"

The door to the office opened, and it was Deputy Dawson, wearing a battered hat with the front brim pinned up. "Everythin' all right in here?" he asked, glancing suspiciously at Duane.

Farnsworth declared: "I was only interviewing the Pecos Kid. He claims that he never fired a gun before in his life. In all my travels, I've never met a gunfighter who had a sense of humor, until now."

The deputy looked at Duane. "Stay out of trouble, boy, or I'll be on you like stink on shit."

Deputy Dawson departed the newspaper office, Farnsworth poured water into his blue porcelain coffee-pot, added ground coffee, and placed it on the stove. "You'd better watch out for poor Deputy Dawson. He has something to prove, and let's hope that he doesn't try to prove it with you."

Jake Russell, ramrod of the Lazy Y, rode down the main street of Titusville, a bent cigarette sticking out beneath his black handlebar mustache. A wide-shoul-dered man of thirty-two, his head throbbed with pain, and he was nauseated due to too much food, drink, and carousing during the night. Now, in the cold light of day, the town had been reclaimed by churchgoers from miles around, who'd come to hear the customary Sunday fire-and-brimstone sermon at the New Titusville Church of Jesus.

Russell dismounted before the Carrington Arms Hotel, threw the reins over the hitching rail, and headed for the lobby. *I wish that son of a bitch Yankee would leave me alone.* Russell felt that Petigru didn't know anything about ranching, but always was giving orders, changing his mind, and devising impractical far-flung plans. But Russell never complained, because he liked the extra twenty dollars a month he earned as foreman.

He crossed the lobby of the hotel, where a few guests were passed out on the furniture, bottles in hands, cravats untied, frock coats covered with spilled food and drink. The desk clerk nodded knowingly to Russell as the latter turned toward the stairs.

He came to the third floor, walked down the corridor, and knocked on the door at the end. Petigru, attired in a purple silk robe, a notepad in one hand, pencil in another, opened it. "Come in," he said with a flair. "Fix yourself a drink."

Russell headed for the bar, and wondered how a man could find happiness doing numbers, for that's generally what occupied Petigru whenever Russell was called on the carpet. The foreman poured himself three fingers of whiskey, and sat on a plush chair beside Petigru's desk. Petigru added the columns as if unaware that someone else were in the room. Luxury always made Russell uncomfortable, as if it were *too* soft and pampering. *Looks like a goddamned woman's gown,* Randall thought of Petigru's robe.

Petigru finished adding the column of numbers, then put his pencil down. "Now what did I want to speak with you about?" he asked.

Russell was astounded. *He called me in all the way from the ranch on a Sunday, and he doesn't know what he wants to palaver about?*

Petigru stuck in his finger into his cheek. "Oh yes, I remember. Did you see the shooting last night?"

"I seen the second one, but not the first. I got into town late."

"Then you know who Duane Braddock is, the so-called Pecos Kid. What'd you think of him?"

"He nearly got his ass blowed off."

Petigru stiffened in his chair. "But . . . I thought he was a fast gun from the Pecos country!"

"He's just a dumb kid who got off a lucky shot. Pecos Kid, my ass."

"Do you think it's true that he never fired a gun before?"

"Can't say fer sure, but Clyde Butterfield showed him what to do, and the other cowboy was nearly out on his feet. But I'll say one thing fer the kid. He was steady under fire, and that ain't easy."

Petigru leaned toward his foreman. "I've hired Duane Braddock, and he'll report to you in the morning. But there's just one problem. He claims that he doesn't know how to ride a horse."

At first Russell wasn't sure that he'd heard correctly. "Are you a-sayin' that you hired a cowboy what cain't even ride?"

"Maybe you can teach him—he seems like a bright lad." Petigru winked conspiritorially. "Put him in a line shack in the middle of nowhere, or give him something difficult to do. He pretends to be dumb, but he might be a humbug. If the side of a building fell on him, it wouldn't bother me. Know what I mean?"

* * *

Duane headed for the Cattlemen Saloon, found a table, and looked blankly at a painting of maidens cavorting in the palace gardens atop the bar. A waitress in a low-cut dress took his whiskey order, and then he lowered his eyes to see his companions of the afternoon, the usual gamblers, political debaters, drunkards, but the ranks were greatly thinned, without the tumult of the previous evening.

His eyes fell on the group at the bar, and he was surprised to see Saul Klevins looking back at him. The waitress returned with the glass of whiskey, and Duane sipped smoothly. A few tables away, men played cards with such concentration, it reminded him of prayer vigils in the monastery. What is it about poker that interests them so?

He swallowed the contents of the glass, inhaled through his teeth, and wiped his mouth with the back of his hand. He thought about resuming his search for Lester Boggs, when he noticed Saul Klevins heading toward him, a bottle of whiskey and a glass in his hand. The fastest gun in the county sat opposite Duane without asking permission, pulled the cork out of his bottle, and filled Duane's glass. "Here's to the Pecos Kid," he said out the corner of his mouth.

Duane couldn't refuse to drink to himself. Both men swallowed whiskey, sizing each other up at close distance. Duane thought Klevins looked like a hateful, spiteful demon, while Klevins loathed the sheer lines of Duane's jaw. Both men gazed into each other's eyes, and it was flint on steel.

"Did you jest get in over yer head last night?" Klevins asked. "Or are you in my line of work?"

"It was a lucky shot."

"That's what I figgered, but some people say yer really a fast hand from the Pecos country."

"A newspaper reporter dreamed that up. I was born in the Pecos country, but that's about it."

Klevins bent to the side, so he could see Duane's six-shooter. "You had good moves fer a man who never fired one of them things afore."

"Beginner's luck."

"Don't believe in any kind of luck," Klevins allowed. "You had a fast hand, but you act like a stupid kid. I don't get it."

Duane realized that he'd been insulted, but wasn't ready to die. "I'm not stupid, but I'm not an experienced gunfighter, like you. I guess everybody in this saloon is afraid of you, including me."

Is this kid trying to challenge me in some sneaky way? Klevins asked himself. This is just how he set up that cowboy last night. Something told Klevins to back off. "Maybe some other time," Klevins said, arising from the table. "God only knows."

He reminds me of a snake in the grass, Duane evaluated, as he watched Klevins return to the bar. The most dangerous man in town, the last person I want to know, and he doesn't like me. I wouldn't be surprised if he killed me one of these days.

Duane stared into the depths of his whiskey, as if it were a crystal ball. I'd better start practicing with the Colt, as soon as I finish the whiskey, he thought.

"I've been looking all over for you!" Clyde Butterfield sidestepped among the tables. "You're drinking pretty early in the day, aren't you?" The ex-gunfighter pulled back a chair. "I've got a message from a certain lady. She said she's sorry about last night, and she'd like you to stop by at your convenience."

"I wonder what changed her mind?" Duane asked, mystified.

"She'd thought that you were the Pecos Kid, but I set her straight on that score."

"But how do you know that I didn't bamboozle *you*, Mister Butterfield?" Daune asked perversely.

"Come to think of it, you were pretty good for a kid who said he never fired a gun before."

"You saw how scared I was, but you doubt me anyway?"

"You didn't seem *that* scared." Butterfield leaned closer and gazed into his eyes. "Who are you really, kid?"

"Even Saul Klevins thinks I might be the Pecos Kid."

"You have to admit that it was an awfully good shot."

Demoralized, Duane shook his head and sighed. "Everybody prefers an interesting rumor to the boring truth. There never was a Pecos Kid. I'm amazed at how gullible all of you are."

Butterfield pulled out two cheroots. "Care for a smoke?"

Nobody had ever offered Duane a cheroot before, and he'd always wanted to blow smoke rings in the air. He accepted one, and Butterfield lit it with a match. Duane's mouth filled with tobacco, as it scooted down his throat and felt like fingernails clawing his lungs. He burst into coughing, and Butterfield slapped him on the back. "The goal is not to produce the maximum amount of smoke."

Duane tossed the cheroot into the nearest cuspidor. "I thought I'd get some target practice, and maybe you can give me a few pointers."

"There's a place on the east side of town. We can go there right now."

"Can I meet you in an hour?"

As Duane and Butterfield made plans for shooting practice, the outlaw called Hardy entered the saloon, his collar up and hat low over his eyes. Nobody paid any attention to him, and he appeared to be just another cowboy suffering from a hangover as he meandered toward the bar. He ordered a whiskey, then turned around and scanned faces. He picked out Duane and Clyde Butterfield at the corner table almost immediately.

Hardy and the rest of the gang had just arrived in town, and were searching for Duane. Now he'd been found, but Hardy had no intention of taking him on himself. He tossed whiskey down his throat, then headed for the door, to tell his outlaw brothers the good news.

Len Farnsworth sat at his desk, writing a new story:

PECOS KID THREATENS
PUBLISHER OF SENTINEL
Duane Braddock, killer of a cowboy named Dave Collins on Saturday night, brought his special brand of intimidation and brutality to this office today, when he threatened to kill Leonard Farnsworth, publisher of Titusville's only newspaper.

The door behind Farnsworth opened, and he spun in his chair, expecting to see the Pecos Kid standing there, but instead it was the major investor in the *Titusville Sentinel*, wearing a Brooks Brothers suit, carrying his briefcase. "I've been meaning to speak with you about today's headline," said Edgar Petigru. "What do you think you're doing? We don't want people to think that this is a lawless town. I thought we were in agreement on that."

Farnsworth raised his forefinger in the air. "A colorful character like the Pecos Kid can make a town famous. People will come from all over the world to see him get shot, and maybe some will stay."

"The point," Petigru began, "is that nobody wants to get shot, least of all I myself. Please . . . no more stories about violence. We want people to think this is a place where they can bring their families."

"But Mister Petrigru," Farnsworth replied, his eyes glittering with journalistic enthusiasm, "I can make the Pecos Kid as famous as Buffalo Bill. His story has all the ingredients—he's young, he's a killer, he was a priest, he . . ."

Petrigru's ears perked up. "I didn't know that he was a priest."

"Well, he wasn't exactly ordained yet, but . . ."

Petigru stared at him with undisguised contempt. "Farnsworth, you wouldn't know Truth if it fell on you, but I'm a busy man, and don't have time to argue with you. You print one more article about the Pecos Kid, or any other fighting in this town, and I'll have to fire you. Understood?"

"But, sir," Farnsworth protested weakly, "what about freedom of the press?"

* * *

Vanessa examined herself in the parlor mirror, and saw faint wrinkles at the corners of her eyes, but they looked like major excavations in her critical view. The little bump on her nose had always been a problem, her complexion was losing its luster, and her body going soft here and there. I'm going to be an unhappily married woman for the rest of my life, but it's better than six nights a week at the Round-Up Saloon, she reasoned.

She had books, but didn't feel like reading them, and the *Titusville Sentinel* was a bad joke. Vanessa knew that every lonely cowboy in Texas would love to spend the day with her, and sometimes felt like giving herself to one of them, but cowboys were irresponsible drunkards, and where could it lead?

Vanessa wanted resolution of her problem, not temporary distraction. The thought of marrying Edgar Petigru depressed her thoroughly. Even if I move to New York, and attend the opera every night, I'll still have to go to bed with him, she thought.

Something gleamed in the street, and she sat straighter in her chair. A tall figure in black pants and a black hat with silver conchos strode amid frolicking children. It appeared that the Pecos Kid was about to pay Vanessa a social call!

She jumped from her chair, inspected herself in the mirror again, and pinched her cheeks to get color. It was Annabelle's day off, which meant she'd have to answer the door herself. She chewed her lower lip, because she was afraid of him, or herself; she wasn't certain which. All I can be is his big sister. What good could ever result from Duane Braddock and me? she rationalized.

His fist banged against the door. She composed herself carefully, then hesitated, took a deep breath, and opened the door. He stood hat in hand, red shirt unbuttoned at the collar, black hair showing on his chest.

"Mister Butterfield said you wanted to speak with me," he said awkwardly.

"I'm so glad you're here, Duane. Please come in."

Duane entered her home, and was seen by Mrs. MacGillicuddy across the street, and Mrs. Washington a few doors down, not to mention Jed Wilson in the barn, watching Vanessa's home in the hope that he might catch a glimpse of her walking around naked. Instead, he saw the outline of the Pecos Kid through the kitchen window. Jed took another sip of whiskey, pulled on his hat, and ran out the back door, heading for the Carrington Arms Hotel.

Meanwhile, in the kitchen of her home, Vanessa was cutting Duane a thick slice of chocolate cake. "I'm so sorry for the cruel things I said last night," she apologized. "Like a fool, I believed what everyone told me. Where did you sleep?"

"On the sage."

"My goodness—outdoors?"

Duane didn't reply, because she knew as well as he that the sage was outdoors. Instead, he sliced a forkful of cake and placed it into his mouth. The rich chocolate frosting burst against his tongue, an entirely new sensation, for he'd never eaten chocolate cake before. "This is really good," he said, scoffing it up eagerly.

She saw the poor orphan boy deprived of special treats, and felt an overwhelming need to care for him, mother him, and even suckle him at her breast.

Whatever happens, I mustn't spoil the special friendship that I have with this unfortunate young man, she tried to convince herself.

"Thank God for Mister Butterfield," she declared. "He certainly set me straight. I'm so embarrassed by the cruel things I said to you last night. I hope you'll forgive me."

"You were just misinformed, like everybody else."

"But you did . . . kill . . . that cowboy."

The worm of doubt gnawed her mind once more. What if he's the most clever trickster to ever come down the pike? Maybe he fooled Butterfield too. What if he's really the Pecos Kid? she pondered.

He perceived her doubt, and his spirits sank once more. "It's a wonder I haven't been hanged yet."

"It's the same for me," she admitted. "I'm considered a scarlet woman, because I sing in a saloon and keep company with Edgar Petigru. He owns this house, he bought the dress on my back, and he pays my salary. It's not the happiest circumstance of my life, but I don't have any reasonable alternatives."

"Why don't you leave him?"

"Where will I go?"

"I'll take care of you."

She laughed sardonically. "But you have even less money than I. You can't even take care of yourself."

"Tomorrow I'll start my new job," Duane said. "Or we could go to another town."

"Let me show you something." She pulled him out of his chair, dragged him to the vestibule, and positioned him before the full-length mirror. "Look!"

They stood side by side, shoulders touching, and she saw a frantic, harried woman of a certain age, standing next to a young frontier Adonis, while his view was of a stunning regal blonde beside a disheveled and surly cowboy wearing a Colt slung low and tied down, gunfighter style.

She could feel his body heat like a horse that had just galloped a long distance, and let her eyes rove shamelessly up and down his body, while he eyed her in the same desirous manner. He knew that he should be a gentleman, and return meekly to the table, but somehow couldn't prevent himself from reaching out and touching his fingers to her cheek.

A thrill passed through her, and she turned toward him, an expression of terror in her eyes. Whatever made me think I could be his big sister? He wrapped his arms around her waist, and touched his lips to her nose.

"Please don't, Duane," she pleaded.

He knew that he should heed her request, but couldn't stop nibbling her ear. She shuddered against him, and a low moan arose from her parted lips. "No . . . Duane . . ."

He touched his lips to her throat, reveling in the strong, lithe body writhing in his arms. This is what he'd dreamed about from the moment he'd met her, and now at last the dream had come true. Overwhelmed by mad animal passion, they sank to the floor, his warm breath on her throat. "No . . ." she uttered, "no . . ."

He ran his hands over her body, and she ground her lips against his. Their tongues touched, his hand roved up the side of her leg, and suddenly footsteps came to them from the porch outside.

They froze in terror, romantic illusions shattering

like delicate crystal. Duane fled to the parlor, tucking in his shirt, while Vanessa readjusted her hair in front of the mirror. The expected knock came, as she composed herself, opened the door, and nearly fainted dead away. "Why Edgar, dear—how kind of you to drop by." She leaned forward and kissed his cheek.

He was flabbergasted, because he'd expected to find her *en flagrante* with the Pecos Kid. "Where is he?" Edgar growled. "I know he's here."

"Of course he's here. Where else would he go in this ridiculous town?"

She took Edgar's hand and led him to the parlor, where Duane arose casually from a chair, holding out his hand. "Good to see you again, sir."

Edgar was trying to recover from not catching them in the expected lewd position, while Vanessa opened a drawer in the nearby cabinet, and removed a handful of coins. "This is for you," she said to Duane, "so that you can hire a wagon, and go to the Lazy Y in the morning. And I'd like you to stay in a decent hotel tonight, so that you don't have to sleep in the open."

"I'll pay you back as soon as I get my first pay," Duane said, backing steadily toward the door. "Good day, Mister Petigru. Perhaps I'll see you at the Lazy Y sometime."

The door closed, and Duane was gone. Petigru noticed that Vanessa appeared agitated, and could understand why a woman might find the young poppycock attractive. He waited until Duane was out of earshot, and then inquired: "Are you having a love affair with him?"

"Don't be absurd," she snapped.

"You wouldn't be the first woman to commit indiscretions with a younger man."

"And you're not the first jealous fool in the world. You ran here in the hopes of catching me in a compromising situation with that unfortunate boy, and I find your manner insulting. If you don't mind, I think it's time you returned to your hotel."

He opened his mouth to reply, but she was already on the way to her bedroom. He heard the door slam, and then her muffled sobs drilled into his ears. He headed toward the vestibule, feeling guilty and defeated.

CHAPTER 7

DUANE WANDERED ACROSS THE ROLLING plain east of town, on the way to his rendezvous with Clyde Butterfield. Alert for Indians, rattlesnakes, and prairie dog holes, he held his gun with the hammer cocked, as his eyes perused the terrain relentlessly. On the azure horizon were bizarre rock formations resembling ziggurat temples of ancient Babylonia, and he knew that the land once had lain beneath an ancient sea, full of fish and gigantic crocodiles.

How multifarious is God's creation, Duane thought, as his mind turned from aquatic life to the mad minute in the vestibule with the singing sensation of Titusville. His flings in whorehouses were mere physical exercises compared to what happened during the all-too-brief rapture with that magnificent lady. If I knew more about women's clothing, I would've had her naked on the floor, he thought confidently. This is what Wordsworth, Swinburne, and Tennyson wrote about—life can be poetry itself! He realized that he was in love for the first time in his life, and didn't know whether to be happy or puke his guts out behind a nearby cholla cactus.

"Good afternoon, sir," drawled a voice to his right.

Duane spun around, aiming his six-shooter. The figure of Clyde Butterfield materialized out of the wilderness, sitting on a low rock, smoking a cheroot. "Lucky for you—I'm no injun," he said. He jumped to his feet, and tramped toward Duane. "How'd the meeting go with Miss Fontaine?"

"I had a piece of chocolate cake."

"Is that what they call it these days?" Butterfield led Duane off the trail. "It may be difficult for you to understand her, because you didn't experience the defeat of the Confederacy. Her world has cracked apart, and nobody's going to put it back to together again."

They came to a row of bottles and cans before a steep red limestone cliff, with a half-full gunnysack lying nearby. Butterfield puffed his cigar casually, and appeared distracted, when suddenly, like a puma, he sprang into action.

Duane flinched, because it all happened so quickly. In a split instant, Butterfield passed from a lazy, dreamlike state to the classic draw. The sage reverberated with explosions, thick smoke blasted, and tin cans flew into the air, as bottles were shattered to bits.

It was over as suddenly as it began, and Butterfield

stood for a few moments like a statue, cheroot still clamped in his teeth, and gun pointed at his last target. Then he flipped the gun in the air, caught it behind his back, and dropped it into his holster. "It's ten percent talent and ninety percent practice. You can learn it all, if you pay attention. Shall we begin?"

Vanessa watched Edgar Petigru recede toward the town that he owned, waited until certain he wouldn't return, then ran to the kitchen, poured herself two fingers of whiskey, and drank it down.

She sat at the kitchen table and buried her face in her hands. What have I done? she asked herself. I nearly threw away everything, because I lost control of myself with that damned Duane Braddock. Another two minutes, he would've had my bloomers off! I was totally lost, and thank God Edgar showed up.

Her face turned red with shame. There I was like the heroine of a cheap French novel, groveling on the floor with a man ten years younger than I. Duane must think I'm a common slut, the way he touched me, and I certainly didn't put up much of a fight. What was I thinking? And Edgar nearly caught us in the act! Oh my God, this can't be happening. Am I in love with Duane Braddock? Have I finally gone totally insane? I must never, under any circumstances, let that happen again. Do you understand, Vanessa, you idiot? Don't ever let yourself be alone with him again, she scolded herself.

But she couldn't forget rubbing against his sinewy body, and when he'd grasped her breast, she'd nearly fainted with delirium. Stop thinking about him, she commanded herself, but somehow her breast continued to tingle for the rest of the day.

Singleton entered the Blind Pig, and saw the gang seated at a round table in the middle of the floor, drinking whiskey and playing cards. They looked up expectantly as he pulled up a chair. "It's worse'n we thought," he uttered. "He's teamed up with Clyde Butterfield, and they're havin' some shootin' practice on the sage. They're both fast, they got good eyes, and I don't think we can take 'em both at the same time."

Smollett's small eyes smoldered with frustration. "We'll wait until Braddock is alone, and then we'll bushwhack him. Domenici, it's your turn to watch him. Don't let him out of your sight."

It was growing dark, as Duane and Butterfield walked back to town. They were silent, arms and shoulders sore. It had been three hours of draw and fire.

"You've still got a long way to go," Butterfield lectured, "and it might be a good idea to stay out of fistfights, because you could hurt your hand, and that can interfere with a clean draw."

They arrived at the edge of the settlement; lamps blazed in windows, streets were empty. Butterfield continued the seminar as they moved toward the saloon district. "Some men wear a glove to protect their shooting hand. I'd advise you to practice a minimum of one hour per day, for it's practice that separates the serious shooter from the joker." Butterfield placed his hand on Duane's shoulder, as if about to supply the most profound lesson of all, and Duane strained his ears to catch every lofty syllable. "I've got to see a man about a horse. Catch up with you later."

The ex-gunfighter reminded Duane of the austere old abbot, as he disappeared into a murky alley. Duane turned around, and saw the Crystal Palace Saloon.

It was nearly empty, as he made his way to the chop counter. He ordered a steak dinner, sat at a table with his back to the wall, and stuffed his face hungrily, while keeping track of everybody's hands.

Butterfield had taught him to listen for the telltale mechanical click of a hammer being cocked amid other noise, and to hit the floor accordingly, regardless of what else was happening. Butterfield had also shown him many useful tricks and ploys of the gunfighter's trade, and Duane had glowed in the praise of his mentor. Now at last he had Mr. Colt to help him cope with the hardship of life in the secular world.

Petigru sat in his office, studying his ledgers. Town-making was more expensive that he'd anticipated, and sometimes he thought that every citizen of Titusville was on his payroll, from carpenters to cowboys, to the president of the bank. If something doesn't happen within the next six months, I'll get a job emptying spittoons at one of my own saloons.

He scratched his armpit nervously, and had a vague unsettled feeling concerning Vanessa and Duane. He'd pushed his way into an ordinary domestic scene, with no evidence of nefarious conduct, but she'd seemed flustered, her normally perfect coiffure slightly awry, a strange glint in her eyes. Something had happened between her and Duane, but what? Surely they didn't . . .

Petigru was getting a headache. He reached for a pitcher of cool water flavored with whatever dead insect had flown into it, as his suspicion deepened like a great abyss. *Were they doing it, when they noticed me coming?*

The more he thought about it, the more the pieces fell into place. *God only knows how many lies she's told me. I'll bet she's making love behind my back with that ignorant twit. Well, I'll fix her, and as for the Pecos Kid, if he's not careful—I'll pay Saul Klevins to put a bullet between his eyes.*

Duane pushed his empty plate away, swallowed his last few ounces of beer, and wiped his mouth with the back of his hand. *I'll go to bed early,* he said to himself. *I want to be clearheaded and alert when I start my first day on the job.*

His eyes roved the saloon, as he approached the door. Any fast move or hostile word would send him diving beneath a table. Butterfield had pounded the truth of life into him relentlessly. *Pay attention, or you'll end up on Boot Hill.*

Duane felt silly to be so extracautious, because one part of him considered Butterfield overly cynical. *It's not that dangerous,* Duane thought. *Stay out of saloons, don't look for fights, and you'll be just fine.*

He pushed open the bat-wing doors, and nearly collided with a cowboy on his way in. "Watch whar the hell yer goin'!" the cowboy with the long lantern jaw and sandy mustache bellowed. "Well I'll be the son of an armadillo—if it ain't the Pecos Kid! Where the hell you been, boy?"

Duane had finally found Boggs, his cowboy pard. "I was having some target practice with Clyde Butterfield. Which way you headed?"

"I was a-hopin' that somebody would buy me a drink in thar," he replied. "You got any money on you?"

"We start our new jobs tomorrow, and should be at the Lazy Y early. I think we'd better find a hotel and get some sleep."

"What the hell you want to sleep fer?" Boggs staggered on the sidewalk, and it was clear that he'd already enjoyed several drinks. "When you die, you can sleep ferever, but now you got to live, cowboy!"

Duane opened his mouth to reply, when he heard a faint metallic click across the street. It was barely audible amid horses snorting and stomping at the hitching rail, conversations in saloons, and hoofbeats on the street. Duane looked at Boggs, and they both hollered at the same moment: "Get down!"

They dove to the sidewalk, as the night exploded all around them, and lead whizzed over their heads, or slammed into the wooden sidewalk beneath them, sending splinters flying through the air. Duane rolled behind a water trough, a bullet blasted through the boards, and water spurted into his eye.

Never before had he been under intense fire from all directions, and he found the experience petrifying, particularly since he hadn't the slightest idea of what was going on. "Keep yer head down!" Boggs shouted, stone-cold sober now, like the sergeant he'd been at Chancellorsvile. "Return their fire!"

Duane drew his gun, thumbed back the hammer, and raised one eye above the trough. A gun fired on the far side of the street, and something warm blew a hole in his hat.

"I said return their fire, goddammit!"

Boggs pulled the trigger, his gun exploded, and smoke expanded behind the trough. Something prompted Duane to look up, and he was astonished to see a man at the edge of the roof, a gun in his hand, aiming down. Duane spun around and fired wildly. The man shot back, and hot lead slammed into the water trough beside Duane, who clenched his teeth, aimed more carefully, and squeezed the trigger. The gun kicked in his hand, and smoke obscured his vision for a moment, but a gust of wind cleared it away, and Duane saw the man roll lifelessly down the eaves, and land on the sidewalk. Duane stared at him, the second man he'd ever killed, and he didn't even know his name.

"I said return their fire!"

Bullets flew through the air like angry gnats, as Boggs perched stalwartly on one knee behind the water trough, firing at targets across the street. Duane emulated his position, as a bullet zipped past his ear, making him flinch. He saw muzzle blasts across the street, aimed at one of them, and fired simultaneously with Boggs. A second later there was a shriek in the night. "I'm hit!"

"Let's get out of here!" hollered a deep rumbling voice.

Duane fired at a murky figure fleeing down an

alley, but couldn't tell whether he'd brought him down. He heard footsteps receding into the distance, and no more guns were fired on the far side of the street. Hoofbeats could be heard in the alley.

"Keep yer head down!" Boggs ordered.

Duane ducked behind the trough, and thumbed cartridges into his Colt. Moonlight fell on the waxy features of the man he'd killed, and he looked vaguely familiar, but Duane couldn't quite place him.

"All clear out there?" asked a voice from the Crystal Palace Saloon.

"'Pears so," Boggs replied.

Boggs's shirt was soaked with blood. He holstered his gun, then sat heavily on the bench in front of the saloon. "Just like the goddamned war fer a moment thar," he wheezed.

Men drifted out of saloons, as Duane kneeled before Boggs. His cowboy pard had been shot in the shoulder. Boggs seemed in a trance, as his life's blood oozed out of him. "The most important duty of a soldier," he murmured, "is . . ."

He closed his eyes, pitched forward, and Duane caught him before his face crashed into the sidewalk. Duane laid him down gently and rolled him over.

"Is he dead?" asked a voice behind Duane.

"Not yet," Duane replied, "but somebody'd better get the doctor real fast."

Deputy Dawson strolled down the center of the street, gun in hand. "What the hell's going on here?"

"Here comes our lawman," somebody said snidely, "late as usual."

Duane unbuttoned Boggs's shirt and bared the ugly wound. Boggs was passed out completely, face pale, whites of his eyes showing. If it hadn't been for this man, Duane thought, I'd probably be dead right now. Will I have to look over my shoulder for the rest of my life, just because I shot some son of a bitch?

CHAPTER 8

DUANE SAT IN THE BUCKBOARD, A SHARPS buffalo rifle cradled in his lap. The driver, a jolly fellow named Hank Atchison, slapped the reins across the backs of the horses, as he drove Duane toward the Lazy Y Ranch. "Injuns gener'ly don't attack less'n they think they're a-gonna win," Atchison explained. "Keep yer eyes peeled whenever yer out here, 'cause if you don't see 'em first, yer daid."

Duane's eyes explored the terrain, as he realized yet again that the world was far more lethal than he'd previously imagined. He longed for the tranquil spiritual life, but could never return to the monastery now. The memory of Vanessa's lithe body warmed him in the cool spring morning, and he looked forward to seeing her in town next Saturday night.

An arduous week lay ahead, because Boggs had told him that a new tenderfoot cowboy would become everybody's scapegoat until he proved himself worthy of their company. If I could plow through Saint Thomas Aquinas, I can handle anything, Duane tried to reassure himself, as the buckboard rumbled closer toward his highest career aspiration.

Len Farnsworth hunched over his desk, writing feverishly.

PECOS KID SHOOTS TWO COWBOYS
OVER "LOOSE" WOMAN
IN TITUSVILLE

Duane Braddock, better known as the Pecos Kid, provided his own special brand of entertainment in our town last night, when he shot two outlaws to death on Main Street, in front of the Crystal Palace Saloon, which is open twenty-four hours a day, and serves exceptionally fine food.

The object of their dispute evidently was a certain "scarlet woman" named

Farnsworth paused, wondering what to call the fictitious woman, because he couldn't mistakenly use the name of a real lady of the night, who might shoot him for cheap revenge.

The door opened behind him, and Edgar Petigru stormed into the office, a scowl on his face. "Don't you dare!" he shouted, as he marched toward the desk.

Farnsworth shot to his feet, as Petigru grabbed the news story that he'd been working on. "Just as I thought!" Petigru said. "You're incorrigible, and the only way to stop you is drive a stake through your heart! I told you to *forget about the Pecos Kid!*"

"But you don't understand," Farnsworth replied, eyes dancing with headlines and deadlines. "We're creating a legend here in Titusville. When I'm finished, folks all across this country will know about this town."

"They'll know it's a place to steer clear of!" Petigru replied angrily. "Have you gone mad? And what's this about a 'scarlet woman'? You're not even telling the truth!"

"If you knew the so-called truth, you'd be on the next stage out of town, Mister Petigru."

The New York tycoon was astonished by this completely unexpected remark. "What're you talking about?"

Farnsworth spat into the cuspidor. "We've got a deputy sheriff who shows up in time to carry the bodies away, and Titusville has become a magnet for every hard case in Texas."

"Thanks to your insipid newspaper stories. The Pecos Kid? Don't make me laugh. You're going to get that boy killed."

"That'd be the best story of all," Farnsworth said, framing the headline in his mind:

PECOS KID GUNNED DOWN

Petigru paced back and forth, hands clasped behind his back. "I simply cannot tolerate any more of this foolishness! The *Titusville Sentinel* is defunct as of right now! I'll send a messenger with your final pay later in the day! I'd appreciate it if you'd clear out of this office without delay."

Farnsworth pulled out his Colt, and said: "My name is on the lease, and it's my press. I brought it here on the back of a mule."

"I've heard that story a hundred times, and it's probably not true, either. Let's not forget that I'm the man who lent you five thousand dollars to get that rag of yours started in the first place."

"Pay you back when I get it, and if I never get it, that's business. I lost my shirt a few times along the road, too."

Petigru looked down the barrel of the gun, the most convincing debating tool of all. "Surely you're not going to shoot me."

"I will, if you don't get out of my office."

"You'd be living in the gutter right now, if it weren't for me."

"But I ain't," Farnsworth replied, thumbing back the hammer.

On a far reach of prairie, the outlaws dug a grave for their fallen comrade, Ken Dominici, shot through the head last night in Titusville. Dominici lay on the ground stiff as a board, his black beard caked with blood, as Hardy worked the shovel.

Smollett sat nearby, his left thigh bandaged. While running away, he'd been clipped with a bullet from behind. The bushwhack had gone awry, due to the arrival of a friend of the Pecos Kid, and Daltry had been shot off the roof. The original gang of six had diminished to four.

Singleton had cut the lead out of Smollett's leg with his knife, and pain throbbed through his body, as he cursed the cowboy who'd diverted the Pecos Kid from the line of fire. Smollett, who was weak and dizzy and couldn't walk on his bum leg, felt as though his luck was running out.

Daltry spelled Singleton at the shovel, and Singleton sipped out of the canteen. Then he put on his eagle-feathered hat and shuffled wearily toward Smollett. "What do ya think?" he asked.

"Maybe we should put this behind us, and move on."

"No matter where we go, we won't find a town with less law than Titusville, and that bank still looks good to me. I say we hit it, and move on."

"What about the Pecos Kid?"

"Next time we'll kill him right."

"I think he's more trouble than he's worth."

"He killed three of my friends." Singleton looked at Hardy, who was pressing his boot against the shovel's blade. "Hey—should we kill the Pecos Kid, or let 'im off the hook?"

Hardy wiped the sweat off his brow with the back of his arm, and thought for a few moments. "Kill 'im," he said. Then he resumed shoveling.

Mayor Lonsdale sat at his desk, eating a crumpet saturated with butter and raspberry jam, while studying a map of Texas. *Maybe, when this is all over, the missus and me'll go to Austin, and become cosmopolitan folks.*

The door to his office opened, and Petigru stood

there, an expression of tribulation upon his distinguished New York features. "Come in, boy," the mayor said, indicating a chair in front of his desk. "Care for a crumpet?"

Edgar flung his arms outward. "How can you talk about crumpets, you fool! We have no law here, and it's time we sent for the Rangers!"

Mayor Lonsdale smiled beneficently. "There's a lot that you don't know about Texas, Petigru. Don't ever call a man a fool to his face, unless yer ready to die." The mayor cocked the hammer of his Remington and aimed at the stylish New Yorker. "Most unhealthy thing you can do."

Petigru found himself gazing down the barrel of a gun for the second time that day. "It appears that the moral climate of this town has been deteriorating rather rapidly during the past several days. My editor has just threatened to kill me."

"Were there witnesses?"

"I was alone, unfortunately."

"If you need a good witness, let me recommend my cousin Carl. He'll go with you everwheres, testify to anything you say, and he'll only cost one hundred dollars a month."

Petigru placed his fists on the mayor's desk and leaned forward. "I think I've got your whole damn family on my payroll, and it's my money that keeps *you* in crumpets, because I've bought most of this town from you!"

"And I researched the titles, too," the mayor pointed out.

"Which means that they might not even have been yours legally!"

Mayor Lonsdale winked. "But I wouldn't worry about it if'n I was you, Edgar, because any doctor'll tell you that worryin' does no good for the liver."

Petigru dropped into a green leather chair in front of the mayor's desk. "Sometimes, when my spirits get really low, I think that you and all the others in this town have swindled me. I've supported carpenters, lawyers, cowboys, bankers, and even well-diggers. In a sense, this whole town has been a figment of my imagination."

"But think of what'll happen when the railroad comes. We'll *all* be rich."

"What if the railroad doesn't come?"

"Then we'll all move to our next opportunity, that's all."

"But you'll be moving with *my money*, and I'll be flat busted!" Petigru wore a distraught expression, for he was voicing his deepest fears for the first time. Has a bunch of ignorant and uneducated bumpkins bamboozled me out of my fortune, and part of my mother's? They've sold me my own town in the middle of nowhere, and they've let me play king, but what'll happen when my money runs out?

Mayor Lonsdale looked like a fiendish little dwarf as he aimed down the barrel of his gun at Edgar, and closed one eye. "I think I know what's on yer mind, Edgar, and I can't say that I haven't expected it. If yer a-thinkin' about leavin' yer friends and neighbors in the lurch, you got another think a-comin', 'cause we won't stand for it."

This was yet another blow to Edgar's delicate constitution. "Surely you're not going to hold me captive!"

"Hell no," the mayor replied. "You can leave after you fulfill yer financial obligations."

"I'm not paying another dime," Edgar said adamantly. "You can take your damned town back—I don't want it!"

"Neither do we, because if the railroad don't come —this town ain't worth buffalo shit."

The buckboard came to a stop between the barn and the main house. "This is it, Kid," said Hank Atchison. "The bunkhouse is behind the barn. Just do as yer told, don't ask too many questions, and you'll git along jest fine."

They shook hands, and Duane climbed down from the buckboard. Atchison flicked the reins, and the horses turned around in the yard, hauling the buckboard back toward Titusville. Duane stood next to the white picket fence and looked at the big barn.

Not a soul was in sight. He turned to the main house, a large two-story deserted wooden building. I guess that's where Mister Petigru lives when he comes out here, he thought. Duane tossed his bedroll over his shoulder, and headed for the bunkhouse. He had no idea what job they'd give him, and was prepared to shovel horse manure and sweep floors. I hope I can make friends with one of the cowboys, and he'll teach me how to ride, he said to himself.

The bunkhouse was a rectangular shack behind the barn, with smoke twirling from its chimney. Nearby was a hitching rail, a pile of wood, and a privy with a crude half-moon cut into its door. Duane inclined toward the bunkhouse, his new home for the forseeable future.

He opened the door, and a dozen pairs of eyes

drilled through him. He was surprised to see cowboys sitting around, wearing hats, boots, and guns, with barely suppressed amusement on their faces. A bottle of whiskey sat on the table, near glasses and a deck of cards.

A man with a black handlebar mustache stepped forward. "I'm Jake Russell, the foreman. And this is . . . Jethro."

Duane looked into the battered features of the big drunken cowboy he'd fought on his first night in town. Oh no.

But Jethro grinned, as he shook Duane's hand. "You got a helluva punch, boy."

Russell introduced Duane to the other cowboys, and Duane shook their hands. He was suspicious of their apparent affability, because Atchison had said that new cowboys sometimes died under mysterious circumstances, before being accepted by the bunkhouse. If that wasn't enough, Jethro was there as well, but somehow the great hulk didn't seem so antagonistic now that he was sober.

Russell said warmly, "Pick out an empty bunk, and the washbasin's in back. I understand that you don't know how to ride a horse?"

"That's right," Duane admitted. "I don't."

A cowboy nearby guffawed, and covered mirth with his hand. Duane looked at a mean bunch of armed desperados; some carried knives in sheaths attached to their belts, and others had them sticking out of their boots.

"We'll have to teach you," Russell continued, "because you can't do this job less'n you can ride. But there's two schools of thought 'bout larnin' ter ride.

One school says you start with gentle old nags, and work yer way up to the real horses, while the other school says a man should hop on the wildest son of a bitch in the barn, and ride 'em cowboy. Which way d'you want, kid?"

This evidently is the first of their pranks, Duane realized. But I'm not going to break my neck to amuse them on a boring Monday afternoon. "If you don't mind, I'd like to start off with an easy horse."

Russell turned toward his cowboy crew. "Why don't a couple of you boys go to the barn and saddle up Old Ned fer Mister Braddock. We might as well give him his first lesson naow."

Edgar sat behind his desk, but no matter how he figured the numbers, he was deeply in debt to Mayor Lonsdale, Banker Holcomb, Councilman Finney, Judge Jenks, and numerous other citizens of Titusville, and he even owed money to himself as owner of the Carrington Arms Hotel.

He wasn't broke, but it was close. He could borrow more from his mother, but conscience wouldn't allow it. I'm stuck in this town, and my life is danger. The local bumpkins have been swindling me all along, and I underestimated them because they didn't speak like Wall Street lawyers! he chided himself.

There was a knock on his door, and he reached for his Colt. "Come in."

Saul Klevins entered the suite, thumbs hooked in his gun belt. "You wanted to see me, Mister Petigru."

"Yes, have a seat, Mister Klevins. Could I get you something to drink?"

"Whiskey."

Petrigru scurried to the bar, filled a glass with his finest stock, and carried it to Klevins. "I'd like to hire you as my bodyguard."

"'Bout goddamned time you seen the light," Petigru replied. "It's a wonder you haven't been shot by now."

Thank God there are people like Klevins in the world, Petigru thought. "What are your going rates?"

"Fer you, two hundred dollars a month."

Petigru's eyes bugged out of his head, and he felt as though his gut would bust. "Two hundred dollars . . ."

"Guess you ain't innerested," Klevins said. He poured the whiskey down his throat, and headed for the door.

"Wait a minute!" Petigru hollered, jumping up from his desk. "Let's talk!"

"My price just went to two-fifty," Klevins said, gripping the doorknob.

"I'll pay!"

Klevins smiled faintly, as he returned to the desk. "In advance."

"Of course. Certainly." Petigru kneeled in front of his safe, twirled the dial, and opened it up. Inside were stacks of paper money and bags of coins. Petigru counted out the amount carefully, as Klevins contemplated putting a bullet through the back of his head. This Yankee is even dumber than I thought, Klevins said to himself. Maybe I should take it all right now. Before Klevins could make up his mind, Petigru slammed the door shut, and turned the knob.

Maybe some other time, Klevins thought, as he

accepted the money from Petigru's hand. "What'll my duties be, sir?"

"Protect my life and property, as circumstances require. Essentially, you'll be living with me. I'll have the clerk send up a cot for you. And you'll eat at my table, too, of course. There may come a point where I'll want to be alone, and I'll tell you to leave. I hope you won't take it personally."

"I'm a perfessional bodyguard," Klevins replied. "I don't take nothin' personally."

Duane saw a horse in the middle of the corral, with a cowboy on either side, holding the bridle tightly, a bandanna tied around the horse's eyes. Other cowboys sat on rungs of the fence, a row of spurs sticking out behind them.

"Why's the horse blindfolded?" Duane asked Russell.

Russell spat a gob of something brown at the ground. "Wa'al, Old Ned, he likes to get as much sleep as he can, and he can't sleep in the light, so we blindfold him."

They came to the edge of the fence and looked over the slats. Old Ned was coal black, lean, and appeared skitterish, an unusual quality for a horse supposedly docile. The horse's tail swished back and forth impatiently, and he looked like a coiled spring ready to leap through the sky.

Duane was not the fool they thought, and he perceived a cowboy joke in the making. Old Ned is probably the most cantankerous horse in the barn, and these cowboys are here to see me get stomped. But he knew that he had to play along with their pranks to some degree, otherwise they'd never accept him. He looked at the horse's proud head and long, muscular legs. The animal reminded him vaguely of Vanessa Fontaine, with the same excitable energy. He remembered what Boggs had told him about hanging on with his heels, and becoming one with the horse. Duane's youthful optimism came to the fore, as he thought: Maybe I can turn this prank around, and have the last laugh.

Russell turned toward him. "You ain't backin' out, are ya?"

"Hell no," Duane replied. "Let's do it."

He climbed over the fence and walked toward the horse, who perked up his ears and turned in his direction. The closer Duane came, the bigger and younger the horse became, and Duane wondered if he were being incautious. What if this horse bucks me, and I break my neck? he wondered. What the hell've I got myself into this time?

He looked around the corral, where cowboys watched him avidly from grandstand seats. It reminded him of an ordination ceremony in the monastery, with the same portentous gravity. He approached the left side of the horse, as Boggs had taught him. *Swing yer arm fer balance*, he heard the cowboy say in his ear.

Two cowboys struggled to control Old Ned, who appeared raring to go. Duane hesitated, because in a few seconds he'd be riding a cyclone. But he had to learn, and if this was the way God wanted it, he'd see it through. Maybe I can stay on his back if I hold on tight and go with his motions, he speculated.

He touched his hand to the side of the horse's immense neck. "Just hold steady, boy."

Duane heard a snicker behind him, as he prepared to place his boot in the stirrup. If I can ride this horse, my troubles will be over, the orphan thought hopefully. "I'm ready," he told the two cowboys.

"He's all yers," one of them replied.

Duane thrust his toe into the stirrup, grabbed the pommel, swung his other leg up, and settled into the saddle. One cowboy handed him the reins, and the other cowboy removed the blindfold from Old Ned. Duane knew that his hat wouldn't remain on his head long, so he held it in his extended left hand.

The horse blinked his huge eyes at the world that suddenly had reappeared. He'd been worried that he'd gone blind, but now could see again! An uncomfortable weight sat on his back, and he didn't want it there.

Meanwhile, Duane wondered why the horse wasn't moving. Maybe he really is a docile old animal, he conjectured. I don't know anything about horses, and these cowboys wouldn't kill me for a few laughs, would they?

Suddenly Duane felt a violent kick in the butt, and next thing he knew, he was flying through the air. He performed an unintentional somersault, and landed on his head near the slats of the fence.

"Watch out!" hollered a cowboy.

Duane rolled onto his side and opened his eyes. Old Ned cantered toward him, and it was clear to Duane, even with his scant knowledge of horseflesh, that the animal had malice in his heart. He heard cowboys roaring with laughter, as he scooted beneath the fence. Old Ned came to a halt a few feet away, glaring at him through the slats.

Russell slapped Duane on the back. "Not a bad ride fer the first time, eh, boys?"

The cowboys gathered around, gleeful expressions on their faces, and Jethro slapped him on the back so hard, Duane nearly fell on his face. The Pecos Kid turned toward the corral, looked the horse in the eyes, and even Old Ned seemed to be laughing. You'll never ride me, you puny two-legged fool, he seemed to taunt.

Jethro pointed at the horse. "My God—I thank we made a mistake, Ramrod. That ain't Old Ned. That's Thunderbolt—meanest horse we got!"

Russell widened his eyes in mock surprise. "I'll be damned, but I reckon yer right." He turned toward Duane. "Sorry, but the boys got mixed up. We'll take Thunderbolt back to the barn, and bring out Old Ned."

Sure, Duane thought, and the next horse'll be even meaner than this one. These cowboys won't stop until every bone in my body is broken. But maybe, if I really dig my heels in, I can stay on the son of a bitch. "Hold on, Ramrod," he said. "I'd rather learn on a spirited animal like Thunderbolt, instead of a nag like Old Ned."

Ramrod frowned. "I wouldn't push it too far if'n I was you. We had our little joke, and you fell fer it like a ton of bricks. Now we can git one of the tamer horses."

"You said yourself that the best way to learn is to jump on the wildest horse in the corral."

I was exaggeratin'," Russell replied. "You keep after Thunderbolt, he's liable to kill you."

I must impose my will on this animal, Duane realized. He looked into the horse's eyes, and Thunderbolt took three steps backward, then swished his tail and perked up his ears. Duane remembered the words of Lester Boggs, his cowboy mentor:

> Ain't never been a horse, what couldn't be rode.
> Ain't never been a cowboy, what couldn't be throwed.

Duane wondered whether or not he was insane, as he climbed over the fence. The cowboys grumbled among themselves, because the joke was being carried too far, and they didn't want anybody to get stomped. I'm going to ride this horse, Duane vowed, as he jumped to the ground in front of Thunderbolt. "Now take it easy, boy," Duane said soothingly, attempting to approach the animal from his left side.

But Thunderbolt kept changing position, so that he could see Duane head-on. Duane gazed into the animal's immense bulbous eyes, and wondered what kind of intelligence lurked within.

"I wouldn't want anybody on my back, either," Duane murmured to the horse, attempting to pat his mane.

Thunderbolt stood still, and let Duane touch him. It's like Boggs said, Duane mused. You've got to make friends with them. "There, there," he said warmly.

"Watch out!" shouted one of the cowboys.

Thunderbolt craned his huge head around, and tried to bite Duane, who pulled his hand back at the last moment, leaving part of his sleeve in the horse's mouth. Duane became furious at the betrayal of trust, and punched the horse on the side of the head.

Thunderbolt, jolted by the sudden blow, blinked his eyes. Duane took the opportunity to leap into the saddle, thrust his feet through the stirrups, grab the reins, and kick his heels into Thunderbolt's withers. "Come on, horse—show me what you've got!"

Thunderbolt leapt into the air, and Duane's spine whiplashed violently. Duane removed his hat, held it out for balance, and hugged Thunderbolt tightly with his legs, as the horse switched ends, twisted, leaped, and dived.

"Ride 'em cowboy!" shouted one of the men behind the rail.

"Yippee!" hollered another, throwing his hat in the air.

I'm riding him! Duane thought happily, and then found himself lurching into the air. A bird flew past, glancing at him curiously, and then Duane plunged to the ground in the middle of the corral, where he lay still.

"Get up!" hollered one of the cowboys.

Duane opened his eyes. Thunderbolt towered above him, standing on his hind legs, ready to plop his front hooves on Duane's nose, but Duane spun out at the last moment, and Thunderbolt's hooves slammed into the ground, sending up a cloud of dust.

Duane limped out of the way, the horse charged, but Duane switched direction suddenly, and Thunderbolt couldn't reposition himself quickly enough. Duane rushed Thunderbolt's flank, leapt into the air, and landed on the saddle again.

Thunderbolt arched his back at the first impres-

sion of weight, ramming Duane's boots into the stirrups. The horse tossed and bucked frantically, trying
to shake Duane off, but Duane gritted his teeth and
held on. "I can last longer than you," Duane uttered,
"and I'm going to break you!"

Like hell you are, the horse seemed to say, hop-
ping around the perimeter of the corral, trying to slam
Duane into the slats, but the horse's movements were
becoming more familiar to Duane. He held his arm out
for balance, and tried to blend with the tornado
beneath him.

He's tiring, Duane thought, and I've got him figured out. "Hurrah!" he yelled, confident that he was
on his way to victory, but when he opened his eyes
again, he was lying on the ground outside the corral,
and the cowboys were gathered around him.

"Deep cut on his forehead," said one of the cowboys.

Duane felt a canteen at his lips, and took a sip of
water, but his lip coordination was off, and the water
ran down his throat, soaking his shirt. "What happened?" he asked weakly.

"He throwed you," Russell replied. "And you hit
yer head on the fence post. I think you'd better lie
down."

The cowboys appeared concerned for his welfare,
and Duane ached in every bone of his body. He turned
toward Thunderbolt, and the horse laughed at him. I'll
ride you, Duane thought, or you'll kill me. Duane
arose from the ground, and somebody handed him his
battered hat. He poked out the crown with his fingers,
settled it on his head, fixed the neck strap, and placed
his boot on a slat of the gate.

"He'll kick yer brains out, boy," one of the cowboys said.

Duane shook them off, as he climbed over the top rail. No goddamned dumb horse is going to make a fool out of me, he said to himself. Thunderbolt watched with increasing apprehension on the far side of the corral. The cowboy appeared enraged, and Thunderbolt neighed, as he backed toward the fence. Duane stood in front of him, crouched over, bared his teeth, and lunged for Thunderbolt, who darted to the side. Duane leapt on top of him, settled in the saddle, and grabbed the reins. You asked for it, Thunderbolt thought. You want to die—you've come to the right place. He snorted, jackknifed, and went straight in the air. When he landed, he jerked to the left, twisted to the right, switched ends, and tried to ram Duane into the fence.

But Duane hung on, realizing that a horse has only a certain repertoire of movements, and once you understand them, you just work with them. His arm jerked up and down as he bounced in the saddle, his legs kicking the sky. I can do this all day, he thought. It's fun, once you get used to it. "Yippee!" he hollered. "Ki-ti-yo."

Meanwhile, Thunderbolt was getting tired of the exercise. No other cowboy had ever stayed on so long, and he knew that he'd be broken eventually, like all the other horses in the corral. The horse slackened his efforts, and Duane's heart leapt with anticipation of sweet victory. I've done it, he thought, his chest swelling with pride. He grabbed the reins and pulled them back firmly. "Whoa, now."

Thunderbolt stopped, and shook his great head

from side to side. It didn't make sense to buck and toss with so little possibility of success. He snorted in disgust at his poor performance, and hung his head low in shame.

"Why don't we be friends?" Duane asked, patting Thunderbolt's mane. "Maybe we can have some fun together?"

The cowboys gathered around Duane, smirks on their faces. "That was one helluva ride, Kid," Russell said. "I guess you was a-funnin' when you said that you never rode a horse before."

"But I never did," Duane replied.

Russell winked knowingly. "Sure, just like you never fired a gun a'fore. We understand, don't we, boys?"

"Right," they agreed in unison.

"Let's go inside and have a smoke," Russell said. "We done enough work fer today."

"You seem out of sorts tonight, Edgar," said Vanessa Fontaine.

The richest man in town looked at her dolefully, as he raised a spoonful of chicken soup to his mouth. They were seated across the table in her dining room, and it was early evening. "I'm fine," he said gruffly. "You're imagining things."

"Something's bothering you. If you can't tell the truth to the woman you claim to love—then you mustn't trust her very much."

"Stop being sanctimonious, Vanessa. We both know that the only reason you have anything to do with me, is my money, and if I ever went bust, you'd probably never speak to me again."

"How can you even *think* such a thing?" she retorted indignantly. "I don't believe I've ever been so insulted in all my days! Why, you make me sound like a greedy witch."

"Well, if you insist on knowing—I'll tell you. There's a very strong possibility that I, in fact, *will* go bust within the next six months."

She burped, swallowed hard, and wanted to scream: *If you go bust, what'll happen to me?* But she caught the words in her throat, and swallowed them down along with a portion of a chicken's leg. "Has something actually happened, or is this another of your vague, unreasonable fears?"

"Quite a number of dishonest people reside in this town," he replied, "and they've persuaded me that sufficient investment would draw the railroad, but now it appears that they greatly exaggerated that potentiality."

"Who needs the railroad?" she asked cheerfully. "The town seems to be doing fine without it."

"You don't understand," he replied, an edge to his voice. "*I'm* keeping this town alive almost single-handedly, and I pay everybody's salary, including yours, and now even the Pecos Kid is on my payroll. It's entirely possible that I've been the victim of a colossal swindle."

Vanessa stared at him in horror and disbelief. She didn't know anything about business, disapproved of it on general artistic principles, and never had analyzed the economics of Titusville. "I thought that the gambling and saloons made a lot of money."

"Not enough to keep the whole town going."

"What about your cattle?"

"They're worth something in Kansas, but not much in Texas. The hotel and nearly everything else is mortgaged. If I lose my ranches, my cowboys will move to other jobs. The money is merely circulating from me to the cowboys and back to me, with a funnel at one end going to my creditors."

"But what will you do?" she asked, panic coming to her voice.

"I have no idea, and life may get rather dodgy for both of us in the weeks to come. You might be well advised to make the acquaintance of Miss Ellie, just in case."

Saul Klevins and Jed Wilson sat opposite each other in the barn behind Vanessa's home, their faces illuminated by the single candle in the middle of the table. They ate in silence, as the carriage gleamed in the dimness nearby.

Klevins fumed with barely suppressed vitriol. He'd anticipated dinner with Miss Fontaine, and hoped to work his charm upon her, because he knew that many women enjoyed kissing the lips of death, but instead, Petigru had banished him to the barn like a common servant.

Meanwhile, on the other side of the table, Jed cast quick glances of appraisal at his dining companion, and perceived poison bubbling beneath the surface. Jed was obsessed with Vanessa Fontaine, and constantly thought of ways to seduce her. He wasn't quite sure how to bring that about, but knew that the more turmoil in Titusville, the better his chances would be.

When Vanessa was desperate for money, Jed would help her—for certain considerations, of course.

"Sometimes I wish I was Mister Petigru," Jed threw out, like an angler's worm, "and I was there in the main house with Miss Vanessa, but I guess if she had her druthers, the man she'd be with right now is Duane Braddock."

Klevins stiffened at the sound of the name. "What the hell does he have to do with it?"

"Why, he's a-screwin' the pants off Miss Vanessa. Comes here at night through the back door. Sometimes, when the wind is right, I can hear her screamin' like a cat in heat. The Pecos Kid must be a great stud."

Klevins pushed his plate away. "I'm sick of hearing about the Pecos Kid. All he's ever done was get off one lucky shot against a drunk cowboy, and you'd think he was the governor of Alabama. And as fer Miss Fontaine, she's nothin' more'n a high-class whore. A woman like that would screw anything."

"I don't know about lucky shots," Jed said apologetically. "There's some that says the Pecos Kid just acts dumb to put people off."

"He don't act dumb—he *is* dumb, but some people around here don't get it. Besides, I got better things to talk about than that damned little rat."

Jed wanted to say: *He's taller'n you,* but Klevins put on his hat. The door slammed, Jed rushed to the window, and saw Klevins sit on a barrel outside, pulling out his bag of tobacco.

Klevins puffed a cigarette in the darkness, unaware that he was being observed. I'm the fastest hand in town, he told himself, yet I have to eat with the carriage driver, while everybody's talkin' about the Pecos Kid. I really ought to shoot that little bastard, so that people around here can see what fast really is.

CHAPTER 9

A GROUP OF RIDERS LEFT THE LAZY Y LATE next Saturday afternoon. Led by their Ramrod, they headed toward Titusville for their big night on the town.

Their jeans had been washed, shirts ironed, hats brushed to rid them of dust and dead grasshoppers. Each man had bathed, shaved, and wore clean underwear, so he'd be suitably presentable for the prostitutes of Titusville.

Duane rode among them, astride Thunderbolt. After a week in the bunkhouse, Duane had learned that prostitutes were the cowboys' main interest and topic of conversation, but when they worked, they wasted no words, and always cut to the core of whatever they were doing. He always found their cowboy logic unassailable.

The cowboys had accepted Duane after he'd ridden Thunderbolt, and evidently believed that he really was the Pecos Kid, even giving him grudging respect despite his tender age. He'd become another face in the bunkhouse, and his fondest dream had come true, more or less.

He'd learned that the cowboy's life was arduous labor on the hurricane deck of a horse, dawn to dusk, and if you went on a cattle drive, get ready to sleep on the ground for three months. The bunkhouse was even more uncomfortable than the monastery, where penance through harsh living was the goal. Once more Duane resided in all-masculine society, but missed the female touch. He'd learned the basics of roping and working cattle, and his spare time had been spent with shooting practice. He considered himself nearly as good as any man in the bunkhouse.

During the course of innumerable bullshit sessions, he'd learned that Edgar Petigru was the dupe of just about everybody in the region, including the cowboys. They'd all conspired to convince Petigru that a hot investment opportunity existed in Titusville, and the ignorant Yankee didn't know any better. The Lazy Y was run in a haphazard fashion, and evidently didn't have as much cattle as Petigru thought. Now even Duane was part of the humbug.

Like the others, the Pecos Kid was spruced for his night on the town, and had even polished his boots, plus cleaned his gun and loaded it with five fresh cartridges. His gun belt was stuffed full of ammunition, and so was an old black leather U.S. Cavalry cartridge case affixed to his belt.

He felt like a man, and even knew how to ride a

horse! He and Thunderbolt had developed a tentative friendship, but Duane sensed Thunderbolt's dissatisfaction with captivity, and always tethered him carefully. Duane leaned forward and patted Thunderbolt's lustrous mane. "Someday, if I get some money, I'll buy you for myself, and turn you loose."

Thunderbolt snorted skeptically, and sometimes Duane had the impression that the horse was attempting to communicate. Duane pulled out a small bag of tobacco, for the cowboys had taught him to smoke, and his fingers were yellowed by nicotine. He rolled a cigarette, spilling half the tobacco onto his lap, lit it with a match, and let it dangle from the corner of his mouth, like all the other cowboys.

He felt as if he'd fulfilled his favorite dream, as he rode confidently toward the distant city glowing on the plain like Sodom and Gomorrah in the night.

Deputy Dawson sat behind his desk, looking out the window at the darkening street. He dreaded Saturdays, knew there'd probably be shooting, and wondered if he'd be alive when the sun came up on Sunday morning.

He'd heard townspeople talking behind his back and giggling up their sleeves about his inability to make a dent in the violence that had plagued Titusville recently. He always showed up after the shootings were over, because he didn't want to walk into the middle of a gunfight. Let the bastards kill each other if they want to. That had been his philosophy until now.

Deputy Dawson was the poor relative of Mayor

Lonsdale, and suffered feelings of deep inferiority. He didn't have a wife, and if it weren't for the largesse of the mayor, he'd have to get a cowboy job. Everyone thought he was a joke, and it was starting to rankle. He had to take a stand against lawless behavior in Titusville, or else resign, he decided.

Sure hope it's quiet here tonight. I don't want to die just because a bunch of cowboys can't hold their likker, he told himself.

Smollett, Hardy, and Singleton rode down the main street of Titusville, peering about cautiously. They were men with prices on their heads, and never knew when they might be recognized. Their hands rested near their guns. They looked as though they'd been sleeping in their clothes, but didn't appear significantly different from other cowboys in town that night. Their plan was to come up behind Duane Braddock amid Saturday night crowds, and put three bullets into his back.

Smollett rode in the middle, his wounded leg bandaged with an old rag. It ached fiercely; pus oozed out the gash, and it was turning green around the edges. "I'm going to see the sawbones," Smollett said, "and you boys can start looking fer the Kid. When you find him, one of you stay with him, and the other report to me."

Vanessa sat in front of her bedroom mirror, preparing for her evening's performance at the Round-Up Saloon. She'd lost weight during the past week, her complexion had gone pale, hence more cosmetics than usual were required to make her acceptable to the crowd of cowboys and gamblers who'd come to ogle her. No matter how heavy her heart, the show must go on.

She'd spent most of the week in a cloud of gloom, worried about her future, and recalled Petigru's advice to speak with Miss Ellie. Edgar didn't realize it, but his words had plunged terror into Vanessa's heart. If it comes to prostitution, I'll kill myself first.

She raised her skirt, and pulled the derringer out of her garter. Two ugly snouts looked her in the eye, and all she need do was thumb back the hammer, point at her temple, and pull both triggers at the same time. Then she'd never have to worry about prostitution or anything else ever again.

It bothered her that she hadn't been aware of Petigru's true financial situation. I'm a child, and don't know anything about business, she realized. It's easy for men to take advantage of me, because they know I'm needy. I'd marry the devil himself, if he'd buy me a house. But you can't trust men. All they want is one thing, and they'll say anything to get it.

She applied rouge to her cheek, and reflected upon Duane Braddock touching her breast in the vestibule downstairs. She had to admit, despite everything, it had been an extremely exalting moment. She knew that the Pecos Kid would come to town that night, and if he was the man she thought, he'd show up at the Round-Up Saloon.

Why shouldn't I have a taste of love before I die? she thought wistfully, placing Beauregard's daquerreotype in the bottom drawer of her dresser.

Edgar Petigru sat at his window, looking into the main street of town. It was filling with the usual Saturday night riffraff, and he didn't want to go out.

The week had been increasingly difficult, as the true depths of his predicament became increasingly clear to him. He couldn't simply declare bankruptcy, and ride home in a carriage, because home was nearly two thousand miles away, and an Indian might slice his genitals off, and stuff them into his mouth.

Edgar owed substantial amounts to local citizens, and they wouldn't let him leave until they were paid, or he was milked dry. In essence, he was a prisoner, except for his bodyguard, Saul Klevins. But how could he trust a hired gun? Edgar saw Klevins napping on the sofa, his hat covering his face.

Sometimes Edgar had the notion that Klevins didn't like him, and might even shoot him in the back. Edgar had no firm basis for these thoughts, but experienced them nonetheless. Klevins carried an aura of untrustworthiness about him, which made Edgar distinctly uneasy.

Although Klevins appeared to be sleeping, he actually was wide awake, peering at Edgar beneath the brim of his hat. Klevins had laid plans throughout the week. On Monday evening, before Edgar locked the safe for the night, Klevins would slit his throat, steal the money, and be in another jurisdiction by the time Edgar's body was found.

Klevins knew that Edgar would go to the Round-Up Saloon later, to see Vanessa Fontaine. But this time he won't git rid of me so easy, he told himself. I'll have me a talk with the bitch, and maybe she and me can come to terms, especially when she finds out that I'm a-comin' inter a large sum of money. Klevins smiled confidently beneath his hat. Her eyes'll light up when I tell her about the money, because whores have got cash boxes where their hearts are supposed to be, he concluded.

Duane crouched in the alley, watching the carriage approach on the darkened street. He was in the quiet part of town, far from the saloon district, waiting along the route Vanessa usually traveled to the Round-Up Saloon.

He wore his black pants, a black shirt, and a yellow U.S. Cavalry bandanna that he'd bought from one of the cowboys. Atop his head, at a jaunty devil-may-care angle, sat his hat circled with silver conchos. The carriage drew abreast, and he sprang out of the alley, dashed into the street, and jumped onto the running board. Vanessa pulled back in horror, one hand over her breast, for suddenly there he was, the identical person she'd been thinking about on her ride to work.

He opened the door, swung inside, and sat on the seat beside her. Their eyes met in the darkness, she hesitated, but Duane leaned forward and touched his lips gently to hers. She was shocked, enchanted, thrilled, overjoyed—a clutter of confusing emotions sweeping over her.

"I've been thinking about you all week," he said.

"I've been thinking about you, too," she replied, the words out of her mouth before she could stop herself. He touched his hand to her breast, and she didn't slap his face, as she knew she would. "Oh, Duane," she breathed.

Their tongues touched, and he squeezed her breast gently. It was small, firm, pert, and his thumb could make out the outline of the nipple tucked away beneath layers of fabric.

"Don't do that," she begged. "We'll be at the Round-Up soon, and we can't be seen like this."

She made perfect sense, but he couldn't remove his hand, as though it were stuck by the strongest glue known to mankind. He felt her grace and strength, as their tongues did soft combat. She melted in his arms. His other hand roved beneath her dress, and she breathed heavily, as she tried to talk sense to herself. *He's a young bull, he can't stop himself, but I'm more mature, and I'll have to do it.* His hands were driving her mad, but somehow she was able to draw together her last remaining fiber of strength. "*Please,*" she begged. "We can't do it here."

He heard the helplessness in her voice, and somehow her predicament reached the depths of his feverish brain. Reluctantly, he let her go, moved a few inches away, and his trembling hand pulled out his bag of tobacco. She adjusted her clothing in the darkness, her breast still heaving. "How long have you been smoking?" she inquired, as though they were taking a casual ride in the park.

He spilled half the tobacco onto his lap. "Do you think we can meet after you're finished work tonight?"

"I'll be home, and if you found time to visit . . ."

Duane despaired of rolling the cigarette, because he was far too maniacal. He threw the paper out the window, and said ruggedly, "I'll see you then."

He pecked her cheek, caressed her breast again for good measure, and was out the door. She watched from the window of the cab, as the Pecos Kid disappeared into an alley on the far side of the street.

Dr. Robinson examined the man lying with his face on the table, a bullet hole in his leg. The slug had been removed crudely, but the wound was badly infected. The man had ridden out of nowhere, and claimed to've been shot by an Indian, but not many Indians had guns, and although Dr. Robinson's suspicions were aroused, he was bound by the ancient oath of Hippocrates to offer medical care to anyone, even possible outlaws.

Dr. Robinson was only twenty-six years old, with curly brown hair, and a diploma from the St. Louis School of Medicine. He leaned back, wiped his pus-stained fingers on his white apron, and said, "Too bad you didn't see me sooner, because it's quite infected. I can cut away the diseased flesh, and we'll see if it heals."

"What if it doesn't?" asked Smollett apprehensively.

"Well," said the doctor, "it might mean amputation . . . or your life."

Smollett swallowed hard. "When you cut that infection away, you'd better make sure you get all of it."

"Do my best," the doctors aid.

"You'd better do better than your best."

The menacing tone in Smollett's voice was unmistakable, but no surprise to the doctor, who regularly was threatened by patients. "Would you like me to get started now?"

The door opened, and a young man in black pants stood there, wearing a silver concho hatband. "Can I see Boggs?"

"He's in the same bed," Dr. Robinson replied, "and much improved."

The young man passed through the office, and entered the next corridor. Smollett swung his legs around, stood, and pulled up his pants.

"Where are you going?" asked the doctor.

"Something I've got to do," Smollett replied.

Duane entered the small room, and Boggs appeared asleep in the darkness. The curtains had been closed, and Duane reached for the chair. "Hold it— you son of a bitch," croaked Boggs. "I got me gun aimed right 'twixt yer eyes."

"It's me," Duane said.

There was silence for a few moments, then Boggs uttered, "You shouldn't creep up on a man like that."

"I didn't want to awaken you." Duane reached into his pocket, and flipped out a bottle of whiskey. "Have one on me, pardner."

Boggs snatched it out of the air, and the blanket fell off his chest, revealing the tattoo of an eagle. He pulled the cork, leaned back, and guzzled noisily. "Best medicine in the world," he said with satisfaction, as he handed the bottle back. "You sure look like yer full of piss and vinegar tonight. What's goin' on?"

"It's Saturday night in Titusville, and the town's wide open. Can you walk?"

"A few steps."

"Let's go to the Round-Up Saloon."

"Don't know if I can make it that far. Last time I took a walk with you, I got shot." Boggs made a few unsteady steps across the floor, and reached to the wall for support.

"I'll help you get over there," Duane said. "Put your pants on."

Jed Wilson entered the Round-Up Saloon through the back door. He detected the fragrance of Vanessa's perfume, for she'd walked through just a few moments ago, on the way to her first performance of the evening. Jed stepped into the main room of the saloon, slipped into the shadows, rolled a cigarette, and contemplated what he was about to do.

Certain tricks cause amusement, discomfort, or discord, but other tricks can get somebody killed, and it was this latter category that he was about to spring. His eyes roved toward the front tables, and he spotted Edgar Petigru sitting with Saul Klevins. I shouldn't do this, Jed thought, as he moved away from the wall. But I can't resist.

They looked up as he approached, and Petigru's complexion appeared a faint shade of green, his collar undone, eyes glowing with unholy light, while Klevins's hand slid down to his gun.

"I got news," Jed said to Petigru. "Mind if I sit down?" Without waiting for a reply, Jed dropped to the chair opposite them, and placed his hands on the table, where Klevins could see them. "You asked me onc't to tell you if the Kid ever came sniffing around Miss Vanessa again, and . . ."

Jed let his sentence hang in the air, as Petigru turned a deeper shade of green. "Well?" he asked testily. "What happened!"

"While I was a-ridin' down the street, the Kid jumped in back with her, and if I din't know any better, I'd say he give her a screw right thar in the backseat."

Edgar felt as if someone had reached into his chest and torn his heart apart. He was losing everything, and now even Vanessa was being unfaithful! Just like a rat deserting a sinking ship—the bitch took everything I gave her, but now that I need her, she's gone.

Edgar had been on thin ice all week, and was cracking beneath the strain. Somehow her treason loomed larger than his incipient poverty, because poverty harmed only his wallet, while this cut to the vitals of who he believed himself to be. He was vain, filled with false pride, and as he arose, he swore that he wouldn't let her get away with it this time. He stormed to her dressing room, knocked twice, and opened the door.

She sat at her mirror, and flinched in surprise. Annabelle jumped three inches in the air.

"Leave us alone," Edgar said to Annabelle.

The servant left the room, as Vanessa scowled. "I've told you that I don't want you bursting in here like that!"

He pointed his trembling finger at her. "I ought to kill you!"

"Try it!"

Edgar was astonished to find himself staring into the two dull eyes of her derringer. It was the last thing he'd expected, and his mouth went dry. He tried to reply, but he'd never learned, in fashionable New York society, what to say to a woman pointing a gun at your heart.

"Get out of here," she said, "and if you ever come at me like that again, I'll shoot you!"

He pointed his finger at her, and it trembled more than ever. "I know about you and the Pecos Kid—don't think I don't. So you just screwed him in the carriage, eh? I always knew that you were a dirty rebel slut beneath your ridiculous Southern belle pretensions!"

Her eyes narrowed angrily, as her finger squeezed around the trigger.

"No!" he screamed.

The night exploded suddenly with volleys of gunfire.

Ten minutes earlier, Duane and Boggs had emerged from the doctor's office, and were heading toward the Round-Up Saloon. Boggs's arm was draped over Duane's shoulder, and Duane held Boggs by the waist, as they moved along the sidewalk like strange upright Siamese twins.

Duane explained his cowboy week to his spiritual advisor. "I remembered all the things you told me, and they were a big help when I was riding that horse. I just dug in my heels and never let go."

"I'm proud of you, boy," Boggs said, deeply moved. "You was a good larner, or a good liar—I don't know which. There's a lot've people around here what thinks yer a humbug, y'know."

"They think I'm the Pecos Kid."

"Ain't you?"

"You arrived with me on the stagecoach, Boggs—don't you remember?"

Boggs cocked an eye suspiciously. "How do I know that wasn't part of yer game? I don't mean to insult you, pardner, but for all I know, yer bullshit all the way down."

Even my own spiritual advisor doesn't believe me, Duane realized. Everybody thinks I'm a dangerous person, and it does no good to argue. I wonder how many other famous people were fabrications. Is Buffalo Bill really Buffalo Bill? he questioned. They approached the saloon district, and cowboys made way for the crippled man and his escort.

"What happened to him?" somebody asked.

"Maybe," another voice replied, "he drank some of that turpentine at the Blind Pig."

Like last Saturday night, streets and sidewalks were crowded with cowboys carrying guns, passing bottles, laughing, arguing, lying, and enjoying recreation on their way from one saloon to another, with stops in between at the whorehouses and cribs. Biggest crowd of all was in front of the Round-Up Saloon.

"Good evening," said a voice in the night, as Len Farnsworth, publisher *et al.* of the *Titusville Sentinel*, approached.

"Get away from me," Duane said. "I've got nothing to say."

"I meant no harm, sir," Farnsworth said, tipping his hat. "Just wanted to ask your opinion about Saul Klevins. Do you think you're faster than he?"

Boggs pulled his Colt, and aimed it at Farnsworth's

face. "Leave this man alone, or I'll blow yer fuckin' head off."

Duane heard a mechanical *click* behind him, and for a moment was surprised, because Boggs was beside him, but then the full import of his sensory perception came through, and he dove toward the sidewalk, carrying Boggs along with him, as Boggs inadvertently fired his pistol in the air.

Duane rolled out when he hit the ground, as the street reverberated with gunfire. He landed on his belly, raised the Colt, and saw a heavyset man behind him, gun in hand, taking aim. The planked sidewalk exploded beside Duane's face, but Duane held fast and fired point-blank at the man's shirt.

Smollett felt as if someone punched him on the chest, and it was the last sensation he ever had. His lights went out, and he fell in a clump beside Duane, who glanced around excitedly, heart pounding in his chest.

The street and sidewalk had become deserted, except for four bodies sprawled about. Duane looked to his left and right, holding his gun ready to fire, because he was certain that somebody was drawing a bead on him. He'd killed one of his assailants, and one of the bodies was Boggs, but who shot the other two?

A tall, lean figure emerged from the nearby alley, twirling a gun around his forefinger, a cheroot sticking out of his grin. "How're you doing, Kid?"

"What the hell happened?" Duane asked, rising to his feet.

Clyde Butterfield removed the cheroot from his mouth. "I was walking along, minding my own business, and saw a stranger draw on you, so I shot him."

Butterfield flipped his gun into the air, caught it behind his back, and dropped it into his holster.

Duane kneeled beside Boggs, rolled him over, and placed his ear to Boggs's chest.

Boggs said weakly: "This is the . . . second time I took a . . . walk with you, and second time . . . I got shot. Remind me . . . to take walks with . . . somebody else . . . from now on."

"What the hell's goin' on here?" asked Deputy Dawson, strolling onto the scene, gun in hand.

A hoot went up from a nearby alley. "It's Deputy Dawson—late as usual."

A laugh rippled on the far side of the street. "You can always count on Deputy Dawson to show up after the last shot was fired."

"I said, what the hell's going on here!"

"Wa'al," Butterfield said, removing his cheroot from his mouth, "these cowboys here drawed on young Mister Braddock when he wasn't looking, but I happened to be walking by, and we managed to hold them off."

Dr. Robinson arrived in a rush, carrying his little black bag. "It's one of my patients!" he cried, recognizing Smollett sprawled on the sidewalk. He knelt beside the outlaw, listened to his heart, and it was still. "Guess I won't have to amputate his leg."

"This man's still alive," Duane said, indicating Boggs.

The doctor mumbled about rebellious patients as he examined Boggs, while a few feet way, sitting behind the bullet-ridden water trough, his suit soaked with water, Len Farnsworth wrote his next headline:

PECOS KID STRIKES AGAIN!

"How's he doing, Doc?" asked the Pecos Kid.

The doctor examined the wound in Boggs's ribs. "He may live, and he may not."

"Nothing like specificity," Butterfield declared, removing the silver cigar case from his breast pocket, and holding it out to Duane.

"Don't mind if I do."

The doctor grabbed Boggs's feet, and a cowboy standing nearby took his arms. The unconscious cowboy was carried off, followed by other men lugging dead outlaws. Meanwhile, Duane's brow wrinkled with mystification, as he stared at Butterfield puffing his cheroot.

"What's on your mind, Kid?" Butterfield asked.

"I was just thinking about something odd, Mister Butterfield. Whenever I'm in trouble, you seem to show up in the nick of time. If it hadn't been for you, I'd be dead right now."

"I'd do it for anybody. Let's have a drink."

"I wonder who those cowboys were who tried to kill me."

"Once a man gets a reputation with a gun, he tends to attract skunks."

"I want to see how Boggs is doing," Duane replied. "I'll meet you later for that drink." He broke into a trot, following the procession to the doctor's office, and all eyes followed him down the middle of the street.

"He's prob'ly the fastest gun we've seen in these parts," somebody said, "'cept maybe fer Saul Klevins."

Maybe? Klevins asked silently, standing in the shadows beneath the eave. *How can these fools even compare that kid to me? Why, fer Chrissakes, it was Butterfield who did the killin', not the kid.* Muttering to himself about the fickleness of the human race, Klevins drifted toward the door of the Round-Up Saloon.

Vanessa returned to her dressing room, sat in front of the mirror, looked at her face, and tried to make sense out of what had happened. *Why are all these people trying to kill Duane?*

There was a knock on the door, scattering her thoughts. "Who is it?"

The door opened, and Saul Klevins entered, hat cocked low over one eye, smiling confidently. She rose to her feet.

"I didn't say that you could come in, sir."

He shrugged, as if he didn't care what she said. "I figgered it was time you and me had a talk."

She was flabbergasted, because she couldn't think of anything that she had in common with Saul Klevins, whom she'd seen at a distance, and knew to be a gunfighter. "I'm sorry, but I'll have to ask you to leave. I must prepare for my next performance, and there isn't much time."

Klevins made no motion toward the door, but instead hooked his thumbs in the front pockets of his jeans and looked her in the eye. "Let's me and you understand each other, Missy. That Yankee boyfriend of yers is just about tapped out in this town, and he might even get killed, at the rate he's a-goin'. I was a-thinkin' that you might need somebody to protect you, and I'm a-plannin' to come inter big money in a few days, git my drift?" He made an obscene movement of his lips.

She was aghast at his insinuation, and fell speechless for a few moments. "I'm afraid you've made a miscalculation, sir. I am evidently not the woman that you think, and I'd like you to leave."

He raised his eyebrows skeptically. "Don't play the highfalutin Southern belle with me, Missy, because you ain't a-foolin' nobody in this town. When you gets hungry enough, you'll screw a snake fer the price of a potato. It's about time you got serviced by a man, instead of that silly Yankee, or that tenderfoot kid." He raised his nose in the air, and turned toward the door.

"Even if I were dying," she said to his back. "I wouldn't let you touch me. If you ever come near me again, I'll call the deputy."

"And I'll put a bullet in his head."

The door slammed behind Klevins, the flimsy walls rattled, and Vanessa felt as though she'd just been dragged in muck. Once I was a rich man's daughter, she reflected, and if a man ever talked to me like that, my father would kill him. When the militia fired on Fort Sumter, and I cheered along with the rest of South Carolina, how could I dream it would end like this? she questioned with sadness.

Saul Klevins made his way to the bar, pushing cowboys out of the way. Klevins was furious, the corners of his mouth turned down, and he had a cruel expression in his eyes. The bartender set a glass of whiskey before him, then quickly stepped away to serve another customer.

Klevins placed his foot on the rail and looked at himself in the mirror. An ugly toad wearing a cowboy hat peered back at him, and that's how he felt following Vanessa rejection. He sipped whiskey, and it stoked his flames, humiliated by a woman whom he considered basically a whore. My money ain't good enough fer her? When Petigru is dead, and she's all alone in this town, she'll come a-beggin' me fer help, and I'll make her eat them words, and a few other things, too, afore I'm finished with her. She'll regret the day she ever threw me out, so help me God, he told himself menacingly.

CHAPTER 10

DUANE WALKED BACK TO THE ROUND-UP
Saloon, ready to draw and fire. For all
he knew, other skunks were lurking in
the shadows, ready to blow him away. At the
monastery, in his wildest flights of whimsy, he'd never
conceived that such a fate could befall him. A trip to
the cribs and a careless word had led to massive blood-
shed.

If I never went to the cribs in the first place, this
dispute could've been avoided, he admonished himself. Boggs wouldn't have two holes in his flesh, and
I wouldn't be the Pecos Kid. The truth of Catholic
doctrine smacked him between the eyes. My lust for
female companionship has brought me to this sorry
pass. If I'm going to live in the outside world, I've
got to find a nice, stable woman, and settle down in

the sacrament of marriage, he decided.

The street and sidewalk were crowded with men washed in the light of oil lamps streaming from saloons, while horses were lined at the curb, standing silently like ranks of soldiers, bored beyond comprehension. Duane was on his way to the Round-Up, for his promised drink with Butterfield. *There's something he's not telling me, and I'm going to drag it out of him if it takes me all night.*

"It's the Kid!" said a voice nearby.

Duane noticed people looking at him curiously, and all he could do was walk stalwartly among them, ready for anything. He came to the herd of cowboys in front of the Round-Up, and they parted for the Pecos Kid, providing a clear path to the door. Duane strode among them, shoulders squared, spine straight, hat low over his eyes, with a cigarette dangling from the corner of his mouth.

He pushed open the door, and it was wall-to-wall men, except for the tiny stage. Duane was taller than most, and searched among the multitudes for Clyde Butterfield, finally spotting him at the bar. Duane tried to move in that direction, but too much living flesh separated them.

A man in striped pants and a black frock coat stepped onto the minuscule stage. "Ladies and gentleman," he said, "I am proud to present at this time— the beautiful lady you've all been waiting for—The Carolina Nightingale—Miss Vanessa Fontaine!"

The saloon filled with raucous masculine applause, as Vanessa advanced onto the stage. She wore a pale blue dress that reached the floor, a pearl necklace, and pearl earrings. The man in striped pants sat at the piano and fingered the keys, as she basked in the adulation of her admirers.

Duane pounded his hands, as he stared at her with love, lust, compassion, and tenderness, forgetting Clyde Butterfield and the monastery in the clouds. In the soft glow of lamps, through the haze of smoke, she looked like a visitor from celestial realms. Duane remembered the ride in the carriage, and she'd been a wild she-creature from a far-off Amazon jungle. You never know a woman until you taste her love, he realized.

The maestro finished his musical introduction, and Vanessa launched into her first song, about a brave Confederate cavalry captain leading an impossible charge against foreboding odds, and being cut down in the flower of life, like a cherry blossom falling to earth.

Duane listened to the melodious verses, moved by the tragedy of the officer's death, which he knew to be symbolic of the tragedy of the South. Duane had read arguments for and against slavery, and agreed that it was a sin; even the pope had said so in a special encyclical, but yet Duane also knew that many innocent and decent people on both sides had been swept along by events beyond their control, soaking the soil of America with the blood of heroes in blue and gray.

He felt like a child before Vanessa, for she had lived through that epoch as a young woman, while he'd been a mere child in the monastery. He realized once more than she was much older than he, not merely the twelve paltry years, but in experience as well. I'll ask her to marry me, Duane thought, and if she says no, I'll go back to the monastery, unless somebody else kills me first.

Vanessa sang the song of the brave young cavalry officer once every evening, and it never failed to please her audiences of ex-soldiers. She'd written the words and music herself, and it was about Beauregard, her long-dead fiancé. As far as she was concerned, there was a bit of Beauregard in every man standing before her, and she loved them all in a special way.

Whether they were cowboys, carpenters, gamblers, or drunkards, most of them had placed their necks on the block for Bobby Lee and dear old Dixie. She understood them, and they loved her back. Their faces seemed to glow, as she reminded them and herself of more noble and gracious days, in the beautiful hallucination of lost paradise known as The South. No matter how dark the world had become, at least they could come together and draw on that special magic.

She looked every man in the eye at least once, so that she could communicate her affection directly, considering every veteran a hero worthy of her deepest veneration. And then, when she least expected it, her eyes fell on *him*, the Pecos Kid himself, standing near the door. She was surprised to see him there, but kept her voice modulated, and no one noticed the slightest change in her demeanor.

She knew that he'd return to her, for he was trapped in her web, as she was trapped in his. It appeared that the young man standing near the door in black clothes and his fast cowboy hat was her destiny in a strange and incomprehensible way, as though he were the reincarnation of Beauregard, and they were one and the same.

She sang of Beauregard's nobility in the face of implacable odds, and knew that Duane possessed the identical fire. Tonight he'll be mine, she thought confidently, as she belted out the tune.

Meanwhile, at the bar, Edgar Petigru saw the subtle interaction between Vanessa and Duane, and knew with sinking heart that he'd lost the game. But Edgar wasn't intrinsically evil, and his misery was directed not at Duane, but at himself.

A man must recognize his limitations, he realized with a crooked, semiphilosophical smile. I was a muddling cretin with a high opinion of myself, and looked down my down at people fleecing me alive. I actually thought I could buy a woman's love.

In the shadows at his feet he saw the world's most ridiculous fool. They laughed at me behind my back and even to my face, and I didn't see it. I was blinded by false pride, because I graduated from Columbia College, lived on Fifth Avenue, and belonged to the Union Club.

He realized that he was basically a prisoner of the people whom he'd held in contempt. They'll keep me here until they've sucked me dry, like an old cow, he predicted, and I hope they leave enough for transportation to the nearest telegraph office, where I can contact Mother. I've invested in properties that I knew nothing about, and violated the first rule of business. I should've put my money in Brooklyn, he chided himself.

If I ever get out of this mess, he thought hopefully, I'll have fabulous stories to tell the gang at the Union

Club, but they probably won't believe me. I might even become the talk of the town for a few weeks, before sliding back to the commonplace obscurity where a man of my talents belongs.

Farther down the bar, Saul Klevins also observed the silent but obvious interaction between Vanessa Fontaine and Duane Braddock. Unlike the New Yorker, Klevins didn't have a philosophical bone in his body. He tended to believe that a well-aimed slug of lead could solve most problems, and wondered how to plant one in Duane's vitals.

Klevins still smarted from Vanessa's rejection. She'd made him feel like a bug when she'd told him to leave her dressing room. Klevins wasn't accustomed to being rebuffed by women, because the women he generally associated with were prostitutes who flattered men as part of their sales promotion. He was extremely sensitive in a contorted, malignant way, and had the urge to shoot her, but shoot a woman in a small Texas town, you'll hang, he reminded himself.

Now he realized why she'd rebuffed him. Like every other scatterbrain in Titusville, she's gone loco over that damned kid. I really ought to kill him, to show the bitch who's the better man.

The medley ended, and Vanessa bowed beneath a hail of coins, as Annabelle rustled about the stage, gathering wealth assiduously. The air filled with cheers, hoots, the pounding of hands, and the chant: "More! More! More!"

Duane fastened his eyes on the long, lean blonde on the stage. What does she see in me? he wondered. Does she feel sorry for me, because I'm an orphan? He remembered the wrestling match in the carriage, and realized that it wasn't pity that she'd displayed, but raging feminine lust totally out of control.

Meanwhile, on the stage, Vanessa perceived unhappiness on Duane's face. To reassure him, the impulsive creature touched one long elegant finger to her lips, and graciously pointed to him, holding the pose for a full three seconds.

Every eye in the house followed that finger, and it pointed to the Pecos Kid standing in the shadows near the door, thumbs hooked in the front pockets of his jeans. When they realized who he was, they gave him more room, and a path opened between him and the stage. He took one step forward, and then she bowed low to him, spreading her skirt as if to say: *Whatever I am, I surrender to you.*

The saloon was silent as a tomb, except for a drunk snoring beneath a table. Duane was frozen to the floor, with no idea what the occasion required. So he did nothing. The incident passed, she rose to her feet again, skipped lightly toward the wings, and was gone.

At the bar, Saul Klevins narrowed one eye. Her display of affection for Duane, immediately after rejecting Klevins, was too much for the gunfighter's lethal tendencies. He reached toward his holster, eased the gun out an inch, then let it slide back. He knew that a heavy gun settles into a holster, and it helps to work it loose if you're planning to brace somebody. At the far end of the bar, someone handed the Pecos Kid a glass of whiskey, although Klevins had to pay for his. I think it's about time these people found out who's who and what's what, he vowed.

Klevins walked down the length of the bar, and afterward cowboys would say that he'd worn a certain murderous cast in his eyes. He approached Duane, and Duane noticed him closing the distance. To judge from the expression on Klevins's face, it appeared that the gunfighter's boots were too tight, or his last meal hadn't agreed with him. Klevins came to a halt a few feet from Duane, and cowboys gave him space at the bar.

"Can I help you, Mister Klevins?" the mutton-chopped bartender asked politely.

"Whiskey."

The bartender poured the drink, as Klevins looked Duane in the eye. "I hear folks say that yer a real fast hand."

He's looking for a fight, Duane thought, and panic began its ascent up his throat. "Not my fault, what people say."

"You callin' me a liar?"

"I never said a bad word about you in my life."

Klevins flung the glass of whiskey into Duane's face, and men dove to the floor, jumped over the bar, or plowed through the doors. The glass bounced off Duane's nose, and whiskey spattered his face and shirt.

Suddenly, without warning, his life was on the line once more. The very impossibility of the predicament weighed heavily on his mind, but he lacked time for abstract speculation on the meaning of existence. His main task, as he saw it, was somehow to extricate himself from the presence of the extremely dangerous man standing before him.

Duane placed his drink on the bar, and headed for the door, confident that Klevins wouldn't shoot him in the back with so many witnesses. And Klevins didn't shoot him, not out of fear, remorse, or Christian Love, but he wanted to *defeat* Duane, not merely send him to Boot Hill. It had become a matter of honor to the experienced gunfighter.

Klevins's fury increased as Duane approached the front doors of the saloon. He's insulted me, Klevins thought. Actually turned his back on me. Klevins hitched up his gun belt, and followed Duane out of the saloon. "Somebody better git the depitty," an old man uttered. "There's a-gonna be blood in the street—mark my words."

Duane landed on the sidewalk, his heart racing with rabid terror. He walked away swiftly, heading toward Vanessa's home. I don't need a duel with the fastest gun in the county, he told himself. The street and sidewalk were full of men who'd just left the saloon, and they looked at him curiously. "Seems like the Kid's skeered of old Saul," one of them said.

"You're damned right I am," Duane replied out the corner of his mouth, and cowboys nearby laughed at his heedless remark. Duane didn't realize it, but he won the crowd to his side at that moment, thanks to his natural human response. Where's the goddamned deputy? he wondered.

He heard a voice behind him. "What're you runnin' from, Kid?" asked Saul Klevins, standing in the light emanating from the Round-Up Saloon.

Public humiliation was the weakest link in

Duane's chain, and he stopped cold on the sidewalk. Swallowing hard, he turned around and faced the fastest gun in the county.

Klevins spat at the floorboards of the sidewalk. "If it's one thing I can't stand—it a coward! Are you a coward—Mister Pecos?"

Duane struggled to keep his voice under control. "Mister Klevins, you're a famous gunfighter. What have I done to you, that you want to kill me?"

Klevins couldn't articulate that he was jealous of Duane, and wouldn't admit it anyway. "I don't like liars, I don't like backshooters, and I don't like men who talk about me behind my back, and then call me a liar. You skinny piece of shit, I'm a-gonna give you three seconds, and then I'm a-gonna kill you, so make yer play."

Duane raised his hand nervously. "Now just a minute."

"One!"

"But . . ."

"Two!"

Klevins dropped into his gunfighter's crouch, and Duane became paralyzed with fear. I'm going to die, he thought. His throat constricted so tightly that he could barely breathe.

Someone spoke, and Duane thought it the final clap of doom, but then realized the voice came from across the street. "He doesn't have a chance against you, Klevins. It's like shooting a chicken with his wings cut off."

Klevins spun around. "Who said that?"

A tall, cosmopolitan figure in a frock coat and wide-brimmed hat sauntered into the moonlight, Clyde

Butterfield, puffing his cheroot. "Me," he said laconically.

"Wa'al, if'n it ain't the old washed-out son of a bitch himself. You want some lead tonight, Butterfield?"

"I was just suggesting, sir, that you shouldn't draw on a boy with so much less skill than you, because it'd be murder, not a fair contest in the least."

"This kid insulted me, and he's got to pay the price, but if you think you can stop me . . ."

"Let him apologize, Mister Klevins. Like you said, he's just a kid."

"He's old enough to know what he's sayin, and there's some 'pologies you don't accept. But I'll tell you what—since he's such a sorry-ass little bastard—if'n he comes over here and kisses my boots, one after t'other, maybe I'll let him off the hook *this time*."

Everyone looked at Duane, and he replied with one word: "Never."

"Then I'm a-gonna kill you."

Klevins dropped to his crouch again, and held his hand over the ivory stock of his gun. "One!"

"That's enough!" shouted Butterfield.

Len Farnsworth, intrepid reporter, wrote furiously on his notepad as he described the tall, spiffy, Clyde Butterfield strolling into the middle of the street. Klevins eyed Butterfield with undisguised contempt. "Wanna die?" he asked, an acidic tone in his voice.

"You'd kill a boy to show what a great man you are, but why don't you fight me?"

Klevins leaned back and laughed. "You're washed up, Butterfield. Be no contest at all."

"I never shot a boy because I was jealous of his woman."

Klevins paused, and his mouth settled into a grim line. "Yer a-gonna git a bellyful of lead."

Klevins moved toward the middle of the street, and so did Daune, because he didn't want Butterfield to die for his sake. "I'll fight my own battles, Clyde. Step out of the way."

Butterfield looked into his eyes. "If I've ever meant anything to you, get out of the street this instant."

Duane stepped back to the shadows, overcome by the fervency of the plea. Butterfield turned toward Klevins. "You two-bit small-town third-rate assassin— say your fucking prayers!"

"I got nothin' to pray for. *You're* the one who'd better say the prayers, you tired old horse's ass. Fer chrissakes, yer just a joke around here."

Duane would never forget the next few seconds for the rest of his life. Butterfield went for his gun, but before he took a grip, Klevins's barrel already was clearing its holster. The first shot hit Butterfield on his left shoulder, spinning him around, and the second caught him on the back. Butterfield dropped his gun, leaned backward at an impossible angle, and collapsed.

Duane ran into the middle of the street, knelt beside Butterfield, and a trickle of blood oozed from the corner of the former gunfighter's mouth. Both men looked at each other. Butterfield's face was ashen, his breath came in gasps, and it looked like he wasn't going to make it. Finally Duane was able to get the words out. "Don't make me guess for the rest of my life, Clyde! Why'd you do it?"

Butterfield coughed somewhere deep in his chest, and a gob of blood burbled out of his mouth. "You . . . know why. Yer old man . . . in the old days . . . we was . . . pards . . ."

Butterfield went into convulsions, as red foam appeared on his lips. Duane knew the party was over for the ex–staff officer. "Clyde, please tell me—was my father a good man?"

Butterfield made one last effort. "What's . . . a . . . good . . . man?"

"Why didn't you tell me that you knew him?"

"Best . . . you . . . don't . . . know . . ."

Life deserted Clyde Butterfield, and Duane felt it fly away. A voice came to him from the far side of the street. "I'm a-waitin' on ya, kid."

Duane's mouth hung open, and his face was streaked with tears. He looked down at Butterfield, who tried to save the son of his pard, although he was badly outclassed and way past his prime. Duane took a deep breath, rose unsteadily to his feet, and turned toward the fastest gun in the county. "I'm ready."

"Then let's git it on!"

Both men moved to the middle of the street, and Duane was ready to go all the way. He knew he didn't have a chance, but maybe, just maybe, with a little help from God, maybe . . . He took one last look at the world, then spat into the dirt, spread his legs, and took the gunfighter stance that had been taught him by the man lying dead a few away. "I'll count to three, so make your big move whenever you feel comfortable, Mister Klevins."

A new voice entered the arena. "Now just a moment!" It was Deputy Dawson, and he carried a double-barreled shotgun into the middle of the street. He'd been watching from the crowd, and realized that if he didn't at least attempt to control the evening's bloodbath, they'd laugh him out of town. He aimed the shotgun in the general direction of Klevins, and then toward Duane. "Clear the street!"

A gun exploded, a cloud of smoke billowed, and Deputy Dawson was thrown to the side, where he tripped over his feet, and fell in a puddle of mud. Everyone stared at the deputy, but he didn't move. Titusville had become a lawless town.

"If'n I need a deputy," Klevins said, "I'll ask fer one." He holstered his gun, then returned his attention to Duane. "This is it, Kid. I'm tired of playin' with you."

"Just listen to this, Mister Klevins," Duane said, between clenched teeth. "You're the fastest gun in the county, but I'm right, and you're wrong, and if there's a God in heaven—you're going to die."

Duane got into position again, and afterward the old-timers would say that he looked like the angel of death in the moonlight. But then out of the darkness of the crowd, a long black cape appeared, topped by golden hair. Vanessa Fontaine walked toward Saul Klevins and stopped a few feet away. "Mister Klevins," she said, trying to hold her voice steady, "I'll do anything you say, if you'll let him go."

Duane heard her voice, and shook his head angrily. "Vanessa—get out of the street!"

She pretended that she didn't hear, and continued to plead with Klevins. "I apologize if I've hurt your feelings. I know that it was callous of me. Let the Kid go, and we can leave this town together."

Duane turned toward the crowd. "Will somebody please move this woman out of my line of fire."

A group of cowboys from the Lazy Y grabbed Vanessa and pulled her back. She tried to fight, but they were strong and in such numbers, they swept her off her feet and carried her away.

"I'm tired of fuckin' with you, kid," Klevins said, and went for his gun.

Duane darted to the right, and drew his Colt simultaneously. He snapped the barrel up, and steadied his aim, but Klevins fired first. The bullet whizzed past Duane's left shoulder, but the Pecos Kid bit his lower lip and pulled the trigger.

His gun exploded, the street filled with smoke, the crowd could barely see. Vanessa shrieked in dismay, because she thought she saw Duane go down, but he was only stepping forward, for another shot at the figure reeling up the street.

Saul Klevins had been hit in the pancreas, and foul excretions spilled into his bloodstream. The street spun around him. He was completely disoriented, and he tried to imagine what had happened, but didn't even know his name. What am I doing with this gun in my hand? he wondered, as black curtains fell over him.

Daune was aghast, as the famous gunfighter dropped before him. Duane's right arm was extended, Colt pointed at Klevins, who vomited blood onto the ground. I won, Duane thought, and felt as though a tremendous miracle had occurred, for how could he, a mere novice, shoot the fastest gun in the county?

He looked up, and saw the Milky Way blazing a path across the heavens. When he'd drawn his Colt, once again he'd experienced the uncanny feeling that somebody had been behind him, the man with the black mustache, and in that blinding moment he knew that his father had rendered personal assistance from the depths of the spirit world.

Then he lowered his head, and his eyes fell on Clyde Butterfield lying in a pool of blood and dank water. Duane knelt beside him. Gore was everywhere—the jaunty ex-staff officer a lifeless corpse, his hat fallen off, and thinning dark blond hair tousled on his head. Duane leaned forward, and tenderly closed his friend's eyes. "I'll never forget what you've done for me, Clyde," he whispered. "May the Lord have mercy on your soul."

"Here you go, Kid," said a voice above him.

Duane saw a glass of whiskey proffered. He accepted, knocked the contents back, and looked around at cowboys from the Lazy Y, the gunsmith he'd met when he'd first come to town, Sullivan the shopkeeper, who'd sold him a dead man's boots, Edgar Petigru. Even prostitutes from the cribs had come to the center of town to see the showdown between Saul Klevins and the Pecos Kid.

"Guess yer the fastest gun in the county now, Duane," said crippled Sally Mae.

Duane felt sick to his stomach, now that the full shock of events caught up with him. He turned away from them, and stumbled like a drunken man toward the darkness at the edge of town.

CHAPTER 11

VANESSA FIDGETED IN HER KITCHEN, WON-
dering what had happened to Duane. It
was three o'clock in the morning, and
she'd drunk so much coffee, she could barely sit still.
"I hope he doesn't do anything foolish," she mumbled
to the coffeepot. Absentmindedly, she raised the side of
her robe and scratched her bare leg.

Two beady eyes watched, and they belonged to
Jed Wilson. Mouth open and tongue hanging out like a
dog, the Peeping Tom frowned with chagrin as she let
the robe fall, covering her leg once more.

After the shooting, all performances were canceled
at the Round-Up Saloon. Jed had driven her home, put
the carriage away, fed the horses, and then crept to her
window, where he gawked at her like a lovesick boy.
"Looking for something?"

Jed spun around, and found himself facing the Pecos Kid. Jed was so frightened, he couldn't speak. "Please don't shoot!"

"What're you doing here?"

"Just takin' a walk. Din't mean no hurt."

The back door opened, and Vanessa stepped outside. "Is that you, Duane?"

"Your carriage driver was looking through your window."

"I've always thought that he did, but I've never been able to catch him at it."

Duane aimed his gun at Jed's nose. "You're fired, and if I ever see you around Miss Vanessa again, I'll kill you. Now get out of here, and don't ever come back."

For a moment, Jed thought the Pecos Kid was going to put one through his left nostril. He ran away swiftly, and wondered when the next stagecoach left town. Duane watched him disappear into the night, and then holstered his gun. He and Vanessa looked at each other in silence, as a coyote howled mournfully in the distance.

"Care for a slice of chocolate cake?" she asked.

He followed her into the kitchen, where she cut a thick wedge, and served him a glass of milk. He sat at the table, pushed back his hat, and his black hair fell over his forehead.

"I thought a rattlesnake bit you," she said.

"The only rattlesnakes that worry me are citizens of this town."

He placed a slice of cake into his mouth and spoke while he ate: "I thought I'd never see you again. I swear—it was a miracle. May I have another slice?"

So polite, she thought with a smile, as she placed the entire cake before him. "I've always believed in miracles, although they generally happen to other people."

"That's the way it used to be for me, until tonight. Anyway, I thought that I should either return to the monastery, or marry you. To make a long story short, I've decided to marry you."

She laughed nervously. "You shouldn't say things like that to girls, because one of us might believe you someday."

He rolled a cigarette, spilling a substantial quantity onto the floor. "I think we should get out of this part of the country. I'll find a job as a cowboy, and you'll sing in the local saloon."

"But——"

He interrupted her. "And don't give me any horse-shit about the difference in our ages."

She thought for a few moments, not completely surprised by his roundabout proposition. "I won't mention it, as long as you never refer to me as *my old lady*."

"Why don't we go to bed?"

It wasn't the most romantic offer she'd ever received, but she still simmered from his earlier embraces. She wished they could have a little ceremony, with a preacher saying those special words, but life was complex, and sometimes a woman needed a *young* man. "You've got to promise that you'll never lie to me, Duane. That's all I ask."

"You've got my word," he replied, and hoped he wasn't lying.

She led him down the hallway to her bedroom,

holding the lamp like a torch. He hung his hat on her bedpost as she turned down the covers, and he couldn't help noticing the fine subtle curve of her hindquarters. The artery in his throat began to throb, although it was nearly four o'clock in the morning.

She finished her housekeeping, and appeared ill at ease. The time had come for The Grand Encounter, and both recalled a certain tempestuous carriage ride, and a mad grope in the vestibule. Duane hung his bandanna on the other bedpost, then sat on the chair and pulled off his boots. "Aren't you going to get undressed?" he asked.

She blew out the lamp, then untied her red silk robe, letting it slip from her shoulders. It revealed a pink flannel granny nightgown, and she lifted the hem over her shoulders. Duane stepped out of his pants, and perceived her long, slim nakedness in the moonlight.

He thought of all the nights he'd dreamed about her, and now at last they were alone, with all pretensions banished. They reached toward each other, embraced, and electric thrills networked his body. When he touched his lips to hers, he realized that a woman's flesh and blood was an irresistible argument against the cloistered life. They moved toward the bed, dropped down, and clasped each other warmly. He smothered her face with kisses, as she contorted against him. The mattress began to squeak, augmented by little moans and sighs.

He rolled her onto her back, and gazed at her white marble curves and hollows resplendent in the moonlight. Tumultuous lust crashed over him, as he touched his tongue to her nipple. She hugged his shaggy head tightly against her, and felt the stubble of his beard on her sensitive emotions. "Oh Duane . . ."

Her voice trailed into the night, blending with a breeze fluttering the curtains, and choruses of insects singing on the sage. Duane ran his tongue over her body as though she were a big piece of candy.

He opened his eyes in the middle of the night, besotted by love, her cheek on his chest, and he could feel her regular respirations. He turned his head toward the window.

The full moon floated over exotic horizon calligraphy, illuminating a vast, measureless range. It's a great land, and I've finally found my mate, he mused. We'll make it somehow, won't we? He gave her a hug, and she replied with a sleepy kiss against his chest, plus an affectionate little coo.

His eyes grew heavy, as if he were drifting to slumber again, but somehow, inexplicably, in the far-off endless vista, he saw the spectral outlines of two old gunfighters strolling along, sharing a bottle of whiskey, their arms across each other's shoulders, their wide-brimmed hats on the backs of their heads.

Duane couldn't perceive them clearly, but it appeared that the shorter gunfighter wore a black mustache, with silver conchos on his hat, while the lanky fellow maintained a head of thick blond hair, with a certain devil-may-care soldier's stride. Their hearty laughter rang in Duane's ears, as they congratulated each other merrily, passing the bottle from hand to hand. *I don't know who killed you, Daddy, but I'll find out someday. And you laid down your life for me,*

Clyde, so I'll always bless your name.

Joe Braddock waved, and Clyde Butterfield saluted the infamous Pecos Kid, as the two ghosts danced together through the foggy ruins of time.

Jack Bodine is the pseudonym of an author who lives in New York City. This is his second western for HarperPaperbacks.

Saddle-up to these

THE REGULATOR *by Dale Colter*
Sam Slater, blood brother of the Apache and a cunning bounty-hunter, is out to collect the big price on the heads of the murderous Pauley gang. He'll give them a single choice: surrender and live, or go for your sixgun.

THE REGULATOR—Diablo At Daybreak
by Dale Colter
The Governor wants the blood of the Apache murderers who ravaged his daughter. He gives Sam Slater a choice: work for him, or face a noose. Now Slater must hunt down the deadly renegade Chacon...Slater's Apache brother.

THE JUDGE *by Hank Edwards*
Federal Judge Clay Torn is more than a judge—sometimes he has to be the jury *and* the executioner. Torn pits himself against the most violent and ruthless man in Kansas, a battle whose final verdict will judge one man right...and one man dead.

THE JUDGE—War Clouds
by Hank Edwards
Judge Clay Torn rides into Dakota where the Cheyenne are painting for war and the army is shining steel and loading lead. If war breaks out, someone is going to make a pile of money on a river of blood.